DON'T TRUST HIM

EAST RISE SERIES
BOOK 4

LISA CUTTS

BLOODHOUND
BOOKS

Copyright © 2025 Lisa Cutts

The right of Lisa Cutts to be identified as the Author of the Work has been asserted by them in accordance with the Copyright, Designs and Patents Act 1988.

Re-published in 2025 by Bloodhound Books.

Apart from any use permitted under UK copyright law, this publication may only be reproduced, stored, or transmitted, in any form, or by any means, with prior permission in writing of the publisher or, in the case of reprographic production, in accordance with the terms of licences issued by the Copyright Licensing Agency.
All characters in this publication are fictitious and any resemblance to real persons, living or dead, is purely coincidental.

www.bloodhoundbooks.com

Print ISBN: 978-1-917449-9-60

For Carol and Richard Stone,
Here's to books, dogs and beer.

THEN

I knew that I was taking a big chance – a *massive* one – not to mention one with an outcome that could end it all. Potentially my life, *definitely* my freedom. Still, that was why I did it: the rush was like nothing on earth – well, nothing legal anyway.

I had taken my time, watched the premises, scoped the route, timed the comings and goings of anyone likely – or stupid enough – to try to stop me.

I had upped my game, there was no doubt about it. But the trouble with this game was that, not only were the stakes high – so was the win.

Still, it wasn't the first time and it certainly wouldn't be the last.

I sat in the car, tried hard to steady my breathing, and took the key from the ignition. To those scuttling past on the pavement, crossing the road in this shitty little town, right at this moment I was nothing more than a man parking his battered Ford Cortina. No one ever paid me any attention, and, right now, that was exactly what I wanted.

I leaned across to feel beneath the passenger seat. My

fingers grasped the edge of the woollen balaclava before reaching the sawn-off shotgun a couple of inches further away. My nicotine-stained fingertips grazed the surface of the crumb-riddled, black plastic floor mats, the gun knocking the empty cigarette boxes and discarded takeaway wrappers out of the way.

With the blood pumping in my ears and my heart racing, I tucked the shotgun inside my deliberately-too-large jacket and rested the balaclava in my lap.

This was the part where I had to take my time, keep control and focus.

I did all that and more as I ran what was now a well-practised eye over the glass front of the building society.

Bradford and Bingley was my financial establishment of choice, most likely because of their adverts on television. They always seemed to appeal to the right people, the sort who had money.

Once more, I took a few deep breaths, made sure I had a tight grip on the balaclava in one hand. Over the last few months I had perfected the art of leaving the right one free for the shotgun when the time became right.

One last glance up and down the almost empty mid-morning pavement before I got out of the car.

For one stupid moment, it crossed my mind to lock the car, but as there was no one I trusted enough to be my getaway driver, locking it would cost me precious seconds when I'd need them most.

Without giving anything else much thought, adrenalin now off the scale, I cleared my mind of everything that didn't involve executing the perfect armed robbery.

I walked the 250 feet towards the building society, one hand on the balaclava, the other on a loaded shotgun.

I strolled along the pavement, face down, collar up, palms sweating. Even before I opened the door and stepped inside, I knew there were only two customers and one middle-aged woman working behind the counter.

Ideal.

One elderly man stood to my left, busy trying to fill in some piece of paper with a pen chained to the desk he leaned against. A young woman of about twenty stood in front of me at the counter, foot tapping presumably in annoyance at how long her transaction was taking.

That was about to change.

I almost felt sorry for these people: they had no idea what was about to happen; the impact the next few minutes would have on the rest of their lives, wondering if today might have been their last.

Still, I had a job to do.

I stepped forward to the bored customer, getting unnaturally close to her. She was wearing a cheap perfume, something sweet that reminded me of old ladies, all flowery and sickly.

She turned her head, irritation on her face, about to tell me to step back, and then her features changed dramatically as she realised what was happening.

Her mouth opened into a perfect circle, while her eyes grew to the size of saucers, her skin deathly white as she took in my balaclava. Until this point, she hadn't even noticed the shotgun I had pulled from inside my jacket.

Now that I was pointing it at her head, she most definitely had.

'Hands on the counter,' I said to the woman behind the till. She looked terrified too, but that was the point.

'Money, now,' I shouted. The bank teller was mid-forties, attractive in a mumsy way, shaking like a shitting dog.

She fumbled, unsure of what to do, even though her staff training would no doubt have instructed her on how to behave if someone were to come into your provincial branch and point a gun at a customer's head. Supposedly this stupid bitch thought it would never happen to her. Except now it was, and she should get on with it. I hardly had all day.

'Fucking do it,' I shouted at her as I grabbed the petrified younger woman's arm.

I glanced behind me at the old man – pen in his gnarled, liver-spotted hand, his face a mask of horror – then I turned my attention back to the counter.

'Notes only,' I shouted at her again. 'Fives, tens and twenties.'

Fifties were too difficult to get rid of. Keep it simple, always.

I let go of the young woman's arm to pull a Sainsbury's carrier bag from my pocket, then threw it across to the cashier and watched as she stuffed the cash inside.

I lunged across towards the bag, grabbed it by the handle then turned and ran towards the door. My whole body was coursing with adrenalin, making me feel more alive than I ever thought possible.

I ran out of the building, shotgun back inside my jacket, balaclava pulled off my head as soon as my feet hit the pavement.

Then I was back to a brisk walk towards the car, not looking behind, not trying to draw attention to myself. Just a man with his collar up to keep out the cold on a chilly afternoon in the south-east of England, shopping bag at his side, car keys ready to shove in the ignition.

I almost laughed as I opened the car door, threw the bag down next to me and pushed the shotgun back under the passenger seat. I indicated and pulled out of the parking space, driving away, the sound of police sirens growing louder in the distance.

CHAPTER ONE

TUESDAY 5 MAY

The jobs were coming in thick and fast. What had once felt like the world's weirdest but most rewarding challenge now felt to Detective Inspector Harry Powell like the universe's biggest piss-take.

How exactly he was supposed to run an incident room with over half of his staff on restricted duties, reduced hours and flexi-working, he simply wasn't sure. No one seemed to work an eight-hour day any more, most reluctant to do overtime. All except DC Sophia Ireland, who never seemed to turn it down.

Still, as he had always done, he would embrace this new-age way of policing and hope he retired before it went completely belly-up.

It was either that or privatisation, and that would surely be a disaster.

As he sat mulling over how he was going to manage dividing his staff among an over-burdened, under-staffed county, as well as the review of all outstanding Missing Persons he had been volunteered for, his landline rang. The display told him that the deputy chief constable was taking time out of her day to call him.

'Ma'am,' he said. 'What can I do for you on this fine Tuesday morning?'

'Harry,' she said, the warm, polished tones of a newsreader sounding in his ear. 'I hope all is well with you.'

'Ah, I'm happy as a pig in the proverbial.'

He looked to the ceiling, one of his most comforting places for solace in some form. Quite why, he didn't know; it had never worked before.

'Well, Harry,' she continued as he wrapped the phone cord around his fingers, certain something bad was about to follow, 'the thing is, we're sending you another member of staff, so that's good news.'

No, it's fucking not good news, he wanted to shout into the mouthpiece. It was only going to bring him grief: senior officers did not telephone someone many ranks lower than themselves out of the blue, to tell them they were getting a new member of staff. Not without there being inherent problems attached.

He waited.

Here it was.

'You're to get someone really keen and motivated. He's one of the new fast-track detectives, so he's done his basic training and is raring to go. We're all very enthusiastic about this latest project, placing the newest recruits into specialist posts, and I know that you and the guys at Major Crime will make him feel very welcome.'

'There's no vacancies,' he thought he heard himself say, as he wondered if she had actually heard him.

'What?' said Deputy Chief Constable Loretta Bannister.

'I said, ma'am, that we don't have any vacancies. We haven't advertised, there hasn't been a fair and open recruitment process as advertised by Inhuman Resources, and we certainly don't have the budget for another officer. I'm about '

'Look, don't worry about the finer points, okay? I'll send you his resumé and you can find him something to do. And let's be honest about all of this, it doesn't really matter whether you find him some work or not, the important thing is that, on paper, he looks as though he's being gainfully employed.'

There was a second, just one second, when Harry really wasn't concerned about his future, his pension, his job, and then he remembered that he had worked for almost thirty years in a career that had sometimes supported him, but sometimes hung him out to dry.

'Tell you what,' he said, 'you, or someone who's got the information at their fingertips, can send it over to me. You know, the usual – who this person is and his smorgasbord of policing credibility – and I'll find him a job that's right up his alley. Anything else I can help you with today, ma'am?'

He glanced down at his near-white fingertips, phone-wire strangulation taking off nicely. Some things never changed, and they never would.

'No, no. I think that's about it,' she said.

He heard a slight pause in her tone. It might have been her thinking time, but then again, it might have been her PA bringing her a beverage.

'Okay, boss,' he said as he held back a sigh. 'Email me the details and I'll find him a role here.' *On this specialist unit that good detectives wait years to get on*, he thought as he chewed on the inside of his cheek and hung up the receiver.

Whoever was coming was going to be a problem. There was something very wrong about this.

Still smarting, Harry let out a heavy sigh when his phone rang again. This time he saw that the call was from the Force Control Room: this was rarely a good thing. Either something had happened that needed his immediate attention or, horror of horrors, a member of the public wanted to talk to him.

'Harry Powell,' he said, trying to sound a little less miserable than he felt.

'Morning, mate,' said a voice sounding far too cheerful to be employed by the same people who were paying Harry his wage. 'It's John Pinnock over at the FCR. I've got something for your attention on this lovely morning.'

'Well, I'm just the lottery winner of East Rise town today,' said Harry, trying to add the right amount of sarcasm. He knew the calls were recorded, but he also knew Inspector Pinnock well enough that he would appreciate the overtones.

'Let's see,' said John, 'I've just emailed you our CAD 852 of a call to us today. Some workmen who were about to start clearing farmland found what looks to be human remains in a shallow grave, clothing indicating a female. The address and who you need to speak to there are on the CAD.'

There was a slight pause while Harry opened the email and then said, 'Okay, John. Leave it with me and I'll take a look.'

As he gathered his thoughts, Harry went into automatic mode: despite feeling the tension surging through his whole being, this was what he did, and this was what he and his team excelled at.

They investigated murders for a living and almost every member of staff in his depleted incident room would pull out all the stops following the discovery of a body in suspicious circumstances.

There really was nothing that came close to murder.

Harry rubbed his hand across his face as he glanced in the direction of the corridor, sounds of early morning chatter and chinking of ceramic mugs coming from those already at work and eager to begin the day.

He knew that a couple of the team were off today, including Detective Constable Hazel Hamilton, Harry's girlfriend. That thought made him smile. He liked working with her and she never took advantage of sleeping with the boss. Still, he hesitated, deciding whether to forewarn those who were at work that their day was probably about to be severely disrupted or leave them to their existing work until there was actual confirmation of a body.

As he brought up CAD number 852 on his computer screen, scrolling through for the details he needed, he shook his head at the distant memory of being called out in the heavy rain in the early hours – one morning years ago in the driving rain. He had trudged across a field, ruining a pair of almost new suit trousers, water finding its way inside his wax jacket to trickle down his neck, only to shine a torch into the ditch onto the suspected corpse, throw his head back and exhale a long and heavy sigh.

The uniformed officers guarding the scene were about to warn him off sliding down the bank and contaminating the crime scene when he had held out a hand to silence them.

'Cancel the CSI,' he had shouted over the rain and wind to his stunned colleagues. 'It's got fucking antlers. I'm going back to bed.'

It wasn't his finest hour, but at least he had stopped short of calling them all incompetent fuckwits.

Harry had remembered sharing the story the following morning with another of the team, Detective Constable Pierre Rainer. Pierre had cried with laughter, holding his sides and wiping the tears from his eyes.

To his surprise and shame, Harry found himself wiping away his own tears as he thought about Pierre, his colleague and friend. His loss was felt by everyone in the incident room, but by none more than Harry.

Cynical as Harry might be, unenthusiastic about murder he

was not. He raced through the words on his screen, hairs on the back of his neck standing up, certain that what he was reading was the unmistakable beginning of East Rise incident room's newest murder.

CHAPTER TWO

Detective Constable Sophia Ireland was never one to turn down overtime, which was fortunate as there was never going to be a shortage of it.

She paused at the cashpoint, fingers hovering over '£20'. She thought about it for a moment, then pressed '£10', and hoped it would last her until the weekend.

She stuffed her bank card back inside her warrant card, shoved that in her jacket pocket and curled her fingers around the note, all the while wondering if she'd make it through to payday.

As she crossed the road heading back towards East Rise police station, she totted up the overtime she had worked in the last few weeks. She'd not worked as much as she would have liked as the department was frequently running out of money. Some hours she'd done for free just to get the work done. The budget was empty and there was no way she could have left the job half-done. Still, getting paid for it would have been better.

For a moment, Sophia paused outside the sandwich shop. They made the best crab sandwiches. The bread was freshly baked, the crab locally caught. If she spent nearly half of her cash on a sandwich, though, she would most definitely be overdrawn in no time.

Fingers still clasping her cash, she turned and walked away back towards the front door of the police station.

As she got to the bottom of the steps, her phone bleeped. Shaking it free from her pocket with her other hand, her stomach dropped when she saw it was from her mum.

Hi love, hate to ask but any chance of making it £250 this month? Things are very tight. Grandad's care home fees are due. xx

The glass doors slid open as Sophia reached them, fumbling to get her phone back in her pocket. She could have walked to the side of the building and made her way to the entrance there, which took her directly to the Major Crime Department, but she often walked through the front counter, simply to stop and say hello to whoever was on duty.

This morning, it was Ian Davis, busy dealing with the only other person in the foyer. She smiled and waved at Ian. He looked up and gave her a smile in return as the man he was talking to turned in her direction.

Something about him made her slow her pace. She couldn't put her finger on what it was. It wasn't simply that he was handsome; there was something about him.

She had reached the door and was aware that she needed her pass to get through, only she couldn't remember where she'd put it. As she was about to ask Ian to let her through, he called, 'Soph, if you've got a minute?'

'Of course, Ian,' she said, wondering if her hair was now a mess from her trip to the cashpoint.

She took the opportunity to walk the short distance back to the counter and get a good look at the man who was leaning against it. Aged mid-thirties, probably a little over six feet tall, although difficult to be accurate due to the leaning, the mop of black hair flecked grey in places, clean-shaven, polished shoes, no wedding ring.

She stood and locked eyes with the stranger, not fully able to forget that Ian was only a couple of feet away, barely an arm's length across the counter. It didn't escape her notice; it was the same cheap countertop where, over the years, she had stood at and spoken with hundreds of members of the public. Some were victims with physical injuries, who had dripped blood right where the main object of her attention was now leaning. Some had been suspects she had arrested for a myriad of crimes, some as witnesses to those crimes. No one had ever made her stop and stare so unashamedly.

'Soph,' said Ian – not for the first time, she was sure.

'This is Dane Hoopman.'

'Hello, Dane,' she heard herself say.

Then she only just heard Ian add, 'He's transferring here. He's not supposed to start till tomorrow but thought he'd drop in early and say hello.'

'Hello,' she heard herself say, picturing her face reddening.

Snapping to attention, and with some semblance of professionalism, Sophia said, 'Where's he starting? I'd better not let him through without warning. Who should I speak to?'

All the time she was aware that she was talking about someone who was present, and who she really should bring herself to look in the eye. Except as rude as it was, she found she couldn't.

At last, he spoke. The voice she was expecting: a deep, even tone. 'I've been told to ask for DI Harry Powell in Major Crime. I'm on attachment.'

One hand fumbling with her newly located security pass,

the other on the door handle, she said, 'Leave it with me. I'll take care of you.'

Even without Dane's wry smile, she appreciated her own poor choice of words.

CHAPTER THREE

Twenty-five minutes later, Harry pulled his car over in the crime scene's makeshift car park, which was, for all intents and purposes, the entrance to a farmer's field. Thankfully, it was a fairly large area that was currently housing eight other vehicles, including a large marked police van, a CSI van and a white Ford Transit.

Harry clocked the worried, grey-tinged face of the man he assumed had discovered the body. He wore heavy-duty, well-used boots, tatty jeans and a shirt, and, over the top of it, a high-visibility jacket. He spoke rapidly to the policewoman taking his details, constantly crossing and uncrossing his arms over his chest; his left leg, which was slightly pushed forward towards the officer, jiggled as he spoke.

Yep, he had all the hallmarks of someone who had just found a body.

Making a point of a noisy approach, Harry's shoes crunched on the stones as he covered the twenty yards to his witness.

Nodding to the police officer, Harry said, 'Hello, Kate,' before he turned his attention to the man he guessed to be in his early thirties, hands now down by his sides as if he didn't really know what to do with them.

Harry stuck out a hand and said, 'I'm Harry Powell, the on-call detective inspector from East Rise Police Station.' They shook hands, Harry noticing the clammy palms of the jittery workman.

'Paul Tanswell,' he said. 'Sorry about my hands. They're a bit sweaty.'

'Didn't notice,' said Harry. 'How are you feeling?'

He saw Paul lift his shoulders and drop them. It was no doubt the best he could manage under the circumstances of his bizarre Tuesday morning.

'Listen, Paul,' said Harry. 'I'm going to have a quick chat with PC Smith and then be back to speak to you in one minute. That okay?'

He waited for a nod before stepping a few yards away out of earshot, and took a brief summary from the officer who had started to take details not long before Harry arrived.

'In your opinion, how's he doing?' said Harry.

'Not too bad, but I think he may be putting a brave face on,' she said, voice as low as she could make it. 'He said that there should have been two of them here working, but his crew-mate didn't show up. Probably would have done a blokey-type laugh it off thing if he wasn't on his own.'

She glanced down at her notes.

'Before you arrived, I got as far as him telling me he was sure it was a woman. It looked like the hand was sticking up out of the ground, a couple of the fingers chewed off or missing, but the clothing the arm was coming out of had some sort of lace-trimmed sleeve.'

'Doesn't prove it was a woman,' said Harry, scratching at the stubble on his chin. 'Might be Adam Ant on his way home from a gig.'

'No,' said Kate, with no hint of amusement, 'he doesn't live around here. What stuck in Paul's mind was the thin gold bracelet around the hand – or what's left of the hand since the foxes have had a go on it – and the fine blonde hair. He said that he thought it was a woman's hair.'

She scratched at the side of her head with her pen before she added, 'And Adam Ant's got black hair.'

Harry thanked Kate, wondering how she knew so much about an 80s pop icon who was probably on *Top of the Pops* before she was even born, and made his way back towards the witness.

'There's no need for you to come back over to the site with me,' said Harry as he watched Paul let out a slow breath. 'I'll leave you in the capable hands of PC Smith for now, and one of the plain-clothes officers will be in touch soon to get a more detailed account from you.' He gestured towards the policewoman. 'I've been updated on what you found, and while I don't want you to keep going over it, is there anything else that comes to mind before I leave you here?'

Harry watched as Paul looked in the direction of the shallow grave on the edge of a copse, blocked off by police tape.

'Only that it was the last thing I was expecting to see today,' said Paul. He turned back towards Harry. 'Supposed to be having a quick look across the land, checking for anything unusual ahead of the building work that's to start here next week.'

He waved a hand in the direction of the green landscape. 'The field's been sold and we're looking to build new homes here. It was all set to start last summer, but there was some issue with an access road. Anyway, that's not important, but that area of trees where . . . where, well, you know. I could have sworn I checked that towards the end of last year.'

Paul broke off and chewed his bottom lip. 'If I, well, *she* . . . I would have noticed last year, wouldn't I? How long has she been there?'

Harry put a hand up to touch Paul's shoulder. 'It's unlikely that you would have noticed, to be honest.'

'I've no idea who she is, but the thought she's been lying there for all that time, people walking by her, *over* her.' Despite standing in the morning sunshine, Paul shuddered, crossed his arms again, although this time possibly less through nerves and more for warmth.

'There's really nothing you could have done,' said Harry, reluctant to provide further comfort about deterioration of human flesh, the impact of the weather conditions or soil erosion. It wouldn't help Paul and it could taint any evidence he might have to give one day in Crown Court. That was always Harry's end-game – the conviction. That was what it was always about.

Leaving Kate to take care of Paul, Harry trudged along the pathway, the uniformed officer on the cordon pointing him in the direction of a small huddle of police officers all standing and examining an exposed cadaver in a shallow grave.

CHAPTER FOUR

The Boundary pub sat at the corner of an unassuming southeast London street. It had once been a thriving establishment used by dockers, lorry drivers and locals. Historically, its customers came from trade on the Thames, council houses and local markets, but nowadays, the only business came from a select few locals who were unwelcome in most other pubs.

A black Mercedes pulled up outside the building, its occupants all too familiar with the rundown establishment. The gleam of the impeccable car was all the more noticeable against the pub's façade: years of dirt and fumes from goods vehicles on their way to brown sites and breakers yards, plus the hum of daily commuters taking shortcuts through the rat runs, had ingrained filth into the brickwork and rotting window frames.

Two men got out of the car and strolled to the front door of The Boundary as the driver made his way around the corner away from the main road. They didn't have to worry about knocking as the door was flung open the moment they crossed the narrow pavement.

'All right, gents?' said the landlady, harsh morning sun

highlighting every line she had accumulated on her face over her thirty-eight years.

She stepped backwards, holding the door wide with one tattooed arm, gold bangle catching in the sunshine.

'Nice bit of tat you've got yourself there, Sheila,' said the first one through the door, nodding at her jewellery.

'You're a saucy bastard, Sean,' she said as he stopped to kiss her on the cheek. 'You'll 'ave something nice to say to me, won't you, love?' she said to the slightly shorter and younger of the two.

He stood in front of her, placed a hand either side of her face and said, 'You're lovelier every time I see you, sweetheart.' He leaned down to kiss her.

She called to Sean, 'See, he knows how to treat a lady, he does.'

'Don't fucking make me laugh,' said Sean. 'The greedy bastard's after some breakfast, ain't you, Milo?'

She closed and bolted the door behind them before walking to the other side of the bar and leaning towards them, arms folded across her chest. 'What do you boys fancy?' she asked, looking from one to the other.

'How about a couple of nice big baps?' said Milo.

She threw her head back and laughed, her body, not to mention her breasts, wobbling as she did so.

'You can make your own tea,' Sheila said as she moved away from the bar, hands smoothing down the thin cotton of her T-shirt. 'How does a couple of bacon sarnies sound?'

'As lovely as you look,' Milo called after her as she sauntered to the kitchen.

He looked over at Sean. 'What?' he said at the slow shake of his boss's head.

Sean glanced in the direction of the kitchen, sounds of

crockery and saucepans being moved drowning out their conversation.

Keeping his voice down in case Sheila heard, he said, 'I thought you were gonna try and give her one over the bar, you fucking polecat. I said to keep her on side, not bang her.'

'Worth a try,' said Milo with a wink. Then he shouted, 'Sheila, want a hand out there?' before sliding himself off the bar stool and walking behind the bar towards the sound of her off-key singing.

Sean wasn't amused at his employee's behaviour, yet Sheila had been an invaluable source to him over the years. The last thing he wanted to do was rush her into handing over what they'd come for. Still, they didn't really have time for this: breakfast and shagging were all well and good, only not with so much to do.

He turned on his bar stool and ran an eye over the interior of the worn and neglected pub. He was able to almost taste the traffic fumes, despite the now locked doors and distance from the pavement. The place had certainly seen better days. Still, it was ideal for what they had in mind.

Who would be stupid or brave enough to pry into their business in this shit-tip? They were the biggest organised criminal gang in south-east England and they had all corners of the market covered, not to mention contacts in the right places.

CHAPTER FIVE

DI Harry Powell stood at a respectful distance from the hand clawing its way out of the earth. It was less of a hand and more of a gnarled piece of bone. In fact, at first glance, the only thing that really gave away that it had once belonged to a human was the lacy once-white material in the general area of where a wrist used to be.

Harry crouched down for a better look. To himself, more so than to any of the officers guarding the scene or the senior CSI setting up her camera, he muttered, 'Paul did pretty well to even see this. It's not that obvious.'

'Talking to yourself again, Harry?' said Jo Styles as she checked her photographic equipment.

'Get more sense that way, Jo,' he said, smiling up at her.

'I wouldn't kneel down there, by the way,' she said, returning the smile.

'Since when have you ever known me to contaminate your crime scenes?' said Harry, feeling the onset of cramp in his thighs.

'Wake up and smell the urine,' laughed Jo, prompting Harry to spring up from the floor. 'Didn't you wonder what that odour was mingled in there with the warm summer breeze and good old countryside fragrances?'

'Fucker,' said Harry as he glared in the direction of the witness. 'I bloody well asked him if there was anything else I should know. You're telling me that him stopping to take a leak and wazzing all over my crime scene was a detail he omitted to give me? Dozy bastard.'

'He was probably too embarrassed to say it a second time,' said Jo. 'Any chance you can get out of my shot, please?'

'Sorry, Jo,' said Harry as he stepped to the side. 'It's clearly going to take some time to get whoever this is out of the ground.' He looked around to where half a dozen uniformed officers were carrying out painstaking searches in the nearby undergrowth. 'Providing this lot don't turn up a second body, I guess I should head back to East Rise and get some sort of investigation going.'

'First things first,' she said as she pulled an evidence bag from her pocket. 'Want to take this bracelet with you? I've got enough photos of it for now.'

Harry took her camera from her while she carefully teased the gold jewellery from its owner and dropped it into the plastic bag.

Jo held it up to the light and the pair of them stared at it as if it were a thing of wonder.

'We'll call it nine forty-two hours,' said Jo as she checked her watch and produced a pen from her inside pocket. She scribbled the time on the sealed bag, handed it to Harry and crouched down to make a note of what she'd done on her paperwork.

'I'll get this back to East Rise,' he said, folding the bag and securing it in his pocket. 'Chances of DNA from this?' he said, pointing to his pocket where the item was now concealed.

With a minuscule shrug of her shoulders beneath the paper

suit, Jo said, 'As good as anything that's sat out in the elements for weeks, maybe months.'

'Won't hold you to this, Jo,' said Harry, nodding in the direction of the dump site, beyond the remains of the hand, 'but that does look very much like the back of a woman's head sticking out of the ground. Though I'm probably letting the length of the hair stop me from seeing it as a bloke. What do you reckon?'

Jo tilted her head to the side, considered Harry's question as she looked at the slightly raised mound of soil, leaves and twigs before she said, 'My money at this stage would be on a woman. Blonde, obviously. I can't tell much more without disturbing the body, and I need to wait for the others to arrive before I start that. You're the DI, but my starting point would be missing blonde women.'

Harry was well aware of what he needed to do. Something had been niggling at his brain since he'd taken the call from the Force Control Room that morning.

He had a sinking feeling that he knew the identity of the woman lying under a compacted mound of soil, missing some of her digits, with heaven knows what else beneath the surface. That morning's scan of the Missing Persons list had sent a chill down his spine.

Whatever parts of her had been eaten by scavengers and insects was the least of Harry's troubles. He had let this woman down once before; had seen her go to trial for a murder she hadn't committed and, once free, he had failed to protect her.

If Harry wasn't mistaken, the body used to be Jenny Bloomfield, someone his incident room investigated and charged with murder before she walked free from court and straight into her own murder.

CHAPTER SIX

The last year and a half had been trying for DI Harry Powell: his marriage had broken down; his divorce was through; he'd found his friend Linda lying on her kitchen floor, head caved in; and a member of his team had been murdered on duty.

Now it looked as though Jenny Bloomfield's murder was going to bring a shit storm of epic proportions.

'Fucking brilliant news,' muttered Harry to himself as he made his way to Detective Sergeant Beckinsale's office on his way back from dropping the bracelet to the CSI's office for an urgent lab run.

'Want the good news or the bad?' he said as he stuck his head around the door frame to speak to her.

He watched her look up at him: only her eyes moved, and possibly a vein in the side of her head. Though in fairness, it was more of a throb he thought he witnessed as opposed to movement.

After what seemed like minutes, she gave in to his fixed stare, or at least as much as Sandra Beckinsale ever gave in – she raised an eyebrow.

'What I love about you, Sandy,' he said, 'is that you manage to keep your enthusiasm under wraps.'

'As you well know, sir,' she said, 'it's *Sandra*, not *Sandy*, and I guess you're about to tell me about the body that's been found.'

'Either you're psychic or you've seen the CAD too.'

'I looked at the CAD and saw your email telling me you'd already gone out to it. I've stopped a couple of the team from going out on other enquiries in case you need them for a briefing.'

'I'm very grateful,' said Harry, glad that even if she was one of the most miserable individuals he had ever met, she was capable, and took on anything with no complaint, merely a look of disdain.

Harry stepped inside the office, closing the door behind him. He wasn't about to unburden himself to Sandra, yet he had to update her on what he knew, warts and all.

'I've got a bad feeling I know who's lying out in that field,' he said, managing to avoid her eye. 'I think it's Jenny Bloomfield.'

He waited. No adverse reaction.

She reached over for a handwritten green message form.

'I took a call while you were out,' she said, 'and put the details on a green for you.' Sandra pushed the paper across to him and sat motionless while he read it.

'Christ,' he said, 'you spoke to Tanya King, Jenny Bloomfield's daughter.'

Harry took a deep, silent breath and felt his shoulders hunching up to his ears. He would have put good money on hearing the knots in his shoulders tie themselves up.

'We knew that Jenny went missing the day she was acquitted of murdering DI Bowman's wife,' said Sandra. 'You weren't the only one who thought she'd simply legged it.

'Tanya came back from Australia some weeks ago and she's been doing a bit of her own detective work. Somehow she got wind of the body that's turned up this morning and demanded I tell her everything about it. I politely informed her that wasn't going to happen, although I've asked her to come in and speak to me as soon as she can.'

'I'll do better than that,' said Harry. 'I'll go and see her myself. There might be a bit of bad news to break to the family. I'll be the bearer of that.' Harry stood up to go.

'Oh, I nearly forgot,' he added. 'Apparently we're getting a new member of staff we didn't ask for.' Sandra froze, fingers hovering over the keyboard.

'What?' she breathed.

Harry couldn't remember his right-hand woman ever appearing so stuck for words. Often her words were blunt, but never before had he witnessed her struggle to form them.

'A member of staff we didn't ask for?' she repeated, as if saying the sentence again would give it clarity.

'I know,' said Harry. 'I'm hugely suspicious, as every bloody chance I get I ask for money to fund another member of staff, but I may as well be talking to my poxy self.'

He paused, scratched his chin and said, 'I'm either being sent a useless twat or a wrong 'un. With my fucking luck, he's both.'

Harry walked towards his office. He didn't hurry, the toll of the last few months showing more and more each day. It wasn't only the cutbacks and the lack of staff: his incident room had been ripped apart. One of his team, someone under his care, was no longer here.

Harry missed him more and more each day.

And the memories were so painful, not to mention the guilt he felt at letting both a colleague and a friend down.

Sometimes this bloody job simply wasn't worth it.

As he ambled to his boxy office, broken blinds flapping against the grimy window in the breeze, he realised he was mumbling to himself. His girlfriend, Hazel, often scowled in his direction when she thought he wasn't looking. It was only when he caught her head-tilt and the almost imperceptible tightening of her eyes he realised that, once more, he was mumbling and swearing to himself.

What exactly was he supposed to do with a broken fucking major incident room, not to mention a broken fucking team?

A couple of heads jerked in his direction as he passed through the MIR, confirming what he had feared – he was talking out loud.

'Ah, Soph,' he said as he got to his office door and saw one of his DCs loitering in the confines of the corridor. 'Nice that you've taken time out to come and see me.'

He gave her a smile, the best he could manage these days.

She returned it with one almost as pitiful, yet there was something else about her. If he wasn't very much mistaken, she seemed to be blushing, or at least it was a hot flush.

Tactful as ever, Harry said, 'You look a bit red there.

You coming down with something or is it the menop—'

After noticing the look on her face, he considered his next words carefully, and came to the conclusion it would be best if actually there were none. Instead, he gestured towards his office.

She trotted ahead of him, covering the short distance and coming to a stop inside the doorway.

'There's someone here, sir,' she said when Harry was seated. 'Apparently he's new to the team.'

Harry reached up to scratch at an already stubbly chin, facial hair moving faster than his brain.

'He's here already?' he said.

'You're expecting him?'

'I was expecting *someone*,' he said. The look of confusion on Sophia's face had given too much away for the DI's liking. The last thing he wanted was his staff assuming that he had no idea what was going on. They'd already lost enough faith in him.

'Well,' Harry backtracked, 'I was expecting someone *tomorrow*, not today. What's he like?'

He watched Sophia as she smoothed down her skirt and put a hand up to brush away a stray strand of hair. She appeared to become self-conscious of the movement and dropped her arm to her side.

'He seems . . . he seems okay, I suppose,' she shrugged.

Something about Sophia's body language made Harry think there was more to it than she was letting on. If he wasn't entirely mistaken, his DC might be a bit smitten with their newest arrival.

'Best you go and get him, then,' said Harry as he unlocked his computer to find the details of his latest challenge, something he had no time for today.

One thing he did know was that this was going to test what little patience he had left.

CHAPTER SEVEN

'Welcome,' said Harry, a tight smile taking hold of his mouth. Following a brief handshake, he offered his newest detective constable a seat.

Harry tried not to take an instant dislike to the man: first impressions weren't always so accurate.

Dane Hoopman was good-looking, charming, articulate and, as far as Harry could tell, intelligent. So as a man whose complexion made him hide from the sun, who had stubble that had usually advanced across his freshly shaved face by mid-morning, and who'd lost a front tooth to a game of rugby in the 1990s – a match he hadn't even won – Harry was irritated by him.

Consciously, Harry clenched his jaw and ran his tongue along the inside of his veneer. 'I've had a quick look at your short service record,' he said at last, a little more begrudgingly than he had intended.

'Thank you for your time, sir,' said Dane, legs crossed and seemingly relaxed on the first day of a job that, a couple of hours ago, no one in the whole of East Rise Police Station knew about.

'You've taken us by surprise, I have to admit,' said Harry as he pushed back his chair and tried to appear more at ease than he actually felt. 'Deputy Chief Bannister clearly knew you were coming, and it would seem from the email I've just received from HR that they were also aware of your arrival.'

None of this seemed to faze the officer sitting in front of the detective inspector.

'I see you've already worked in a couple of departments,' said Harry, glancing over at his computer screen. 'A number of operations you've been involved with and the various teams you've been a part of all speak positively of you.'

Harry watched him closely: there was something about him he didn't like, but couldn't quite put his finger on. It was probably his own insecurities of late, burdening himself with all that had gone on around him. He was getting older and with it more cynical and jaded. He knew he shouldn't take it out on his new officer.

'That's kind,' said Dane, with what Harry could have sworn was a twinkle in his eye. 'I've really enjoyed my role as a DC and with no family at all or anyone to rely on me, promotion is my aim. I must admit I've always had my sights set on detective inspector; by the time I'm your age, I'd like that to be a possibility.' Harry felt himself bite the inside of his mouth. Normally, he would throw his head back and laugh; share the joke with his audience that he was in fact only fifteen years older. Except he didn't want to share the joke. Not only did Harry not like this imbecile, he didn't want to see the funny side, least of all with him. That had perhaps been the problem of late: too much on his mind and everything weighing too heavily. Whatever it was, his mind was now telling him only one thing – this man was a prat.

'Sorry?' said Dane, forehead creased by a frown.

That surprised Harry: he imagined the newcomer used Botox.

'Sorry? What?' said Harry, worried for a minute that he had actually called him a prat out loud. It wouldn't be the first time he had inadvertently said what was on his mind. He could still remember the trouble he had caused in a Gold Group meeting when 'trawling the ocean bed' had come up on his wank-word bingo card and he'd shouted 'House'. The deputy chief constable had looked very angry.

'Oh, I thought you'd said something,' said the detective constable.

'Perhaps it's my age,' said Harry with a wry smile. 'I'm talking to myself now.

'Anyway, we need to get you introduced to the others on the team; I'll get DS Sandra Beckinsale to do that. She's a decent enough person, bit dry but a bloody good worker. She can get you access to the systems,

HOLMES and all that sort of thing.'

'Keen to get stuck in, but I'm not HOLMES trained.'

'Right. That's going to be a problem, but we can get you access and training later. There's always loads of work, and if you need anything let me or Sandra know.'

Dane clearly took that as his cue to leave and stood up.

'Before you go,' said Harry, 'no one's explained to me why you're here in Major Crime.'

He flashed a smile at Harry and said, 'I asked for an attachment here on my last appraisal, sir. Never thought they'd agree, but here I am.'

'Just one more thing,' said Harry, looking up at this member of staff he knew very little about. 'Anything else I should know? Any problems or welfare concerns?' A grin broke out on the officer's face.

'Nothing at all, sir. An unblemished record. What you see is what you get.'

THEN

Stealing, nicking, choring, whatever you want to call it – I loved it. Why get a job when you can take what you want?

I liked to travel by bus, take in the view, sit at the back and pick out a victim. It wouldn't be long before some confused old coffin-dodger would get on, fumble around with their change and take a seat by themselves.

This particular Wednesday, market day in this one-horse town, I took my seat and didn't have to wait long before I saw the old girl shuffle on, huge shopping bag on one arm, nan bag on the other. That's where she put her purse, inside the nan bag, outside pocket. My job was almost too easy.

I maintained my air of nonchalance, not even giving my target one more glance as I made my way to the door, rang the bell and waited for the stop opposite the Post Office.

As I jumped down, I turned to look in Dixon's window, smiling as I saw her in the reflection struggling to get down the step.

I gave her a tedious three-minute wait until she got across the road and shuffled to the Post Office to get in line and collect her money.

The speed this woman was going, I probably had time for a pint. I glanced across at the pub two doors down from the Post Office. My mouth watered at the thought of a lager, but that would have to wait.

She came out, hairnet and all, and went in the direction of Woolworth's. My favourite shop: it didn't have CCTV and its security guard was not only incompetent but extremely lazy.

My heart surged as she went inside, followed closely by me.

I kept a discreet distance behind her as she made her way to the card section, and I waited patiently while she browsed, picking up card after card and reading every single word.

All the time she was unaware I was getting closer to the pension money inside her unzipped handbag.

I kept my breathing slow and inched ever closer. It was hardly as exciting as pointing a gun in someone's face, but even so, it gave me quite a rush as I bent down to pick out a 'Good luck in your new job' card, my other hand inside her bag.

A few feet along the aisle, a small child was screaming and crying, his mother desperate to placate him. The old woman turned her head to look, giving me the perfect opportunity to grab her purse and slide it inside my jacket.

It felt reassuringly heavy inside my lining.

Pleased I had managed to grab the purse and secrete it in one movement, I congratulated myself on a smooth job as I walked towards the High Street and my well-earned pint.

I liked Wednesdays: most of the old biddies almost burst their colostomy bags to get to the Post Office and to their pensions on Tuesdays, but Wednesdays were much better. The town was busier, and besides, if they could afford to leave it one more day, they didn't need their money as much as I did, did they?

CHAPTER EIGHT

That afternoon, the incident room held the kind of manic that was usual on the first day of a job breaking: Sandra Beckinsale was her own unique mix of terse and blunt, Harry was battling for staff and funding, and the detective constables were torn between a desire to be on a new murder and to continue battling through their existing workload.

Sophia had already made herself available, hoping for all the overtime she could get, and was thinking about who else might be put on the enquiry. Dane Hoopman was new to the team with no apparent workload. It made sense that he would be thrown in at the deep end, and she could act as his lifebuoy.

She gave a little shudder at the thought just as Dane walked through the incident room door.

She watched him scan the room, almost an air of arrogance about him. With his handsome face and what she could only imagine was a toned body underneath the expensive-looking suit, he had every right to appear in control.

First-day nerves clearly hadn't kept him up all night.

The thought of Dane keeping her up all night made her breathe a long sigh, louder than she'd have liked.

'All right there, Soph?' said Tom Delayhoyde from the desk opposite her.

She glanced over at him, momentarily distracted from the current object of her desire, frown creasing her face.

'You want to stop huffing and puffing like that,' said Tom, peering at her over a stack of box files. 'And I'd lay off the gurning at your age too. You can hardly afford any more wrinkles.'

'Fuck off, wank—'

Aware of another presence at the side of her desk, she broke off and looked up into the face of their newest colleague.

'Am I interrupting?' he said, with a smile on his face that Sophia took to be one of bemusement. This wasn't the impression she wanted to make on him. Quite why she wanted to make *any* impression on him, she wasn't yet sure. She wasn't one to have relationships with colleagues: that was a tried and failed method of getting a boyfriend.

Her attraction to him was purely physical, yet it didn't usually take such a firm grip of her emotions. She frequently fancied men she met at work, but never struggled for something to say.

'Dane's talking to you,' said Tom helpfully.

'Sorry, what did you say?' she said, annoyed at herself for behaving like a love-struck teenager.

'I was asking if you can show me Sandra Beckinsale's office, please?' he said, smile still flirting with his face.

Sophia was aware that she was watching his mouth as he spoke. Shaking her head, she said, 'Yes, course I will.'

She pushed her chair back and looked across at Tom, who was staring at her in a worrying way: clearly, she was making a fool of herself.

A sure sign that she needed to get her act together, fast.

'It's down here,' she said, pointing in the direction of the cubbyhole used by three of the detective sergeants. 'I'll show you.'

Very aware that she was in front of him, she wondered if he was checking her out as she walked along the worn corridor, past the ladies' toilets, tiny, filthy kitchen and towards the farthest point of the incident room.

As they approached the door, she called over her shoulder, while attempting to see if he had in fact been watching her. 'Let me know if you're working on the new murder, it'll be a good one to cut your teeth on.'

Once again, Sophia found herself acutely aware of what she'd just said: not everyone shared the same warped sense of judgement as Major Crime when categorising violent deaths.

She stopped at the door, needlessly jerked her thumb in the direction of the sign that read 'Detective Sergeants' and tried to work out his expression.

It wasn't one of horror, so that was a start. If she wasn't mistaken, it was the same amused look that his face had taken on towards her earlier bewilderment and shameful incoherence.

'When I say, "good one",' she said, feeling the need to explain and prolong their conversation, 'I mean that it sounds like an interesting and slightly *unusual* one, so you can get to grips with HOLMES and how everything works.'

He was standing very close; she was sure he had moved towards her and not the other way around.

Expensive aftershave.

'Sophia,' barked Sandra from only a few feet away. 'Bring him in. I've got a briefing in fifteen minutes for this new job. Don't waste your time going to it, you and Dane will be working on something else, though I could do with you both on the murder. Give me five minutes to welcome him and come back with two new investigator's books.'

'I'll leave you to it,' said Sophia, feeling the blush creep up her neck. 'See you in a few minutes.'

She stepped forward, or as forward as she could without walking into him. Instead of going into the DS's office, he moved his shoulder out of the way and twisted his torso so that she had little choice but to brush against him as she made her way back towards the incident room.

That she hadn't imagined.

CHAPTER NINE

'Right then,' said Harry, as soon as everyone was seated in the conference room. 'For those of you who don't know me, I'm DI Harry Powell and I'm the senior investigating officer for this operation.'

He ran an eye over those seated around the table, some brought in from other departments. 'I know that a lot of you have come from elsewhere and have your own workloads you've left behind to be here. We've had to let some of our own staff be released to your departments too, and while it isn't ideal that you won't be working within your own specialist roles, I'm afraid that's the way things are. Thank you for your attendance and continued dedication and professionalism.'

It was all bullshit – they simply didn't have enough officers, so Fraud were working on murder inquiries and Major Crime were working on fraud investigations.

After everyone had introduced themselves, more for each other's sake than anyone else's, Harry got down to business.

'Before we get started on this, a quick update – and thanks for those of you who worked on the kidnap yesterday. The "hostage" – I use the term lightly – was found safe and well.

Safe and well except for the black eye he got from punching himself in the face, taking a photo and sending it to his mum with the message, "If you don't pay £500 into my bank account they're going to seriously fuck me up." He's been charged and remanded for blackmail and his mother's mightily pissed off with him.'

A few laughed and a few tutted at the time and energy they had wasted when they all had work stacking up.

'Getting back to today's business, this morning I went out to the scene where the body, or what's left of one, had been found in a field a few miles from East Rise in Lower Lynton. Early indication is that the body is female – it's badly decomposed, but some clothing and jewellery have been found.'

He paused, gave what was the beginning of an encouraging smile, couldn't find the energy to finish it, and then added, 'We think, but this is not under any circumstances to go outside this room at the current time, that this is Jenny Bloomfield's body.'

Harry once again paused. It wasn't for dramatic effect, but he wanted to let the information sink in. Most of his incident room staff had worked on the murder of former Detective Inspector Milton Bowman's wife, Linda. And each and every officer at East Rise knew that Aiden Bloomfield had been convicted of that murder, while his mother, Jenny, had last been seen walking free from the court after the jury acquitted her.

After he adjusted his tie, blew air through the side of his mouth and couldn't fail to notice the deadpan stares of a few of his staff, he looked down at his iPad and said, 'Sandra is drawing up a list of actions for allocation so please make sure you all know what you're doing. There's an abundance of work to be done, including speaking to Tanya, Jenny's daughter, which I'll be doing myself, but without, at this stage, letting on that we believe we've found her mum. We need to be positive about the identification before we do that, although from the sounds of it she's far from daft and will need to be handled carefully.'

He glanced around the room at his team again. 'It'll probably be another late one tonight while we get some work under way. Our relevant times for verifying movements, CCTV, ANPR, are huge, meaning a lot more work than I'd like. We'll have to go back to the date Jenny Bloomfield walked out of court, right up until the body was found this morning.'

Harry knew this would bring the pains on, but he had no choice.

'The most sensible thing, unless anyone has any other ideas,' he said open-palmed, nodding encouragement to the room, 'is to make the first forty-eight hours after Jenny's disappearance the priority.'

Murmurs of agreement wafted around the table.

'Right then, I'm off to see Tanya King and the rest of the Bloomfield family. I don't expect them to welcome me with open arms, especially as Jenny's been missing for months and they probably feel we've done rock all to find her.'

As the detective inspector *supposedly* rallying the troops, he was aware he was going about it the wrong way.

'I'm going to have to leave you to it,' said Harry. 'DS Sandra Beckinsale's here to sort out the logistics of everything.'

He aimed this last remark at the detective sergeant sitting beside him, who, if she was perturbed at being left in the lurch at the last minute, did not react or show it in any way.

He closed the door on a roomful of people who were now expected to work round the clock if necessary, at least doubling their scheduled hours.

THEN

I waited until dusk – enough light for me to see, but not so much that I could be seen. For several minutes I hung around on the edge of the vandalised kids' park, glancing up at the second-floor flat, double-checking my earlier recces had been worthwhile.

Shitty little council flat in the bad part of town. Neighbours who mind their own business, with no sense of civic duty. Just the way I liked it.

I saw the light go on, movement behind the ill-fitting curtains and the unmistakable flicker of a television screen.

Show time.

I threw my cigarette on the ground among the rest of the litter, stuck my hands inside my jacket and pushed my fingers into the metal knuckleduster.

If he was lucky I wouldn't have to use it, but needs must and all that.

Heart beating a little quicker, I let the wonderful adrenalin rush surge through me as I moved towards the front door.

Fortunately, someone had taken time out of their busy schedule to smash the glass panel, giving me access to the door handle and thus the communal entrance. I was inside in seconds.

The concrete stairway smelled of piss and cannabis. I took them two at a time, finding myself on the second floor and outside of flat number eight right on schedule.

A quick glance towards the only other door on this part of the landing assured me that I wouldn't be disturbed.

I rapped on the door of number eight and stood to the side, counting under my breath, willing the footsteps to hurry.

As he opened the door, the stairwell light timed out, leaving only the weak light from inside the flat.

I swung inside the flat, knocking him to the floor. The last thing I wanted to do was to touch him, but I had to grab his arm to pull him a couple of feet inside so I could get the door shut. Filthy bastard. Smelled like he'd cacked himself too.

'Up', I said. 'Money and drugs, now.'

'What? What dr—'

I didn't have time for this.

As repulsive as he smelled, I leaned down, grabbed him by his greasy cardigan and hauled him to his feet, all five foot five and eight stone of him.

With my free hand, I punched him in the side of the face, a short, sharp connection with his cheekbone.

He cried out, put his hands up to his bleeding torn skin, his bloodshot eyes full of fear.

'I won't ask again.'

The pathetic little man pointed a bony finger towards an open door, edge of a bed visible in the gloom.

Not wanting to give him any opportunity to run for it (unlikely), call the police (*very* unlikely), or pull a weapon on me (laughable!), I dragged him along the nicotine-stained wallpaper to the bedroom.

The entire room reeked of cannabis. My timing, as planned,

had been impeccable: his dealer would have dropped his gear off that morning, meaning a full stash was waiting for me, guarded only by this loser who was off his face.

Pushing him to the floor beside the bed, I grabbed the bags of weed, stuffed them in my pockets and proceeded to empty the nearest drawer from the bedside table.

'Please,' he said, 'don't take my medication.

I've got MS.'

'Tell someone who gives a fuck. Money. Now.'

He pointed to a small wooden set of drawers on the far side of the bed.

Wary that he was slumped between me and the door, I moved around the room, one eye on his now-swollen face.

To my surprise, the drawer contained three rolls of bank notes, each holding a wad of about thirty notes.

I grabbed them, stuffing them inside the front pockets of my jeans, and ran straight out of the flat.

As my feet hit the chewing-gum littered, dog-crap infested pavement, I relaxed and smiled to myself.

Good day's work.

CHAPTER TEN

Sophia was grateful that Dane had offered to drive them to headquarters for their briefing. It gave her time to study him, with little opportunity for him to do the same to her.

He was an extremely good-looking man, yet clearly he knew it.

Her tone remained as matter-of-fact as she could manage as she said, 'So, do you live locally?'

Dane glanced across to look at her, a grin on his face. 'East Rise, born and bred,' he said, before turning his attention back to the road. 'I moved away for a bit, pursued other interests before coming home.'

'Other interests?'

Without taking his eyes off the road this time, he said, 'I outgrew the place at one point, felt I needed to get away, see what the rest of the world had to offer.'

'And?'

'It was interesting, and I can't deny I had fun, but I thought it was time to come home and settle down.'

Sophia felt her heartbeat quicken a little upon hearing this, the now familiar lurch her stomach insisted on doing whenever Dane made remarks he no doubt considered innocent.

'You've still got family here then?' she asked, with as much of an innocent tone to her words as she could muster.

Still studying him, she thought she saw his face darken, his jaw clench, but perhaps that was to do with the stress of heavy traffic as they made their way from the coast towards HQ, Sandra Beckinsale's warning to be on time still ringing in their ears.

'Not any more,' he said, face now unreadable as he turned away from her, peering off to his right, checking for a gap in the steady flow of traffic at the roundabout they'd approached.

Aware that now was probably the time to refrain from asking him any more personal questions, Sophia changed tack.

'I'm not sure why we're going to work on some bloody fraud job while there's a new murder to work on. I can't imagine what the Bloomfields are going through, especially with Jenny's son Aiden in prison. The family – or at least what's left of them – must be so distressed.'

For a few seconds, Sophia thought he hadn't heard her. Before she could repeat herself, Dane said, 'Poor bastard. Poor, poor bastard.'

'Jenny?'

He shot her a withering look.

'No, the son, Aiden. I can't imagine what he'll go through when he finds out his mum's been murdered while he's banged up. It's beyond thinking about.'

A conversation such as this with Tom Delayhoyde, her usual colleague of choice for such enquiries, would have by this stage escalated into a row. Needless to say, it wouldn't have been an argument of any duration and would have most likely ended with Tom apologising and Sophia telling him to 'do one', but this was different.

She wasn't sure how to interpret exactly what Dane meant, and something about the way he said it made her think that perhaps she didn't want to know.

Even so, she wasn't a woman to be stopped in her tracks because someone disagreed with her. Not even when that someone was the best-looking man she had ever seen in the flesh.

'Yes,' she said, somewhat tersely, 'but at least Aiden isn't bloody dead. No, he's incarcerated at His Majesty's pleasure, being fed and housed by an already overworked, underfunded prison service that can barely cope as it is. Just because his mum's been found dead – and we haven't had confirmation it's her – it doesn't mean to say he's innocent or deserving of our sympathy.'

A bemused look appeared on his face as he looked over at her. 'Have I touched a nerve?'

'You could say that,' she replied. 'Sorry, but you weren't here when Harry found Linda Bowman's body. It was a bloody tough murder enquiry, with everyone wondering whether Milton Bowman, one of our own, had killed his own wife, not to mention the ripple effect it had on other officers and the fact their teenage son went to pieces. Life can be bloody unfair.'

He nodded, a slow and measured gesture as if weighing her words carefully. 'Sometimes,' he said slowly, 'life is extremely unfair.'

His words coupled with his expression made Sophia think that there was a story here, something he was reluctant to tell her. Perhaps this wasn't the time. It didn't stop her trying.

'So, what's led you to that conclusion?' A pause, hesitation, possibly annoyance, so she felt compelled to add, 'If you don't mind me asking?'

There was further silence while she inwardly scolded herself for seeming as though she was appeasing him.

Relief hit her when he answered. 'My life hasn't always been, shall we say, *blessed*?' Beautiful deep eyes on her again.

'It's difficult to know what lies behind anyone else's façade,' he said, before turning his attention back to the road. 'Every one of us acts a part, usually more than one depending on the audience. Put simply, Soph, know your audience and you can get away with murder.'

CHAPTER ELEVEN

Harry spent most of the journey to Ron Bloomfield's house muttering to himself, still livid that he had been forced to give up staff to help out the Fraud Department. He was only a couple of streets away when his mobile phone rang.

The name 'Haze' appeared on his hands-free screen and he smiled. Even though, as the senior investigating officer, he had a very important meeting to attend with a soon-to-be-broken family, he wanted to talk to his girlfriend.

'Hi, love,' he said. 'How's your day off going?'

'It's good. How's your day?'

Harry indicated and pulled the car to the side of the road.

'Well,' he said as he gave a long sigh, 'it's been quite a turn-up for the books.'

'That was an extremely lengthy exhalation of breath there.'

'Sorry, darling, been quite a day so far.' He tapped his fingers on the steering wheel. 'We've got a new job in,' he said.

'Okay . . . You going to tell me more or will it wait until tonight?'

'I'm about two minutes' drive away from Ron Bloomfield's house.'

'Christ, H. What's happened to him?'

'Nothing, as far as I know,' Harry said. 'We've found a body. And we think it's Jenny Bloomfield. You remember she was released from court when she was acquitted of Linda's murder? Well, we all thought she'd buggered off with some bloke she'd been shagging. Now, it turns out no one saw her again and it was some time before she was reported as a MisPer by her husband.'

'Want me to come in to work?' said Hazel. 'There's nothing—'

'No, darling, no. You enjoy your day off, besides, you're back tomorrow. Once I'm home, you'll soon tire of me. I'll be bumping my gums about what a day I've had, and you can work some of that Mancunian charm on me.'

'I was calling to see what you fancied for dinner.

What do you want me to do?'

'Eat without me,' he said. 'This could take a while.'

He ended the call and drove towards the Bloomfields' house. When he reached it, he pulled the car over outside the address and walked towards the front door.

He had thought about bringing someone along with him, but this wasn't going to be easy and he saw no reason why another member of his team should be shouted at as well.

He had no more time to think about that before the front door opened to reveal a woman whose world had imploded.

Tanya King's face said it all: anger, despair and hopelessness. Each and every feeling was written on her face.

'Hello,' he said, holding out his warrant card. 'I'm Detective Inspector Harry Powell from Major Crime.'

The broken woman merely nodded at his warrant card and led him into the family home.

Harry followed Tanya into the spacious living room where several other members of the family were waiting. As he entered, they all stared at him. The look was the same: they wanted answers, yet experience told him they wouldn't be any happier once they got them.

No one was going to be able to appease the Bloomfields, who no doubt were seething with the police and everything they stood for at this moment in time. As a professional detective, Harry knew he had his work cut out and would never get them onside. The best he could hope for was co-operation.

The first thing anyone said after Harry had introduced himself to the room hadn't been the opening question he'd expected.

A man Harry placed in his mid-thirties stood to the side of Tanya's armchair, jaw clenched, furrowed brow.

With a strong Australian accent, he said, 'What the fuck are you doing to get my wife's brother out of prison?'

THEN

I was running out of money, so I got to work.

I'd been busy on my evening walks, taking my time and scoping for opportunity.

Here I was, rear of the 1940s semi-detached house, gloved hand reaching over the top of the wooden gate to draw back the bolt before slipping the other side. Without making any noise, I pushed the six-foot-high gate so as not to alert neighbours if they spotted it swinging open.

I ran a well-practised eye over the back of the property, not stepping back too far. You never knew who could be watching from an upstairs window in the adjoining street. It didn't quite have the same nerve-tingling anticipation as strutting into a bank and pointing a gun at someone's head, but it would do. For now.

Needs must, and all that.

The kitchen top window was open a fraction. Wherever possible, I liked to make a discreet entrance: any damage was immediately discovered by frightened, and sometimes furious, owners on their return. I had learned the hard way to keep a low profile.

This house had great potential.

As I looked round the garden for something to stand on, I took in the weeds and general neglect of the place. The back of the house told a very different story to the front.

Perhaps I had this all wrong and there was no money here at all.

I picked up a rusty garden chair, cautious that it would hold my weight, and placed it in front of the kitchen window. Making sure I wasn't about to go through the seat, I climbed on and took a better look at the inside of the house.

The state of the kitchen almost made me gasp. I caught sight of myself in the window, shaking my head slowly.

This was clearly a room that had last seen an update shortly after the war: lurid yellow flowers the size of a newborn adorned the walls, the free-standing cooker, surely a museum piece with its grill at the top, four-ring burner and single tiny oven. The place looked moderately well-kept considering it must have been something like fifty years since it was done up.

Instinct told me to climb down off the chair, go through the gate and forget the place. But something was stopping me.

Old people. And old people usually had loads of cash.

I leaned in through the window and released the catch at the bottom.

The only sound I made was a soft squeak as the sole of my training shoe made contact with the draining board. The only sound I heard was my own breathing.

I crouched on the surface, conscious someone might be home.

Creeping like an actual burglar, I made my way through the kitchen to the hallway. It had a clear plastic runner down its entire length. Something I hadn't seen since I was a child in the 80s, and something I was pretty sure hadn't been manufactured since.

An open drawer caught my eye as I tiptoed along my cheap plastic childhood memory. I opened it to reveal a bank card and seven, no, eight twenty-pound notes. I stuffed the cash into my pocket. The bank card was too risky.

My gloved fingers pulled open the rest of the drawers and cupboards, but there was nothing worth stealing. Disappointed that I was risking so much for a pathetic £160, I froze.

There was definitely someone upstairs moving around.

Well, this house wasn't going to burgle itself.

I took my favourite balaclava out of my pocket, pulled it over my face and headed for the stairs.

CHAPTER TWELVE

Over the years, Harry Powell had broken bad news, been the brunt of families' despair, suspects' anger and been in more volatile situations than he cared to remember. Few came close to the level of hostility that was currently pulsing around Ron Bloomfield's living room.

'You know what my family's been through, do you?' spat Tanya King at him. 'Do you?'

'Yes, I do,' he said, standing in front of her, both of them centre-stage in a macabre theatre of torment neither wanted a starring role in, yet both refusing to back down for wildly different reasons.

'I was the officer who found Linda Bowman's body,' Harry said. He wanted to explain, not make a point, although he saw Tanya's shoulders drop an inch at this. Someone in the room let out an audible breath.

'I wasn't the senior investigating officer on that murder because I was a witness. I knew Linda and her husband.' Tanya kept eye contact with him while rapidly blinking.

'I'm telling you this,' said Harry, as he looked at each of the four people in the room, 'because it's important you understand that we investigated Linda's murder and two people were charged.' He paused.

'Those two people,' he said, now looking straight at Tanya, 'as everyone here knows, were your mother and your brother.'

Shouting broke out among the family, some who had been seated stood up and the angry Australian man took a step towards Harry.

'Enough!' shouted Harry, his face now as red as his hair. 'This is about Jenny, so please listen to what I've got to tell you.'

Ron Bloomfield started to speak, voice almost a whisper.

The Australian opened his mouth to say something.

'Let Dad speak,' said Tanya.

The hush was instant.

'You've found a body . . .' Ron slowly blew the air out of his cheeks, squirmed in his seat. 'Have you found my wife?'

Without being asked, Harry took a seat on the sofa opposite Ron.

'The simple answer is we need confirmation,' said Harry, 'but we have found a body and we believe the body to be a woman.'

Harry turned to his right, addressing the young woman he could now hear blowing her nose.

'You're family too?' he said.

'We weren't related,' she said. 'We were friends for a long time. I'm Cathy Walters. I was at court from time to time. Just wish now I'd have been there for her that last day.'

There was more crying into her tissue.

Once more Harry addressed the family. 'I've seen to it that DNA samples have been taken to the forensics lab as a matter of urgency. They'll then be run through the Missing Persons' Database.'

Harry waited for a second and as Ron opened his mouth to speak said, 'Can I ask, Mr Bloomfield, why you didn't let us know immediately that your wife hadn't returned from Crown Court that day?'

At least he had the decency to avoid looking straight at Harry when he said, 'We . . . er . . . hadn't been getting on too well, and so, I . . .'

'Didn't come to the trial?' asked Harry.

More sobbing and crying.

'Don't you dare upset my dad,' said Tanya, fists clenching and unclenching.

'It would have helped if we'd known straight away that Jenny didn't come home,' said Harry raising his voice. 'You only let us know two weeks after she was last seen leaving court. We've carried out checks on her mobile phone, credit and debit cards and, as you know, they haven't been used.'

'Someone must have seen her,' said Tanya.

Now wasn't the time for Harry to explain that with so many CCTV cameras being lost in the cutbacks and with two weeks wasted, months later they had little chance of ever knowing what had happened to Jenny Bloomfield.

CHAPTER THIRTEEN

Sean Turner had always been ambitious; he simply didn't want to work hard for anything. Becoming a criminal had therefore seemed like natural career progression, only he hadn't expected it to be such hard work.

He came from a long line of people who operated outside of the law: some were alive, some were dead, and some were incarcerated. The most important thing to him was keeping on top of his game and sussing out new ventures. He currently had a couple of very successful enterprises on the go and things were on the up.

The Boundary pub had turned out to be a goldmine. He knew that he could trust Sheila to store the goods, and operating his couriers out of the pub was working like a charm.

'We've got about five minutes until the driver gets here,' said Sean to Milo. In response, Milo used one hand to shove a second bacon sandwich into his mouth and gave Sean a thumbs-up with the other.

'Enjoyed that, then?' said Sean. He didn't wait for a reply before adding, 'I'm going to run upstairs to make sure all's well before we collect the packages.'

'Want me to go, boss?' asked Milo, words partially obscured by the noisy scoffing.

'No, you relax. Let your food go down,' said Sean as he pushed himself off the bar stool. 'Besides, I want to make sure they're all up to speed with what's going on.'

Sean liked to surprise his employees now and again, make sure they were doing as they were supposed to. He paid a reasonable wage, not to mention a little profit-sharing now and again, so he expected a bit of loyalty.

As he made his way through the pub's kitchen towards the staircase, he stopped at the bottom to hear what his three business associates were doing in the living room above the pub. He could hear someone talking, but other than that, silence.

That was a good start.

He crept up the staircase – the old floorboards were creaky, but practice had taught him which steps to avoid. He didn't want to alert them to his approach.

When he reached the closed door he paused again, one hand on the door handle, ear cocked towards the room.

The conversation he heard warmed his heart.

'Hello, there, Mrs Simpson,' said a male voice. 'This is Detective Constable Mark Frinton from East Rise CID. Can I just confirm with you your date of birth, please?' A pause.

'Thank you, Mrs Simpson, that matches the records we've been sent through from your bank about some unusual activity on your account. Now, what . . .'

Sean heard his worker clear his throat before he said, 'I know, I know. That's why I'm calling so that we can sort this out. I work for the Fraud Department and so that I can speak directly to your bank, what I need you to do is confirm which bank and branch you use . . .'

Another pause as Sean opened the door and crept inside.

'DC Mark Frinton' acknowledged him, as did the two women in the room, who smiled.

Sean stood behind his would-be police officer and read the details he'd scribbled down on the pad in front of him.

'Thanks for that,' said 'Mark'. 'Now, before I ask you to read out the long number on your card, I'm going to give you the police CID number for the Fraud Department. Okay, so write this number down and call straight back and ask for Detective Constable Mark Frinton on extension 3838, and they'll put you through to me so you can be reassured you're actually speaking to the fraud team.'

With a smile, Sean wandered over to the table piled high with packages. As he heard the unsuspecting Mrs Simpson hang up the telephone to supposedly dial her local police station, Sean opened a couple of the boxes. Rolex watches peeked back at him.

He glanced around, amused by how gullible people could be as the bogus police officer handed the phone to one of his accomplices. She waited until Mrs Simpson had finished pressing the numbers on her keypad, expecting to connect to the police, but instead, the open line merely put her back through to a shitty little living room above a terrible pub in south-east London.

'East Rise Police,' said the woman now holding the phone. 'How can I help you?'

The simplicity of it was breathtaking, yet more lucrative than selling drugs, not to mention with better clientele.

'DC Mark Frinton, extension 3838,' she said with a well-practised warmth to her voice. 'Yes, madam, he's certainly one of our fraud officers. He's right here on the police system. I'm putting you through now.'

She hit the mute button, handed the phone back to the man

sitting next to her and pulled on a pair of rubber gloves before sifting through the pile of bank cards in front of her.

Sean waited while Mrs Simpson gave her home address, the PIN number of her debit card, confirmed her daily limit and promised to wait in for the courier sent by her 'bank' who would collect the card so that a replacement could be sent out the same day.

Phone call finished, Sean said, 'Nice. Going okay?'

The three nodded enthusiastically until the woman sitting nearest to him, long blonde hair swept into a ponytail, the only one not to have spoken so far said, 'It's only the third one we've managed this morning, though. Two didn't call back and one told us to fuck off.'

The change in tension in the room was immediate. Sean perched himself on the edge of the table, stared at each of them and said, 'Best you all pull your socks up, then. If you don't get on with it and get me ten grand by the end of the day, I can always find you jobs as my couriers.'

No further threat was necessary. Three pairs of worried eyes looked back at him and three heads nodded with more enthusiasm than was necessary.

'Stella,' Sean said to the fake police switchboard operator, 'are those cards you've got there any good?'

'I'm about to bag them up for the next cash-point run,' she said, reaching across for a pile of envelopes, pen at the ready to write the PIN number on the inside flap of the respective envelope. 'He'll be here in five minutes.'

Sean stood up again and walked over to the Rolex watches. Picking one up, he pointed to its face and said, 'Well, he'd better hurry up before these cards are burned. Even old Mrs Simpson isn't so stupid that she'll leave it days before she calls her actual bank.

'Pass me one of those carrier bags, Stella,' he said. 'It's not often I drop by to see you all, but now I'm here I may as well do a bit of shopping.'

He took the rubber glove offered by Stella and picked up six or seven watches, three Mont Blanc pens and threw in a diamond ring for good measure.

With a final glance across the pitiful room, paint peeling from its brown ceiling, a threadbare carpet and £30,000 of fraudulently obtained goods, Sean wished them a lovely day and added, 'Don't forget, I want ten fucking grand by the end of today.'

Several seconds later, Sean was back down in the bar.

'We're off in a second, Sheila, love.'

She stood behind the bar drying her hands on a tea towel. 'Don't forget to give us a kiss goodbye,' she said to Milo.

They made their way to each other across the ten feet or so of unpolished, dusty wooden floor, Sheila now with the tea towel over her shoulder and Milo with his arms out.

'Fuck's sake, you two,' said Sean as he headed for the door, 'it's like a poor man's *Love Island* in here. Pack it in.'

He unbolted the door and looked cautiously out into the street. It didn't pay to attract attention to the place, and it certainly didn't much lure in paying clientele, even when it was supposed to be officially open.

'Motor's here,' shouted Sean over his shoulder, no desire to look round and see the antics going on. 'Take this carrier bag and see you in the car.'

He walked out and jumped into the front passenger seat of the black Mercedes.

'Silly bollocks'll be out in a moment,' said Sean to the driver as they sat, hazard lights blinking, driver tapping his fingers on the steering wheel.

Milo climbed in the back and earned himself a glance from Sean.

'I take it after all that bloody nonsense you at least managed to pick the carrier bag up?'

'Course,' said Milo.

'You're going to have a busy couple of days knocking that lot out,' said Sean.

Milo opened the bag, rummaged around and pulled out a small black box. He gave an appreciative whistle as he set eyes on the diamond looking back at him.

'Nice,' he said, 'and worth a fortune.'

'It is,' said Sean, 'and I know the perfect buyer.'

THEN

Knives, I liked knives. The blade was always the understated means of frightening the absolute fuck out of someone, and so nice and quiet.

In a quintessentially English village, there was nothing quite like a rural, isolated Post Office. There was nothing quite so bloody vulnerable either.

I couldn't risk getting the bus to this one, as its far-flung location meant there was only one every hour. Someone would remember me.

Instead, I drove to a nearby lane, jumped out of my car and changed over the number plates with a set I'd nicked that morning from a car at the train station.

Keeping my breathing steady, palms sweating a little more than I'd have liked – knives were so up-close and personal, downside being I had to touch people – and I was ready.

The feel of the mask in one jacket pocket and the serrated hunting knife in the other made my heart rate soar as I drove back towards the Post Office.

The glass-fronted shop told me that it was empty, all except the middle-aged woman arranging copies of *My Weekly* and

The People's Friend, blissfully unaware of what was about to happen.

Perhaps it was time for a real challenge.

Still, I parked a few feet from the door so I was out of her immediate eye-line, pulled the Halloween mask over my face and burst through the front door, knife held out in front of me.

She screamed, naturally.

I smiled, although it was wasted as she couldn't see my face behind the devil's mask. She could, however, see the glint of the blade.

'Money, now,' I shouted.

She froze, started to say something.

'Fucking now,' I hollered, making a grab for her putrid mustard jumper and almost lifting her off her feet towards the counter.

'Timer,' she stammered as she tried to turn her head to look at me.

'Eyes front,' I said, losing it with her now. How long did she think I had?

'It's on a timer,' she rasped as I dragged her behind the counter towards the safe.

'Open it,' I said, knife at her throat.

'Please, please,' she said as she felt the metal threaten to pierce her skin. 'It's on a timer and won't open until my husband comes down this afternoon.'

'Till, till,' I said, unable to believe that she'd risk having her neck sliced open for money that wasn't hers, although annoyed that this wasn't going the way I'd wanted.

Her fat little fingers frantically pressed the buttons to open the till drawer behind the completely redundant security glass.

It opened to reveal about four hundred pounds. At this rate, I'd be doing this again in a day or two.

It was probably time to go back to burglaries.

CHAPTER FOURTEEN

The motorbike courier knocked on the door, gloved fist banging on the glass.

The occupant, Mrs Simpson, a woman in her late fifties, got up from her kitchen table, hands shaking slightly as she walked towards the tall figure casting a shadow into her hallway.

Everything in the house, including the house itself, was bought and paid for after her husband died, leaving her comfortable but heartbroken.

She was still in the grieving process, which was probably why she'd been caught off-guard when she answered the phone to DC Mark Frinton that morning.

Another rapping on the door as she moved towards it, the outline of a motorcycle helmet clear through the frosted pane.

She picked up the envelope containing her bank card from its place on the occasional table by the front door.

With a deep breath, she opened the door and attempted a smile at him.

The man standing in front of her was dressed in black, the black motorbike helmet only letting her see a flash of his white, youthful face. Their eyes met for the briefest period before he took the padded envelope, stuffed it inside a bag he wore across his chest and strode away towards his motorbike.

Heart pounding in her chest, Mrs Simpson watched him drive down the street before closing the front door. The relief was too much, and as she steadied herself against the table, the two detective constables who had been waiting upstairs ran down to catch her before her knees buckled under her.

'Come and sit in the kitchen,' said one of them.

'You did brilliantly,' said the other.

Mrs Simpson looked up into their concerned faces, hands supporting her as they guided her back into the kitchen.

'Is there anyone we can call for you?' said the younger of the two men. 'You look a little shocked by this and I don't want to leave you here on your own.'

She felt the sting of tears form in her eyes and searched her trouser pockets for a tissue.

'My kids will think I'm a stupid old woman for falling for that phone call this morning,' she said, unable to stop herself from crying.

'No, they won't,' said the older one. 'Firstly, I reckon they'd be more annoyed that you didn't want them here. Secondly, what'll make them proud is that you quickly recognised it as a scam and called your bank, cancelled the card and dialled 999.'

The three of them sat in the kitchen, a ticking clock and restrained crying the only sounds for several seconds.

'I know you've explained this once,' Mrs Simpson said, 'but what happens now?'

'The courier is only a small part of it all,' said the older police officer. 'To tell the truth, we're not all that interested in him. We follow him and he leads us to whoever's behind this.'

'How often do you catch the people behind it all?' she asked as she dabbed at her eyes. Even through the tears, she couldn't fail to notice the looks the policemen exchanged.

'In all honesty, Mrs Simpson, not that often.'

CHAPTER FIFTEEN

Dane had been noticeably quiet since they'd walked out of the Fraud Department's briefing at HQ. Sophia had driven them back to East Rise in near silence, the couple of attempts at conversation being stifled by her colleague's refusal to be drawn into talking to her.

As she reversed into a parking space at the police station, she suddenly felt a bit sorry for Dane. He didn't have much service in the police, was one of the 'new breed' of fast-track detectives, and was probably feeling way out of his league.

'Are you okay?' she asked him as he went to open the door as soon as the car had come to a stop.

He gave a shrug. 'I thought I was coming here to work on murders and I feel as though I've been shafted with some bloody telephone scam crap just to keep the new boy out of the way.'

'Aren't you forgetting something?' she said, edge to her voice she hadn't intended.

He paused, the door open an inch or so. 'Sorry, sorry,' he said. 'And you've been even more stitched up by babysitting the newbie.'

Sophia laughed, and then said, 'I'm sorry, but you do look very pissed off. It's not ideal for me either, you know, but at least it's something different.'

Dane threw himself back into his seat, ran his hands through his hair and said, 'But why all the mystery? That briefing was pointless. We don't even know where the target premises are, they didn't even seem to know the names of the people behind it all. It was less of a briefing and more of a game of Guess Who?'

'Look,' she said, 'fancy grabbing a coffee and talking it through? Fraud's something I'm not too familiar with either. After ten years at Major Crime it's hardly my area of expertise, but whatever we're investigating, the process is very similar.'

He looked over at her, hands now down on his thighs. He gave her a smile and said, 'Better than that. How about a proper drink? On me to say thank you for showing me around today and putting up with my crappy mood.'

'You're on,' she said. 'I'll just take my paperwork and the car keys back to the office.'

'Would you mind taking my notebook too?' he asked. 'I need to make a quick call before I leave.'

It seemed unreasonable to say no. Sophia was, after all, about to go back inside the building, yet she would have thought he'd want to say goodbye to his new colleagues in the office on his first day.

He smiled again. It reached his eyes.

She took the book he held out to her and walked back inside the police station while he stayed in the yard, mobile clamped to his ear.

It wasn't a date, she knew that, yet it had been over two years since someone had last taken her out for a drink. Perhaps it was about time she got over her terrible break-up and got on with life. Shaking her head at the memory of the screaming and shouting when it had finally all gone wrong, Sophia swiped her card at the scanner and let herself into the office. What exactly had she been doing in such a dire relationship?

She wandered along the corridor to the banks of desks, said goodbye to the couple of people still around, threw the paperwork on her desk and hung up the car keys on their hook.

Dane was good-looking, seemed bright and had a steady secure job. It appeared foolproof. She might even enjoy herself and have a few drinks.

Sophia made a detour to the ladies'. As well as wanting to brush her hair, reapply her foundation and a spray of perfume, she wanted to make sure her almost-to-its-limit credit card was tucked safely inside her warrant card.

It wasn't much use, yet she didn't want Dane to pay for the drinks if they stayed for more than one.

She checked her appearance in the mirror, looked herself in the eye and muttered, 'Don't sleep with him on the first date. You've waited over two years to have sex, so another month won't matter.'

One final glance in the mirror and Sophia walked out of the toilets and to the car park in search of Dane.

He wasn't there.

For a second she wondered if he'd gone back inside after all, but dismissed that as he had no reason to. The yard was a reasonable size; it held over fifty vehicles when full, yet she could see pretty much all of it, and it was empty of people.

Sophia took her phone out to ring him and then thought better of it. If he'd disappeared, she most certainly wasn't going to run after him. She might not have been on a date for a very long time, but she wasn't about to be treated like this.

She'd walked to work that morning to save herself both petrol and parking costs, so the twenty-five-minute walk home would do her good. By the time she arrived home, she would have worked off her anger. To think she had actually felt sorry for the prick.

Letting herself out of the side security gate, Sophia glanced up and down the road.

Dane was leaning against a wall, watching her.

There was no smile, no attempt on his part to make his way to her from across the street.

For a moment, she thought about turning and going straight back inside, or just walking home.

'Well?' she shouted at him, anger showing in her voice, irked that he had made her so furious. 'Are we going for a drink or not?'

She knew he could hear her. Even though they were on separate sides of the street, not only was she hollering at him, there was no traffic, no background noise and he was looking straight at her.

When he pointed to his ear, shrugged and said, 'What?' it was the final straw.

Fuming, she turned and walked back towards the rear gate of the police station, scrabbling in her handbag for the security pass she'd had in her hand only seconds ago.

Sophia's offended senses blocked out the sounds of Dane's heavy footsteps as he raced across the road towards her.

Hand briefly touching her shoulder, not to stop her from leaving, just letting her know he was there, he said, 'Sorry, Soph, I really am. I've got a terrible sense of humour and I'm messing this up. One more chance?'

She turned to look at him, then indicated they move to the farthest point of the pavement away from the police station's public entrance.

'Listen, arsehole,' she said. 'I do not need the likes of you dicking me around, okay? I'm tired. I work long hours and if you want to go for a drink, that's fine, but don't for one second think that pissing me about like some bloody love-struck teenager is going to either ingratiate me into your heart, or anywhere else for that matter, or make me want to work with you ever again.'

On a roll now, she saw the start of a smile appear at the corner of his mouth, so carried on. 'Don't try to mug me up, and definitely don't laugh at me or I'll have your bollocks on a spike. Good-looking you might be, but it doesn't make you any less of a wank-stain.'

She paused, more for breath than effect.

'Firstly,' he said, 'I'm so sorry. Secondly, drinks are on me, plus cab fare home. Thirdly, no one's ever called me a wank-stain before, so shall we celebrate that with shots?'

Sophia looked away, her turn to hide the start of a smile.

'You'd better be sorry, good you're paying, and finally, Jäger bombs, and I know just the bar.'

Ensconced in a booth at the back of Sophia's favourite bar – and the only one in East Rise that made anything like authentic cocktails – she watched Dane order their drinks. Downing shots with him was not going to be her most sensible move, but it was one she knew, with a sigh, was inevitable.

True to his word, Dane bought the first round and came back with a tray containing four shots and a jug of lager.

'Who else is coming?' she asked.

'Thought you might want to pick which one you want, you know, so you don't think I've spiked any of the shots. The ones you don't want, I'll drink first.'

'Bloody hell,' she said. 'It's not hard to tell you're a copper. Worked on many rapes, have you? The only blokes who'd think like that are police and sexual predators.'

'How do you know I'm not both?'

'You probably are.'

He shifted over to her in the booth, propped his elbow on the back of the seat and said, 'Seems a bit dangerous to come for a drink with me in that case.'

'It's always a good idea to get to know your colleagues,' she said, lowering her gaze to the tray of drinks. 'You can have that one and I'll have this one. You go first.'

Dane grabbed hold of the glass, lifted it to his mouth and downed it.

She watched him lick his lips before she took her turn.

'Lager?' he said.

She shook her head and picked up another shot. And then the fourth.

'You're buying, right?' she said. 'But prosecco now, please. I don't want to get too drunk. I've got work in the morning.'

Once again, she watched him walk to the bar, a warmth spreading throughout every part of her body. She was pretty sure it wasn't caused by the alcohol.

THEN

The risk that came with holding weapons to people's heads in banks was putting me off. Technology was starting to improve and the financial world was getting wiser in its attempt at protecting itself, and – just as annoyingly – at alerting the police. Even they seemed to be getting their act together. I wasn't sure what to make of it all, so until something else came up, houses it was.

Even though breaking into houses didn't give me the same thrill as armed robberies, it was a safer option.

As much anguish as it caused me to admit it, I loved being armed. Why wouldn't I? I went from *being* the most important person in the room to everyone else *knowing* that I was the most important person in the room.

Kudos.

It wasn't all about that, of course: it was also about the money.

I could make a few thousand from an armed blagging, yet the risk was great. I wasn't entirely stupid – get caught with a gun and the result was going to be a lengthy stretch. Going to prison didn't frighten me, but I felt too much pride at knowing I hadn't, as of yet, got caught. That was the main thing.

An unblemished record.

The thought made me smile as I sauntered along the side of the faux-country house, which tried to give off the impression that it was a stately building, but had all the hallmarks of being designed by someone with more money than taste.

With minimum effort, I was over the fence running side-on to the eyesore of a house, and into the garden. It was already getting dark and I had seen the young couple go out some time ago. My recce meant that I knew they lived alone, didn't have a dog and the burglar alarm could be overcome in seconds. Besides, the house was in the middle of nowhere.

Something told me this was going to be very lucrative.

Five minutes later, having found a ladder in the unlocked shed – *careless* – I had sprayed foam into the alarm box, propped the ladder next to an open bedroom window and was about to make my big entrance.

All without breaking a sweat.

I literally shimmied up the metal rungs of the ladder, lifted the window and stuck my head through the gap.

Holding my breath, I listened.

Nothing.

All I could hear was my own heart thudding. It was still exciting, even if I didn't get off on it as much as waving a weapon around.

Deciding it was now or balance precariously on a ladder all night, I squeezed a shoulder through and leaned down to grab the handle on the larger of the windows.

For a minute it didn't budge, and I had visions of running back down the ladder and smashing a panel in the kitchen door.

My panic was short-lived, however, as the handle turned and the window opened.

It took another minute or so of manoeuvring myself a few rungs down so I could get inside the bedroom, dirty footmarks on the windowsill, probably on the floor too as I dropped to the thick carpet.

It wasn't to my taste, none of the decorations of the vast house were, but I could tell expense when I saw it.

This was clearly a guest room and not where the good stuff would be.

I made my way from room to room, confident that turning on lights with my gloved hand would not attract attention from non-existent neighbours.

Then I hit the jackpot. A study with a safe.

Usually I wouldn't waste my time with a safe. I had neither the skills nor the equipment to break into one.

What I did have, however, was a tremendous amount of luck: the key was in the lock.

I tiptoed across to the safe – quite why I felt the need to in an empty house, I couldn't fathom – and I turned the key then the handle.

Still unable to believe my good fortune, I doubted there would be anything inside.

Some days, it felt good to be so wrong. Piles and piles of cash sat in front of my eyes. Mostly fifty-pound notes, along with stacks of twenties and, as if an afterthought, a handful of tenners thrown in for good measure.

I sat on my haunches, gloved fingertips drumming the side of my head.

I was torn, *so* torn: if I took the lot, I was probably looking at £250,000. The problem was, I didn't think I could carry it to the car hidden about a mile away. I'd need to grab some bags, or possibly even pillowcases to put it all in, but then the risk of being seen would increase enormously.

For a second, I played along with this fantasy in my head, and then I did the sensible thing.

Grabbing a couple of bundles of the fifties and five bundles of the twenties, I estimated that I had about £50,000 or so.

My hand hovered over the remaining wads of cash. This was the big one – I knew it. And it wasn't that I had any qualms about taking money from the smug prick who owned this monstrosity if I thought for one foolish minute that I might get away with it. If I was a desperate man, he might even be the sort of person I'd think of working with. Whatever he was up to, it was lucrative, and I wouldn't mind being in on it.

The desk next to the safe was probably worth more than all the money in my one-bedroomed flat. He might not even miss the money.

I was sweating like a bastard now and I badly needed to piss.

Getting away from here and hoping that my exploits remained undiscovered was never going to work, even if I retraced my steps and made it look as though I hadn't actually got inside. The owners would know I'd foamed the alarm.

I didn't have time for this. I knew the chinless wonders who lived out here in the middle of nowhere wouldn't be home for hours, but I needed people to see me miles away. It paid to be cautious. It was why I was good at this.

Fifty grand would suit me just fine, for now anyway.

I crammed the cash inside my jacket and decided to run down to the front door and leg it. It seemed an easier option than trying to climb back down the ladder, especially with my pockets bulging with cash.

For caution's sake, I stuck my head out of the study and waited. Just to make sure.

So far, so good.

I got to the top of the stairs, appreciated the ornate wooden balustrade and polished escape route, barely had time to run an eye over the portrait of the couple whose money I had just stolen and made it to the door.

On full alert, I heard a car in the distance.

I froze with my hand on the front door.

Did I open the door and dare that, in the cover of darkness, even if my luck had now run out and this was the early return of the owners, I could still make it into the shadows and to safety?

It had to be worth it, and I had surprise on my side.

Only flaw in my plan – the door was locked.

The headlights shone straight at me through the glass window, causing me to duck. I frantically looked up and down for a key, a bolt, anything to unlock the fucking door.

Then I remembered, I'd left the lights on upstairs. I figured I had only a minute before they came through the front door.

I wasted valuable seconds in the hallway as the car's headlights lit up the staircase. There was only one option left to me: go back out the way I'd come in.

I took the stairs two at a time, grabbing at the handrail, woollen glove failing to get any purchase from the polished surface, but wanting to steady myself. If I fell, I was going to prison, or possibly worse.

The kind of person who kept a quarter of a million in their home wasn't an average person.

Racing up the stairs to the back bedroom, I thought about whose house this actually was. I had no doubt bitten off more than I could chew.

For a spilt second I hesitated at the doorway, unsure whether to turn the lights off, but I dismissed it as a bad idea. They might just assume they had left them on before they went out for their somewhat brief soiree.

I ran across the room to the still-open window, prayed that

neither of them would go straight to the back of the house, put the downstairs light on and see the ladder against the wall.

Knowing I had only a few seconds now, I climbed up onto the windowsill, made a grab for the ladder and froze.

I could hear a key in the front door, then voices.

'Why 'asn't the alarm come on?' said a cockney-accented man.

Fucking great – a gangster.

'Christ if I know,' said the female equivalent. 'Did you set it?'

'Of course I set it. You watched me do it.'

The voices were carrying up the hallway, across the bedroom to where I stood perched on the windowsill, one hand on the ladder, the other on the window.

It was now or never.

He knew he had a ridiculous amount of cash in his safe, and I knew he would go straight for it.

I all but threw myself out of the window, clambered down, missing out rungs as I went, chancing that I wouldn't break an ankle as I jumped the last four feet into the darkness.

That was when they grabbed me.

CHAPTER SIXTEEN

The bar was getting busy and Sophia and Dane no longer had a quiet corner all to themselves. Other drinkers were encroaching on their space, meaning that when Dane tried to ask her something, he had to lean across and put his mouth to her ear.

A shudder ran through her as he touched her.

'Shall we get out of here?' he said. 'Get something to eat.'

She felt herself nod without really thinking it through. Food would do her good, not to mention prolonging the time she got to spend with Dane.

He stood up and cut a path through the throng towards the door. Twice he glanced back to make sure she was making her way out of the crowd. When he reached the door he held it open and waited for her to step outside.

'Still my treat,' he said. 'Where do you want to go?'

She swayed a little in the cool evening air, aware she was probably about to slur her words.

'This time of night we'd be lucky to get anything,' she said, now over-enunciating every syllable.

'Come on,' he said, 'we'll find somewhere open.'

After twenty minutes of wandering around and finding

places were either full, about to close for the night or looked a bit of a health hazard, they opted for two portions of chips from a roadside van and wandered in the direction of the beach.

The two inebriated off-duty detectives sauntered along the pebbles towards the sea, away from all signs of life.

'I don't want to walk much further,' she said, unsure now that she stood with her cooling chips in her hand, looking across to where France was supposed to be. She'd be damned if she could find it after four shots, two large beers and glasses of prosecco she hadn't been sober enough to count.

'Hold these,' said Dane as he passed her his chips and took off his jacket. He placed it on the pebbles and held out a hand as he clumsily sat down.

'Not the most comfortable of places, but at least we can have a conversation without someone being able to overhear us.'

Her head turned sharply towards his voice; she was unable to see his features clearly in the gloom.

'That sounds a bit paranoid,' was the only thing she could think of to say.

'I really didn't want to end up on the beach with you,' he said. 'When I thought how tonight might have gone, it was going to be nothing like this.'

'What were you expecting? This is East Rise not the West End of London. It's pretty slim pickings here on a Tuesday night at ten o'clock.'

'It's not where I thought we'd end the evening.'

Sophia was only aware that her legs had started moving of their own accord when she heard the sound of her feet losing their purchase on the pebbled beach.

'Are you all right?' he asked as he put out a hand to steady her.

She handed him back the two packets of chips and lowered herself down on to the shingle, the noise giving away that she was finding it more difficult and a lot less elegant than she would have liked it to be.

At least in the gloom he couldn't clearly see her ungainly descent.

She heard the clear signs of Dane sitting down beside her on the makeshift blanket. From the lack of body heat, she guessed that he was moving that bit further away.

'Your chips'll be getting cold,' he said as he held one of the bundles, white paper the most defined part of his movements.

'Thanks,' she said, resisting the urge to cram a handful into her mouth so she could ask him a question.

'Why did you come here?' she said.

There was a rustle of paper, then a waft of salt-and vinegar-soaked chips.

'To eat these,' he said.

'No, you cretin,' she laughed. 'I mean East Rise nick. Why here? Why now?'

'More a case of being sent here. I'm new and it seems a bit of a project to keep posting the fast-track detectives in all sorts of departments under the guise of development. Major Crime seemed a natural progression. And, of course, there was a vacancy.'

'Pierre,' she said to herself.

'What?'

'Never mind,' said Sophia. 'We lost an officer and it seemed to set in motion a kind of mass exodus.'

'Oh, I'm sorry. Were you close?'

'Not really, but he was a lovely guy. It's always tough when someone you saw every day simply isn't there anymore.'

'How did he die?' said Dane. 'If you don't mind me asking.'

Sophia found she was holding her breath, and then said, 'He was murdered. On duty.'

She heard the shifting of pebbles again and heard a change in his voice – a tone to it that hadn't been there before.

'Must have been devastating for you all, especially Harry.'

Sophia hesitated then, the breeze and strangeness of the situation sobering her up and sharpening her senses. It struck her as an odd remark to make.

'Why did you mention Harry?' she said after a considerable silence. 'He didn't have anything to do with it. It wasn't his fault.'

'I didn't say it was,' said Dane. 'Last thing I was suggesting was that he was to blame, but he's the detective inspector and it's his incident room. He must have felt responsible, whatever his actions, not to mention that every member of his team looks up to him as their boss.'

Sophia wasn't sure if it was the cool evening breeze rolling over her or something else.

Dumping her chips on the pebbles, she pushed herself to her feet.

'We've got an early start, Dane. I'll see you in the morning.'

The noise she made as she scrambled back towards the promenade coupled with her fury meant it was impossible for her to hear whether Dane made any effort to call her back or simply let her walk away.

CHAPTER SEVENTEEN

WEDNESDAY 6 MAY

The atmosphere in the incident room at East Rise had not been anything resembling normal for some time, and this particular morning it was more strained than ever.

Sophia wasn't used to having to wonder whether she should talk to her colleagues or ignore them: usually she either chatted or got her head down when the work required her undivided attention. Today, she was unnaturally quiet, something that Hazel Hamilton seemed to home in on straight away.

'You've not said much this morning, Soph,' she said from her desk across from Sophia's.

'Everything okay?'

'I'm fine, thanks, Haze,' she smiled back.

'Did you have a late night?'

Sophia's head snapped up from the statement she was pretending to read that was clutched in her hand. 'Why do you say that?'

As soon as the words were out, she recognised how they sounded. So much for trying to play last night's antics close to her chest. She was going to give herself away at this rate.

'No reason,' said Hazel, a frown creasing her forehead. 'You don't seem to be yourself, that's all.'

Hazel glanced around the room, lowered her voice and said, 'And I wasn't sure how pairing you up with the new guy was going to go down. What do you make of him?'

With a shrug, Sophia said, 'He was reasonable company, although he seemed a bit put out to be working on a fraud investigation. He clearly expected Major Crime to be a bit more glamorous.'

As Hazel opened her mouth to say something else, Harry appeared in the incident room, coffee mug in hand.

'Where's Dane?' he asked as he scanned the blank faces of his team.

No one answered; no one wanted to admit that the new boy was late on his second day.

The door from the main part of the station opened, and all heads turned towards the noise of someone making an entrance, two boxes of Krispy Kreme doughnuts held aloft.

'Really sorry I'm late,' he said. 'As I was running a few minutes behind schedule anyway and knew I'd need to make amends with doughnuts, I thought I might as well do it in style and stop and get the good stuff.'

He offered the room a glimpse at his wares and smiled in Sophia's direction, an action that didn't escape Harry's notice.

Dane balanced the boxes on the edge of a free desk and said, 'I'll get a round of drinks in then. Who wants what?'

The silence was broken by the stampede of officers hoisting their cups on to the table next to the sugary snacks, unable to turn down the chance of not only having someone make them a hot drink so early in the day, but bringing them the staple food of all police stations.

'When you've done that, Dane,' said Harry, 'would you and Soph come through to my office for a minute, please?'

'Thanks, you two,' said Harry when the three of them were settled in his office. 'Events of yesterday pretty much superseded any chance I had of speaking to you at length, Dane. I know it's far from ideal that you're both working with an entirely different department and have been roped in to help Fraud, but it's out of my hands.'

There were a couple of seconds before anyone spoke.

'Can't say it's not a huge disappointment to feel as though I've missed out on working on a murder, sir,' said Dane. 'Sophia's been a great help though.'

Sophia felt as though her cheeks were on fire and prayed that the air of nonchalance she was adopting was working, although she severely doubted it.

'We've been briefed about the job and have to get back to HQ today,' she said, wanting to steer the conversation away from any potentially dangerous mention of their late-night drinking, or the fact she'd stormed off at the end of the night. 'We've been given this morning to sort anything before we're loaded up with work. There are some early-morning warrants across the county, arrests, that sort of thing we'll be helping out with.'

'Okay,' said Harry. 'Don't forget that if you need anything give me a call. I wasn't keen to give up any staff, but I had no say in it. So thank you for going along without complaint.'

'By the sounds of it,' said Sophia, 'I think we'll be working with them for a few weeks. Unless, of course, you can pull any strings?'

He smiled at them both and said, 'I'll do my best, but I think anything I have to say will fall on deaf ears. That's about it unless you've anything else you want to raise?'

They both shook their heads at him then got up to leave.

Dane indicated to Sophia that she should go first, but as she reached the door, he said, 'Oh, there was one other thing, sir.'

She hesitated in the doorway and Dane said, 'It's okay, Soph, nothing for you to worry about. I'll catch you up.'

Despite feeling a little perturbed at her dismissal, she stepped into the corridor as Dane reached across and pulled the door to behind her. Curiosity made her want to stay and hear what they were talking about through the paper-thin walls. Manners stopped her, so she ambled back to her desk to gather her paperwork for the day ahead.

A few minutes later, she watched Dane and Harry walk into the incident room, side by side, sharing a joke about something. Last night, Dane's opinion of Harry hadn't been a very positive one, so the camaraderie struck her as somewhat false.

She dismissed her own thoughts as nothing more than a product of her hangover, hunger and annoyance that she had ended up spending money on a cab home. A fare she could ill afford.

Even so, she watched Dane as he chatted to Harry: he was full of smiles and nods in the right places, yet there was something calculated about his demeanour.

Sophia had been a police officer for nearly half her life and she was used to seeing the worst in people.

Surely that was what she was doing now? The self-preservation thing she had so easily taken to over the last couple of years. That skill she'd developed of avoidance every time a man talked to her, tried to get to know her. Somehow she would always find a way to convince herself not to get involved.

Perhaps it was time for her to put those feelings aside and take a risk.

Dane threw his head back and laughed at something Harry said that Sophia couldn't hear from where she was. From the shaking of Harry's shoulders and the mirth on his face, he was clearly sharing the joke. Something that she rarely saw him do since Pierre had been killed.

There was a chance that Dane wasn't such a terrible risk to take after all.

THEN

First rule of waking up in an unknown location, when the last thing you remember is being grabbed and knocked unconscious, is surely, try not to move and pretend to still be unconscious.

'Wakey, wakey, you fucking maggot,' said a voice close to my ear as I lay on the concrete.

Keeping still earned me a kick in the ribs. I winced and opened my eyes.

The light made me want to shut them again, and they probably would have remained that way had it not been for the bucket of cold water tipped over my head.

Forcing myself to sit upright, despite the pounding in my brain and the urge to vomit, I took in my surroundings. A set of concrete stairs to the right of me led to what I guessed was the ground floor of a house. I hoped that a house was a good sign rather than a lock-up or disused remote building somewhere, which would surely have meant that I wasn't getting out alive.

In the meantime, two enormous heavies, pumped up on steroids by the looks of their terrible skin and lack of neck, stood between me and the stairs.

Not to mention the further problem who stepped out of the

shadows straight in front of me – the bloke whose house I had just broken into.

From the self-indulgent portrait in his hallway, I recognised him straight away.

'Oh,' I said.

'Oh, indeed,' he replied. 'This is what we in the business call a little bit of a clanger.'

'Business?' I said in a voice I hoped wasn't giving away my fraught nerves.

'The family business,' he said. 'The type that makes problems disappear.'

He left the words hanging there.

I needed to talk myself out of this one, or a sore head and boot to the ribs were going to be the least of my problems.

I looked up at him from the floor, moved back against the wall, and with as much casualness as I could muster, I rested an elbow on my bended knee. It was now or never. 'When it comes to stealing, I've got a very good set of skills. How about I work for you?'

His face instantly took on a frown. From the corner of my eye I saw his two musclemen's shoulders tense.

'We caught you escaping,' he said. 'Clearly you're not that skilful.'

He started to turn away from me, and with a nod in my direction said to his minders, 'Deal with him.'

'Wait,' I said, instantly regretting it as he paused and with a swift change in direction, reached for my throat, strong fingers cutting off my air supply.

'*Wait?*' he said, specks of spit hitting me in the face.

I tried to prise his hands off me, but the lack of oxygen was making me panic. I was going to die here in his cellar. The blackness started to creep in on the sides of my vision.

I was taking greedy gasps of stale air. Then I realised my

own hands were on my bruised neck, trying to convince my brain that the danger had passed.

He stood over me. 'You've got some fucking nerve breaking into my home then asking for a job.'

'What if I told you that I could provide you with very useful information about all sorts of criminal activity,' I said, watching his reaction. 'Not to mention allowing you to stay one step ahead of the police?'

'I haven't got all day.'

I was trying to think fast. I gave it my best shot.

'I've got a job interview for a CCTV operator,' I lied. 'Once I get the job, I pass along all you need to know about black spots and who's doing what in your town.'

He threw his head back and laughed. The sound died in the cold basement, which was exactly what was going to happen to me if I didn't think fast.

'That's only the start of it,' I said. 'I've been avoiding getting myself nicked for years.'

He had no idea if I meant it or not – that was clear from his expression. My heart rate quickened as he took a step towards the stairs. It was back to me now.

For one second, I thought he was going to leave me down there with four steel-toe-capped boots for company.

With a glance over his shoulder, he called out, 'Come on then, let's hear the rest of your plan. If I'm not happy when you're done, *you* won't be happy when I'm done.'

I nodded at the gargoyles and followed him out of the basement into his house.

CHAPTER EIGHTEEN

EVENING OF WEDNESDAY 6 MAY

A large part of Harry's day had been taken up by meetings explaining to senior management where the murder enquiry was heading and, of course, asking for more funding and staff.

He flicked through the HOLMES database, glancing at how many outstanding actions there were to be completed, and wondered how they ever managed to convict anybody. As a detective inspector, his job was a managerial one, but it wasn't beneath him to go out and visit witnesses.

One in particular struck him as being a previously untapped source of information. He punched the name of Jenny Bloomfield's friend, Cathy Walters, into his keyboard and trawled through everything the police system held on her. It wasn't much, but he wasn't about to go round her house without looking into her first. No one was that stupid.

A movement in the corridor outside his office caught his eye.

'You still here, Sandra?' he said.

'I'm about to head off,' she said, leaning against the door jamb. 'Need anything from me before I go?'

'No,' he said, easing himself back in his chair. 'I was about to go out and see Cathy Walters, but you can lock up and set the alarm if you like.'

'She's the friend who's crawled out of the woodwork now her bestie, Jenny Bloomfield, is dead, that right?'

'Very cynical, yet accurate,' said Harry as he put his hands behind his head. 'I've had a look and she didn't feature in Linda Bowman's murder at all. If she and Jenny were such great mates, I'd have thought her name would have cropped up somewhere.'

'Want me to come with you?' asked Sandra.

'Nah, I'll be fine,' said Harry as he stood up and pulled his jacket from the back of his chair. 'I wanted to speak to her tonight because tomorrow we'll need to go back and update the family. I want to find out what Cathy's got to say before the grief hits them full-on.'

'Night, then,' said Sandra.

'See you in the morning.'

Harry grabbed his paperwork and switched off the light, mindful that the witness he was on his way to see might have had a very good reason to stay out of the way up until now.

The traffic was heavy for the time of night and it was after 8 p.m. when Harry pulled up outside the modest terraced house that belonged to Cathy Walters.

He saw a light on through the bedroom window and hoped she wasn't already going to bed. Keen not to miss his opportunity to talk to her, Harry got out of the car and rapped on the door.

A face appeared at the window to the left-hand side of the front door. Cathy's expression was one of surprise, although Harry could have sworn he saw a flicker of annoyance flash over her features. Perhaps it was her long brown hair scraped back into a ponytail on the top of her head that made her look a little harsher than the last time he'd seen her.

Harry waved his warrant card at her and shouted, 'Hi, Cathy. It's DI Harry Powell. We met yesterday.'

She disappeared and he heard the sound of footsteps as she rushed to open the door to him.

'All right, all right,' she said, glancing up and down the empty street. 'Please don't holler that the police are at my door.'

'Sorry,' he said. 'Most people we deal with couldn't care less. Can I come in?'

With a noise that sound like a humph, Cathy stood back and let him in.

He was pleased to see that she was wearing trousers and a T-shirt, not pyjamas.

Once seated in the front room, the offer of coffee declined, Harry said, 'Thank you for speaking to me. I wanted to see if there was anything you could tell me about Jenny that might help.'

She fiddled with her ponytail, pulling her hair over one shoulder.

'Is it her then? Is it definitely her?'

'We're still waiting on confirmation,' said Harry tactfully. 'We hope to have some results soon.'

Cathy stared at him. Perhaps she could tell it was a lie, but Harry wasn't budging on this one. Family deserved to know news like that first.

Eventually Cathy said, 'We were at school together. We weren't really friends then, but years later I bumped into her in Waitrose.' She gave a hollow laugh.

'Usually I shop at Aldi or Lidl, but I was on my way home from a job interview.' Cathy looked down at her bare feet on the worn carpet. 'I was feeling optimistic, so I thought, why not? I had on a brand-new and quite expensive dress, so afterwards when I thought back to the conversation Jenny and I had over the curly kale, I figured she probably imagined I was doing a lot better for myself than I actually was.' Harry gave her an encouraging smile.

'Well, we had a "let's do coffee" conversation and met up a couple of days later.'

She broke off again, twirled her hair around her fingers and tucked her feet under her legs.

'It wasn't easy to tell her that I was flat broke,' said Cathy, 'but Jenny was so lovely and said she'd help me out, keep her ears open if she heard of any jobs coming up. I'd worked for years for a kitchen firm – anyway, you didn't come here for my life story.

'Jenny was great, and we met from time to time. She always paid for lunch or drinks – I felt as though I was taking advantage, but she would never take a penny, even when I was back on my feet.'

None of this was helping Harry and he was just about to think he was wasting his time when Cathy said, 'The lunches and drinks stopped when she started the affair.'

Harry hoped his expression didn't show surprise. There had been a suspicion that Jenny had been having an affair, yet he was expecting to have to subtly weave it into the conversation.

'Do you know who he was?' said Harry.

A shake of the head.

'No, but she seemed pretty smitten,' said Cathy. 'She wouldn't ever tell me, although I didn't want to pry. It was nice to see her . . . you know, happy.' She gave a miserable little shrug.

'Do you think he had anything to do with her disappearance?' asked Cathy.

'I don't know,' said Harry, 'but if he did, trust me, we'll find him.'

Harry sat forward in his seat.

'Cathy, this is important. You need to tell me everything, and I mean *everything*, that Jenny ever told you about this man. Leave nothing out.'

CHAPTER NINETEEN

Sophia wasn't quite sure how the day had ended this way. It had started normally enough, before she and Dane were told that two volunteers were needed for out-of-county enquiries, which would probably mean an overnight stay somewhere.

Neither she nor Dane had seemed all that keen and she felt nervous about spending an entire night in his company. Her feelings towards him were still very much mixed, and she couldn't fathom whether he was deliberately quiet with her on the journey because he didn't enjoy her company, or if there was another reason.

Having spent most of the afternoon travelling across the south coast, and then the early evening taking statements from traumatised victims of telephone fraud – those who had unwittingly handed over their personal information, bank account details, PIN numbers, and then their debit and credit cards – Sophia and Dane were exhausted.

The first reasonable hotel they saw, they stopped to see if they had two available rooms.

Sophia sat in the bar of the Premier Inn, watching Dane as he strolled towards the smiling barmaid who was leaning across the counter, appearing a little too ready to welcome him. Try as she might, Sophia couldn't help but notice the attractive, slim server was also about ten years younger than she was, with that cheery air of optimism that the drudgery and disappointment of life had yet to squash.

Whatever it was that Dane said to her made her laugh, lean against the nearest beer pump and put her hand on her hip. He definitely had an air about him, and it wasn't all down to looks.

Still, Sophia hoped she had a better chance with him than the barmaid.

She shook her head at the idea. She looked up to see Dane standing in front of her.

Slightly flustered, she stared at him, not expecting him to have fetched the drinks so quickly. Then she noticed his empty hands.

'Something wrong?' he asked.

'No, no. I just remembered something, that's all,' she replied, wondering what he'd returned to the table for, if not to deposit their drinks.

'Well,' said Dane, 'the barmaid, who looks a little bit young to even be working here, asked if you wanted ice and lemon with your vodka and tonic. I told her that I wasn't sure and as I'm still in the early days of trying to impress you, I thought I'd better check.'

Sophia had to admit that the line was corny, but it made her laugh.

'Lots and lots of ice and one slice of lemon, please.'

As he turned to walk away, she called, 'Oh, and Dane, if you really want to impress me, a straight glass. And ask about a table for dinner.'

Ninety minutes – and three rounds – later, Dane and Sophie had only moved as far as the bar to get more drinks. The meal they'd talked about eating, having lost much of its importance, was probably past the point of sobering them up, and no one had yet told them their table was ready.

'So, tell me,' said Sophia, speech not yet slurred, but displaying signs of inebriation, 'what made you join the police?'

Dane ran a hand through his hair and took a pull on his pint before smacking his lips and saying, 'It was the glamour and the hope that, one day, I'd meet the perfect woman.'

'You're so full of shit.'

'I've yet to find her, so if you've got any fit mates . . .' he said with a smile.

'You're lucky I'm in a good mood,' she laughed.

'Seriously, what made you want to join?' For a few seconds, Dane considered her question.

'I suppose,' he said at last, 'I'd spent years drifting around working different dead-end jobs. A couple of years ago, I decided I wanted to do something positive, and like all of us I had this starry-eyed notion that I'd help lock up villains. The reality, of course, was immediately obvious: that I'd spend longer doing the paperwork than these wankers would spend banged up. I was beginning to think that I'd wasted my time until I came here, to Major Crime, but now that I've got the chance to work on some more serious stuff, I think things are looking up. What about you?'

'Similar to your story, although I have to confess, do you want to know the one thing that kept me here rather than throwing in the towel and getting a sensible job with structured hours and better pay?'

'Go on.'

Sophia gave a sigh and said, 'Job security and the pension. Now, I'm fucked. I've got to do this bollocks for another twelve years longer than I ever expected to, paying in fourteen per cent to a pension scheme I may never see a penny of. And for what? Constant criticism from the public, the politicians, the media. We all join with a notion of "making a difference", but the reality of the situation is that we can't win. It's relentless; we simply carry on and do the best job we can.'

'What are you going to do, then?'

'Dunno, if I'm being honest.'

She drained the rest of her vodka and tonic, pushed the empty glass towards him and said, 'Is it your round?'

'Strictly speaking it's your turn, but as you're knocking them back quicker than me, I don't mind getting you another.'

Sophia raised her eyebrows at him; she wasn't entirely sure in her alcohol-befuddled brain how she was supposed to react to that comment.

'All I meant,' he said in response, 'was that judging by two consecutive nights of plying ourselves with alcohol, you've clearly got a stronger constitution than I have.'

As she was about to answer him, she felt her stomach growl. Not one to usually act so irresponsibly, especially where the dangerous mix of alcohol and men were concerned, Sophia got up to go to the bar.

'I really don't mind getting you a drink,' he said.

'I'm going to check on our table,' she said. 'It's been ages since you asked them.'

'She said she'd let us know when it was ready.'

Without waiting to debate it further, Sophia walked to the bar and spoke to the barmaid, who looked even younger at a close distance.

She smiled at her and said, 'Sorry, but my friend asked for a table some time ago. I was wondering how much longer it'd be, please?'

Sophia saw a frown on the young woman's face and then a

smile as she said, 'I told him there's one ready whenever you are. Just go on through; it's reserved.'

Having managed to mumble a 'thank you', Sophia made herself hold it together to gesture to Dane that she was going to the ladies'.

Exactly what was he playing at? Neither of them had had time for lunch once they'd been told where they needed to go and had got their paperwork in order. She'd had three vodkas on an empty stomach, all while Dane had deliberately kept her drinking instead of eating.

Now she came to think about it, he had been the one buying the shots last night too, and it was his suggestion they go down to sit on the beach.

If she wasn't very much mistaken, she was being played.

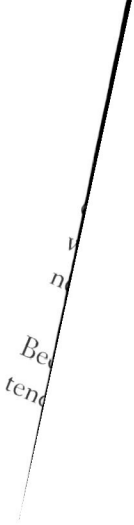

CHAPTER TWENTY

THURSDAY 7 MAY

Detective Inspector Harry Powell had hit the ground running again today. His morning had started earlier than most of his team, with a call out to an attempted murder. Two drunks had found themselves staggering home in the early hours, when one of them had staggered into someone else. That someone else hadn't taken kindly to it and had punched him in retaliation. That one punch put the victim into a coma.

Without a doubt, Harry knew that this latest job to break in his incident room would never be the highlight of any of his team's investigative career. Nevertheless, it was still a tragic waste of two lives: both that of the now brain-dead young party-goer, and the reckless young man who had now ruined his own life with one punch.

Still, the matter needed a mountain of paperwork and lots of inquiries to result in a conviction at court, not to mention the work to support the victim's family and managing the offender's nearest and dearest.

He made sure he was back in his office before Sandra Kinsale arrived. That was no mean feat in itself, as she used to arrive earlier than most of the others. She wasn't going to be very impressed to hear they had picked up another job. Although, in fairness, she wasn't very impressed by anything.

Harry heard her making an entrance into the office, smoker's cough and all.

He was ready at her office door, cup of tea held out to her as a peace offering.

She scowled at him.

'What's gone wrong?' she demanded.

'And good morning to you too, Sandra,' he said, stepping after her into her office.

She eyed him with well-placed suspicion. 'What do you want?'

Even though he knew he wasn't fooling her, Harry tried his best.

'Can't I simply greet my favourite DS with a cup of tea without wanting anything?'

'But you do want something.' she said, coat now off, bag down and sat at her desk.

'Biscuit to go with that?'

When he couldn't take the gurning any longer, Harry said, 'I've been out to a new job: it's an attempted murder at the moment, although the fella isn't likely to pull through.'

He continued through the noise of Sandra blowing air out of her cheeks.

'I need a team to brief, including a case officer, an officer to take a statement from the other drunk witness once he sobers up, two to interview the suspect in custody and a Family Liaison Officer. Well, you know better than I do who we need. CCTV person and outside enquiry officer, too.'

Now she looked furious.

'We'll make it a nine a.m. briefing,' he said, sensing it was time to retreat, 'and thanks in advance for sorting it out.'

He knew when it was time to give his staff some space, and

that time was definitely now. Harry recognised a crumbling organisation when he saw one, and he was in the midst of the biggest crisis he had seen in all his years of service.

Even so, they had a job to do, and he was well aware that he needed to visit the Bloomfield family and break terrible news to them. He had already lost two members of staff to the Fraud Department, so before he did anything else, Harry wanted to make sure the staff he had left were safe and well, even the ones who were currently seconded elsewhere.

Sophia he trusted implicitly. Dane, not so much.

Harry picked up his phone to call Sophia and check everything was all right. As he did so, he noticed the time: it was a little after seven-thirty. Was it too early to call? Their duty time started in twenty-five minutes so they should be up and on their way to work.

He rang Sophia, who answered on the fourth ring.

'Soph,' he said, 'it's Harry. Everything okay?'

'Mmm, thanks . . . It is. What's up?'

'Sorry, sounds as though I've woken you up?'

'No, no,' she insisted, sleep still weighing her words and tone.

'Look, I'm sorry if you think I'm interfering, but after Pierre and everything . . .'

Harry heard her sigh, or perhaps it came from him, it was difficult to tell.

'I was only trying to make sure that everything was going okay with you, and that you're getting on well with Dane.'

'Yeah, yeah,' she said. 'I've got to go. We were out of county on enquiries and stayed over in a hotel. We arranged to meet downstairs for breakfast.' With that she hung up.

If Harry wasn't very much mistaken, through the sound of what he interpreted to be the rustling of bedclothes, he heard the noise of someone else in the room clearing their throat.

He wasn't sure whether to be surprised or disappointed that Sophia had given in to Dane's charm.

CHAPTER TWENTY-ONE

Sophia ended the call from Harry and shut her eyes. She had lied to her boss. Harry was decent, as decent a guv'nor as anyone could ask for, and she hadn't been honest with him.

Dane's arm snaked across her waist, reminding her that she was still in bed with him. She had lied to her boss and shagged a member of the team. She was really racking up the good moves this week.

She felt his mouth kiss her bare shoulder, his hand as he moved it higher.

'We should probably get dressed,' she said. 'You know, do some police work, that kind of thing.' By now, Dane had worked his way to her ear.

'Really?' he whispered. 'Police work? Why would you even think of something so sensible and boring.' She pushed him back to the other side of the bed.

'Because it's our job and what we get paid for. We're supposed to be on duty in less than half an hour. We haven't showered or eaten and we're nowhere close to checking out.'

Dane shifted on the bed, propped himself up with one elbow, hand under his head. She couldn't fail to notice his toned chest muscles, try as she might to keep her eyes locked on to his.

Amusement flickered across his face.

'What?' she said, sitting up and pulling the duvet up to her neck. 'What is it you're finding so bloody funny?'

'I love how serious you are about everything: we're away in a hotel and you won't even start your tour of duty half an hour late. Do you ever do *anything* wrong?'

'Depends on what your definition of wrong is? I don't take the piss, I don't throw sickies and I do my job to the best of my ability.'

'Look,' he said as he moved to sit up next to her, 'I know we get paid, I know some people have much tougher jobs than ours, but let's be honest, we don't exactly get an easy time of things, do we? When did we last have a pay rise, for a start?' Sophia shrugged.

'Your future may be certain, but I've got to work for decades to make ends meet. I've only got, what, two years in this job. I'm at least going to make the most of it.'

'So, Dane,' she said, 'what's your suggestion?' It was his turn to shrug.

'I don't know,' he said, 'but let's start with a shower and breakfast.'

With his final word on the subject, he threw back the covers, got out of her bed and took his clothes in the bathroom to get dressed.

Barely two minutes later, he was back in the bedroom, standing with his hand on the door handle. He gave her a look she couldn't read and said, 'I'll meet you downstairs for breakfast. We'd better get on and finish this job.'

As Sophia sat alone in her hotel room, she wondered, not for the first time, exactly what she was doing getting herself mixed up with Dane Hoopman.

CHAPTER TWENTY-TWO

Harry's motivation was at rock bottom: he could no longer even pretend to his staff that all of their hard work was worthwhile. Morale was at an all-time low, people were leaving the police at an unprecedented rate, and almost half of the new officers they were recruiting were either leaving within a couple of years or getting fired for behaving like bell-ends. Some of them seemed to bring a whole new dimension to fuckwittery: one had just been dismissed for failing to declare he'd been in prison. Vetting had a thing or two to answer for.

Not for the first time, Harry wondered who else was lurking in the shadows in this job. He got up and peered along the corridor to the incident room. Though he needn't worry about corruption in his department, what with having fuck-all staff, as usual.

He sighed and sat back down, ready to skim-read the ridiculous amount of emails that had filled his inbox overnight.

A shuffling in the doorway made him turn his attention away from his desk.

'Sandra,' he said. 'Am I pleased to see you.'

'Are you?'

'Not really, but come in anyway.'

He attempted a smile at his detective sergeant as she entered and sat down, although she looked more wretched than ever.

'Are you all right?' he said, genuine concern for her showing in his voice.

'I've got something to tell you,' she said, fidgeting in her seat, looking uncharacteristically nervous. 'And before I do, I'm sorry, and it's not about recent . . . Well, you know what I'm trying to say.'

The unwritten rule was that no one actually mentioned the crack that had appeared in the incident room following the loss of one of its integral parts. The crack that was now a chasm, threatening to suck them all into it.

There was the merest of nods from Harry before he said, 'You want to leave.'

He fought the urge to add 'me' to the end of that sentence. This wasn't personal – he hoped.

A shrug.

'Not exactly *leave*, leave.' She looked away, to avoid his eye no doubt, and appeared to watch something out of the window.

'I, er . . .' she began. 'I thought it was about time I got myself promoted.'

This cheered Harry up in more ways than he could have hoped for. He threw himself back in his chair, the creak showcasing both the furniture's age and his own weight gain. 'That's great news. What's brought this on after so long?'

'You know I've had the inspectors' exam for some time?' she said, face arranged in some resemblance of optimism.

Harry had absolutely no idea Sandra Beckinsale had once sat and taken her inspectors' exam.

'Of course, of course,' he enthused.

'I thought it was about time I put it to some use,' she said with either a smile or a grimace, it was hard to tell.

'I'll support you in any way, but you know I'll be utterly gutted to see you go, don't you?'

These weren't empty words. What little order they did have left in the office was all a result of Sandra's dedication to the job. She'd been there for the whole team over recent months, especially the younger members who had found some comfort in her dependability and continued strong presence.

Yes, he admitted to himself, he would actually miss her.

'There's an application I'd like you to endorse,' she said. 'If you don't mind, and have the time.'

'Send it to me and I'll get it done today, as soon as I've seen the Bloomfields.'

She gave him a curt nod and made to get out of the chair.

'Oh, Sandra,' said Harry. 'What is it you're applying for?'

She failed to meet his eye again and said, 'It's an out-of-county opportunity reviewing a series of undetected murders for another force. It doesn't guarantee my promotion, but I'll be acting DI for up to two years.'

He smiled at her. 'Far too good an opportunity to pass up – more money, heading up something that's no doubt high-profile, plus the chance to get the next rank up. Wouldn't blame anyone for that.'

Short of grinning at her like a maniac, Harry couldn't have enthused more at her news if he'd tried. 'Thanks for your understanding, Harry.'

This time, she did get up and leave the office.

Another one fleeing his broken incident room. And who could blame them.

He heaved himself out of his chair, took a few steps towards the office door and strolled the few paces to the main office. A bank of almost empty desks greeted him, one or two occupied by officers tapping away on keyboards, frowning and muttering to themselves.

Without realising quite where he was heading, Harry found himself standing behind the chair his friend and colleague Pierre used to occupy. He reached out a tentative hand to touch the back of the seat, aware that the sound of fingers on keyboards had stopped.

Harry's team knew he was a broken man, yet no one could figure out what to say to him. He was their boss, the one they were supposed to go to for answers to their own problems. Harry's rank didn't necessarily mean he had all the solutions, but he was the conduit for the shit that slipped downhill and he always protected his team from the senior ranks, something they all knew and admired.

That didn't stop him looking like a man about to face his own execution.

As he turned to make his way back to the sanctuary of his own office, the phone on Pierre's desk rang.

Harry bit his lip as an unknown local number flashed up on the phone's display screen next to the words *DC Pierre Rainer*.

His outstretched hand, now shaking, reached for the phone. With his voice as steady as he could manage, he said, 'Incident room. DI Powell speaking. How can I help you?'

For a few seconds, Harry listened to the voice at the other end stutter an apology for calling, especially after so long.

'I . . . er . . . well, I heard about the officer, Pierre, on the news,' he said. 'I'm so sorry. He was such a lovely guy.'

'Thank you,' said Harry, hoping this call would soon be over.

'You probably don't even need it any more, but I'm calling from the jeweller's. I've kept the CCTV he wanted for such a long time. He obviously never came back for it.'

'CCTV?' Harry asked, no clue what the caller was talking about.

'Yes, that's right. Pierre came in last year for some CCTV from our shop front. I downloaded it for him, left the disk, then I was off sick, my staff couldn't find it when he came in, and then he never . . .'

It was several more seconds until Harry felt the air return to his lungs, the race of his heart return to its normal manic beat.

'What was it for?' said Harry. 'The CCTV. What did he want it for?'

A short laugh. 'Not really sure, if I'm honest. It's so old now, I doubt it'll be much good for anything, but it was Pierre, you know. I was clearing out the office and—'

'I'll come and get it,' said Harry. 'Give me half an hour and I'll be over.'

He put the phone down, got his mobile from the office and took a walk into town to pick up CCTV for one of his officers who Harry knew would never have requested it without very good reason.

THEN

I couldn't lie to myself; since I'd talked myself into a job with him, things were going well under my new boss's watchful eye. He didn't exactly trust me – that much was obvious. I was secure enough within the fold that I didn't feel like I was about to find myself propping up the foundations on a motorway flyover, but I still didn't know much about the business, other than the fact we sold snide tracksuits from the back of lorries or ran the odd protection racket. I knew there was a lot more to it, and if I wanted to survive in this new role I had to find out what.

Since talking myself out of being kicked to death in his basement, I had done as I'd promised him. Despite finding it hilarious at the time, he had actively encouraged me to get a job as a town-centre CCTV operator. He even got one of his moody business owners to give me a reference.

It was pretty boring work, but I got to watch attractive women saunter around the town, especially when I was on nights. To my amusement, there were always pissed-up hen parties wandering around in their underwear in the early hours.

The money and prospects weren't up to much either, yet I carried on, rarely even seeing my boss for weeks at a time. Any information I had about what I'd seen happen in the town, I passed over at a weekly meet-up with one of his trustees in the Seagull Pickings, a horrendous cafe in East Rise. The boss himself seemed keen to stay out of the town, although apparently he had a very active interest in some of its residents.

Today I had the pleasure of meeting some bloke called Milo, whatever the fuck sort of name that was supposed to be. I guessed it was to keep his real identity under wraps, yet as soon as he walked in – six foot or so, built like a shit-house door, dark suit and boots – it was obvious what he was.

He ran an angry eye around the premises, earned himself a scowl from the surly waitress, skin the colour of Tango, and sauntered towards me looking like he owned the place. Trouble was, for about a grand, he probably could have. I don't recall ever being in such a dire eatery.

I'd deliberately chosen a table for four in the far corner, and I'd got there far earlier than I needed to so I could sit facing the door.

He came around to my side of the table and, to my surprise, pulled out the cheap metal chair next to me.

Once he'd thrown himself down in the seat and barked, 'Love, white coffee – cheers,' at the waitress, he glanced sideways at me.

'Sitting next to me like that, aren't you worried people will think we're a couple?' I said, fairly confident he wouldn't punch me in the throat in public.

He paused while our stroppy server slammed a white mug of strong coffee in front of him.

'The boss would like you to step matters up,' he said, making no attempt to drink the beverage in front of him. 'Enough messing around.'

'What exactly would he like me to do?'

'It's not what he'd *like* you to do, it's what he's *telling* you to do.'

I was expecting matters to tick along as they were for another year at least. I'd been putting some money away here and there, ready to make my escape when the time was right. A change in direction wasn't part of my plan, although it seemed to be part of the boss's.

I felt my throat go dry.

'What's the matter?' he said. 'Run out of witty retorts?'

'What does he want?'

Milo sat back in his squeaky chair and folded his arms across his chest.

'He wants you to move jobs. CCTV just isn't doing it any more.'

He stood up, took an envelope from his pocket and threw it on the table.

'It's all in there,' he said, before walking outside into what should have been a glorious autumn day.

CHAPTER TWENTY-THREE

Harry's intention was to take Sandra Beckinsale with him to see the Bloomfields. The new incident he had asked her to sort out had put a stop to that.

His detour to pick up CCTV from the town centre had made him half an hour later than he'd intended to be, and the last thing he wanted was to keep the family waiting any longer.

With an eye on the front door, Harry got out of his car and made his way along the garden path.

An ashen-faced Tanya King met him on the doorstep. 'Hello,' he said. 'Your dad in too?'

Perhaps it was Harry's earlier insistence on the phone that he give them the news in person that gave the impression she knew what he was going to say, or possibly she had looked so ill for so long, her face was now permanently haunted.

He waited for her to close the door behind him. She was already crying before the latch clicked into place.

The walk to the living room was short but terse, grief and despair coming off her in waves.

Tanya's husband sat in one armchair and Ron Bloomfield in

the other. Both glared at him with no attempt to hide their disdain.

Harry couldn't really blame them.

Without being asked, he sat down. 'There's no easy way to —' he started to say. Sobs escaped from mouths; gasps caught in throats.

Harry looked at Ron. 'The body found in Lower Lynton has been identified as your wife Jenny.'

Tanya was shaking, holding her head. 'You're sure?' she said.

'I'm sorry, but yes,' said Harry, turning to face her. 'DNA has confirmed it and the clothes are similar to the ones she was wearing.'

'How did she die?' said Ron.

Harry tugged at the knot of his tie. 'The postmortem, which was carried out late last night, revealed her neck was broken.'

'Who would break her neck, for Christ's sake?' said Ron, face now shockingly white. 'How has this happened to me?'

It seemed a very strange thing for the widower to say, but then like Cathy Walters, Ron had hardly put in an appearance at Crown Court himself when his wife and son were both on trial for murder. It had always seemed odd, even if he thought they were both guilty, that he wouldn't have been in the public gallery more often than he had been watching the fate of his family unfold.

Although Harry wasn't entirely convinced that Ron was guilty of murder, there were certainly a few things not right about him.

He would have to keep a close eye on Ron over the coming days.

CHAPTER TWENTY-FOUR

On her journey with Dane back from the hotel, Sophia wasn't sure whether to go for casual and chatty or silent and brooding. Clumsily, she went from one to the other.

'Everything okay?' said Dane after a long silence, breaking into her thoughts.

'Yeah, terrific.'

He looked across at her, concern creasing his brow. 'Did I do something wrong, Soph?'

She let out a sigh and instantly regretted it; coming across as wistful was the last thing she wanted to do.

'What are we doing?' she said.

'I take it you don't mean this fraud investigation.'

'Wow, good-looking *and* smart. I feel as though I've struck gold.'

Sophia bit her lip, instantly regretting her choice of words. Not only had she paid him a compliment, the last thing she wanted Dane to think was that she now felt they were a couple. She wasn't even sure she wanted a relationship with him.

'I'm sorry,' she said. 'It's been a while since I've even looked twice at someone, let alone, you know . . . It's difficult for me to get involved with anyone, or at least it has been for a while.'

Sophia looked away out of the side window, desperate to say more, yet unwilling to leave herself any more vulnerable than she already had.

'Whoever he was, he was clearly bad news,' said Dane. 'And he's left you a warier person for it.' Her head snapped round at this comment.

'Seriously, how are you able to make such a quick judgement?' she said. 'Is it because I slept with you? Does that somehow, in your head, mean that you have insight into my deepest, darkest feelings and, even more impressively, you're able to decipher the entirety of my personal life?'

She finished her sentence breathing more heavily than she would have liked, annoyance surging through her.

'Sophia, I'm sorry, okay. I'm really sorry. I didn't mean to upset you.'

As much as she didn't want to appear like she was surrendering, she nodded.

Dane pointed at the junction ahead and said, 'This is our turning. We'll get the statement done at this address and then we'll talk.'

'Okay,' she said, 'I think we should.'

Sophia knew she'd made a terrible mistake sleeping with Dane and now she'd have to face him at work on a daily basis. The second she had answered her phone to Harry that morning, had felt Dane kissing her shoulder, it had dawned on her that Dane had come along when she was feeling low and vulnerable.

She only hoped he wouldn't turn nasty on her when she told him it was over before it had even got started.

CHAPTER TWENTY-FIVE

The driver turned off at the 'Welcome to Merridown Holiday Park' sign, and from Milo's reaction, Sean Turner assumed it was the last place he expected to be heading.

'Here?' was all Milo asked.

'Here,' replied Turner. 'It's discreet, it's cheap and, best of all, it's full of villains.'

'Haven't been anywhere like this for decades,' said Milo as he looked out of the window at the chalets and the London/Essex overspill mooching around in vest tops and shorts.

They pulled up outside the clubhouse, which according to the sign over the door doubled as both the reception and check-in.

'Stay here with the car,' said Turner to the driver.

'We'll walk; take in the ambience.'

Milo opened the door and got out. Turner walked around the car and joined him.

'You've done a good job for me over the years,' said Turner, taking a couple of steps in the direction of what the sign promised to be a 'Wondrous Nature Trail'.

'Thanks very much, boss,' said Milo, mildly surprised at the unusual praise. He kept up with his employer's brisk pace.

Turner continued walking, following the shingle pathway around the side of the site. The sun was shining down from an almost cloudless sky, birds were singing in the trees, and for the briefest of moments, it appeared to be turning into a beautiful day.

Turner called over his shoulder to Milo, 'I thought I'd show you my latest acquisition.'

When they reached a stretch of a dozen or so of the less run-down chalets on the outskirts of the holiday park, Turner came to a stop, waiting for Milo to join him.

They stood shoulder to shoulder, both looking at the balcony of a holiday let that most wouldn't hesitate to rent if they were planning on escaping to the countryside. Especially with a bingo hall and amusement arcades only an empty beer can's throw away – if that was your thing.

Pacing up and down the far side of the wooden balustrade was a young man dressed in black, shoulders rounded, chewing his fingernails. A motorcycle was parked beside the three wooden stairs, complete with helmet on seat.

As they got closer, the young man halted, turned suddenly and, even from the distance of fifty feet or so, looked startled.

'You and I need a little debrief with our courier here,' said Turner to Milo.

They trudged towards the chalet where the young man, who currently looked as though he was about to wet himself, was standing.

'They didn't get me,' he said as they came to within earshot.

Turner put up a hand to silence him.

'Let's go inside, shall we?' he said, reaching into his jacket pocket and removing a single silver key, with a large metal keyring telling everyone it was '16'.

'Look at this,' said Turner to no one in particular. 'No wonder crime's so bloody high. Who puts their door number on their keys?'

He tutted and shook his head before unlocking the door and going inside.

'Come in,' he said over his shoulder, as he walked into the kitchen-diner area of the chalet. The open-plan living room was empty of other signs of life. There were only two ways in or out, and one of those was the empty balcony they had just walked along.

The other door, leading to what must have been the bedrooms and bathroom, was closed.

Turner faced the reckless young courier who had failed to realise that the police were keeping watch in the very house he had been sent to. He watched him steal a glance towards the door. He had every right to be nervous. Undoubtedly, he had a punishment coming, that much he would expect.

'What's your name, son?' said Turner.

'Caleb,' said the courier, tongue darting out in a wasted attempt to moisten his lips.

'Caleb?' said Turner with a nod. 'Good, strong, biblical name. That'll probably come in handy.'

Turner picked up the kettle and filled it from the tap.

He flicked the switch and, after a couple of seconds, the noise of the water boiling was the only sound in the room.

'Well, I'll leave you two alone now,' he said, standing in front of his failed apprentice. He placed a hand on his shoulder. Pale-faced and sweaty, Caleb recoiled from the touch as if he'd had an electric shock.

'I'll see you in an hour, Milo. Don't make too much mess.'

CHAPTER TWENTY-SIX

Head still reeling from his earlier encounter with Ron Bloomfield and his family, DI Harry Powell sat in an interview room inside the walls of HMP Stanley.

He was unsure whether the man he was visiting would even come out of his cell, let alone talk to him. Regardless, Harry sat with his open notebook in front of him.

Harry perched on the edge of his seat in the tiny room, glass panels either end, one side leading to the inner workings of the prison and the other leading to freedom.

Mesmerised, he watched as a prison officer walked to his cubicle, paused at the door and unlocked it with a key from a bunch chained to his belt. It was the man behind him who caused Harry to stare so intently.

Aiden Bloomfield, a man he had sat and watched in the dock while on trial for murder, who was now serving a life sentence, was peering at him with a look of such intensity that he felt his eyes burning right into him.

Harry saw him hesitate as the prison officer pushed open the door and stood aside.

'A visitor for you,' he said, nodding in Harry's direction. 'Tap on the glass when you're done and I'll come back.'

For a second, Harry thought Aiden was going to start banging on the glass before he had even sat down.

Instead, he kicked out the chair tucked under his side of the table and threw himself down into it.

'What?' he said to Harry.

The transformation of the young man he'd met all those months ago was astounding; long gone was the fresh-faced, scared yet hopeful young man. The person in front of him, quite frankly, just looked cruel.

'Hello, Aiden,' he tried. 'I'm Detective Inspector Harry Powell. We met some time ago at East Rise police station.'

'Yeah, I do remember.' He gave a harsh laugh.

'Harry Powell,' echoed Aiden. 'I'd forgotten your name, but not your face. That was the weirdest fucking time of my life. Still, I get to use the gym every day, I'm studying, and I've even got my own cell now. It's small, but I get left alone, so life could be worse.'

He leaned back in the chair, arms folded across a chest encased in an unflattering grey sweatshirt, yet it was still clear to see that the daily workouts were paying dividends.

Harry took a deep breath, unsure how to broach the main subject without causing the hostile young inmate to storm off, or at least as far as the locked door would take him.

He didn't relish the idea of being trapped with him, he knew that much.

'I'm here about your mum.'

Harry paused, let the seriousness sink in. Aiden was far from daft: he understood the nature of his department's work.

He shifted in his chair, feet tapping, fingers drumming.

'Haven't seen her in months,' he said, eyebrows raised,

expression set firm. 'Now, let me think . . .' Aiden tapped at the side of his head.

'Mmm, oh yeah, that's right. How could it have slipped my mind? The last time I saw my dear old mum was moments after I got sent down for murdering Linda Bowman and she walked away scot-free.'

This time he slapped his forehead and shouted, 'Such a fucking idiot.'

Harry wanted to look away from him, but felt he had to hold his ground.

'No one's seen her, Aiden,' he said, his words barely audible. 'That's the point, no one, not even your dad.' The mention of his father brought forth a scoff.

'It's been, what, six months since the trial ended?' he said. 'Not to mention the time I was banged up on remand, waiting for the trial. And all for something I didn't even do. I didn't hurt Linda; she was my best mate's mum. Anyone with a brain would have been able to see that.' He paused. 'Unfortunately, between you lot, the judge and the twelve fucking idiots on the jury, no one actually did have a brain. To top it all off, the only one who could actually have vouched for me and told everyone that I didn't smash her head in, was my mother. My mother, who I'm pretty sure was having a sordid affair with someone and has now conveniently run off with him.'

The tension ran the length of Harry's spine. Most of the incident room had worked on Linda Bowman's murder, including Pierre. Linda had been married to a police officer and she was a friend of Harry's. In fact, it was Harry who had found her body lying on her kitchen floor. Everyone had been under suspicion at one point or another. Harry knew that some even had their doubts about *him*.

If they'd got it wrong, they had well and truly messed up. It didn't bear thinking about.

'The last time anyone saw your mum,' said Harry, 'was the day she was released from the court.' He let the information sink in.

'There's no easy way to tell you this,' he said to the young man opposite him. 'We recently found her body in some woods.'

Aiden's mouth hung open. He blinked several times, but still said nothing.

'Your mum left the court building that day and never went home,' said Harry in a softer tone. 'She hasn't used her credit cards, bank account or her mobile phone since. Please help us – can you think of anything you know that might help us find who did this?'

Aiden leaned forward, elbows on the table, face a mask of hatred. 'Or what? You'll bang me up for life?'

He gave a harsh laugh, pushed himself up from his seat and said, 'And if I do help you, what then? You put some other poor innocent bastard in prison because they'll fit the bill to solve your fucking murder.'

With that, Aiden Bloomfield hammered on the glass, shouting to be taken back to his cell and away from Harry.

CHAPTER TWENTY-SEVEN

Not for one second was Harry's determination to find out who murdered Jenny fading, but he had to admit he was worn out. Everything seemed to be getting him down and under his skin.

He glanced across his office at his framed certificate of office presented to him along with his warrant card all those years ago at the Magistrates' Court, when he was sworn into the office of constable. Frame after frame of Judge's Commendations, Chief Constable's Commendations and Assistant Chief Constable's Commendations lined the walls. But at the end of the day, what did it all add up to?

It seemed pointless in the grand scheme of things, and it was all marred now whatever the future brought.

It was with a heavy heart that he'd gone to HMP Stanley to speak to Aiden Bloomfield. If Jenny Bloomfield had been murdered as soon as she was released from court, then not only was it unlikely to have been her son behind it, but it meant that they had probably convicted the wrong person.

Even worse, the real killer was still out there.

This was a colossal balls-up of epic proportions. Retiring wasn't even an option if he had any chance of discovering who was really behind it all. Harry knew he wouldn't be permitted to actually head up the investigation, especially if his department had got it so wrong in the first place. But he figured that if he worked it right, then maybe they would allow him to work on the periphery. Even better, he'd work away in secret. By the time anyone knew it would be too late.

There must be something he was continuing to miss throughout all of this. The only problem would be discovering what that actually was.

Perhaps he was being too negative, and with everything that had happened he simply couldn't see the wood for the trees any more. Harry found himself searching for a positive in the current situation. A new member of staff on his team was something to be grateful for. They were always so short of staff, any addition made a difference. Except . . .

There was something about Dane Hoopman, something that Harry couldn't pinpoint. Perhaps he simply seemed too smooth and too blameless.

The guy was either a genius . . . or hiding something.

Harry had seen the way Dane and Sophia had behaved around each other. Perhaps it was as simple as Dane having a wife and kids at home. It wasn't as if these things never happened.

The two of them working at headquarters was possibly a mistake, but he was their detective inspector, not their dad. Besides, he didn't really have a say in it at the end of the day. As long as no one else was murdered, raped or kidnapped in the next couple of weeks, the department would probably last another payday.

He picked up his phone to call Sophia then realised what a daft idea it was. She was on another operation with another department and, above all, Harry trusted her.

Even though he knew he was worrying unnecessarily, he

couldn't help himself. He knew that he had let Pierre down, and he wasn't about to make the same mistake twice.

His death had hit them all, not only because he was such a brilliant, kind and well-loved member of the team, but because it could as easily have been any one of them on duty who never returned home that day.

THEN

Well, the new job turned out to be a right turn-up for the books. Reluctant as I was, I had done what the boss demanded of me: I had mostly kept my head down, hardly nicked a thing and was welcomed into the fold.

At least a couple of the people I was working with were all right, and we all regularly went out for drinks. 'Team bonding', apparently. Fucking laughable, but I rarely turned down alcohol, especially when Hannah would be joining us. I had my eye on her; beautiful, sweet Hannah.

From the moment I met her, I appreciated all of her traits – face, body, personality... gullibility.

We had all agreed to meet in the local Wetherspoons, and once part of the small crowd gathered at the back corner of the Guy Earl of Warwick, I set about positioning myself next to Hannah. It took me two pints to get next to her and even then I had to elbow some other numb-nuts out of the way first.

From the other side of our small circle, I saw Carrie give me a look. She wasn't shooting a glare of longing, at least not in my direction. If anything, my money was on her having the hots for

Hannah. Jealously was unattractive, especially in a woman as old as Carrie.

I gave Carrie my most beguiling smile. Usually it worked, although not on this Friday night in a packed wonderland of noise. I had to admire the business model: fill it full of people on a cheap night out, make sure they couldn't hear, making them shout louder, and as a result drink more to compensate and ease their sore throats. Fucking genius.

Carrie, who had been responsible for teaching me all I needed to know for this new job, shot me a look that would normally have worried me. But not tonight. I knew I was going home with Hannah.

Numb-nuts tried to get in between us again. We were standing in a polite little circle celebrating the end of our training and he was getting me down. I moved to my left, out of the corner of my eye making sure that Carrie was witnessing my generous mood.

She had called me aside once or twice over the weeks and told me that I needed to watch my step, and apparently my attitude.

Stupid bitch.

If anyone should watch their step, it was this bloke trying to push his way between me and Hannah.

I decided to get everyone a drink, including the imbecile who thought he could encroach on my territory. Little did he realise, the pint I ordered for him contained a large shot of vodka, as did the one after that.

There was bound to be a set of stairs or a speeding car between the pub and our next port of call.

CHAPTER TWENTY-EIGHT

Sophia and Dane sat patiently in Mrs Armstrong's living room, waiting for her to tell her pitiful tale.

Several times she broke off to wipe away the tears, almost as many times as she said, 'Sorry, sorry. Daft old fool like me should have known better.'

Her liver-spotted hands twisted away at the handkerchief she held between her fingers, the ticking of a clock on her mantelpiece the only audible sound in the room when she stopped talking and silently cried.

'They were so clever, you see,' said Mrs Armstrong. 'My husband was furious with me, but he was out playing golf with his phone switched off. He said he was from the bank.'

'Please don't blame yourself,' said Sophia, not for the first time. She had noticed that Dane had been unusually quiet. For someone who normally had so much to say, it hadn't passed her by that, once again, he was sitting back and letting Sophia take the lead.

'Fifteen *thousand* pounds,' said Mrs Armstrong, voice wavering. 'We were saving the money for a cruise. Holiday of a lifetime. I'm so ashamed.'

She bent her greyed head forward and buried her face in the handkerchief.

Sophia glanced across at her colleague. He yawned.

An hour later, Sophia and Dane left Mrs Armstrong's house and walked towards the car.

'Shall we go for that chat now?' said Dane as he turned on the engine.

'I think we should,' said Sophia. 'But before we do, tell me something.'

He glanced over at her, hesitated from pulling away and said, 'What?'

'Is this boring you?'

'Is what boring me?'

'I know that when you came to Major Crime you thought you'd be working on murders, so getting stuck working on Fraud with me can't have been what you were expecting. But you don't seem very interested in talking to these victims, and you're not very reassuring.'

'Okay, Soph, not only are you doing a brilliant job getting detail from them,' he said as he manoeuvred the car away from the kerb, 'but I'm still learning. I've got what, two years in? You've been doing this for nearly twenty years. Of course I'm going to watch you and learn all I can.'

Vaguely satisfied with the answer, Sophia's mind flew back to the night before. Something was bothering her about the evening – the bit before they ended up in bed.

'How about we stop at this Starbucks up ahead and talk?'

'Yeah,' she said. 'Good idea.'

As Dane pulled into the car park, she tormented herself as to what she should share with him. She'd already been in one toxic relationship, and she wasn't about to end up in another.

THEN

Our big team night out was even more successful than I'd hoped, and here we all were on our final day of training.

I took in the atmosphere around me, the proud parents, spouses, friends and children, all here to watch their loved ones have praise heaped upon them for months of hard work and dedication.

A different boss took my attention today: he stood in front of us, all lined up waiting to be told how amazing we were, what a great thing we had done and would do over the coming years.

'It is with great pleasure that I welcome all of your family and friends here today,' he said, 'to watch you take the final steps of your journey. And what a journey it has been.'

I drifted off for a second, not really concentrating on what he was saying. My mind slipped back to the night before when I had walked Hannah back to her room. I wanted to grin at the thought of the hours I'd spent with her, but I knew I had to be on my best behaviour. Or at least appear to be.

The crowd was on three sides of us, all beaming with pride as we were congratulated for completing months of training.

I had no one rooting for me.

Still, it had been that way for years and, truth be known, it suited me. I'd asked my real boss, Sean Turner, if he wanted to come along and make sure it was all legit. He had laughed – a lot.

I stood still, listening as everyone's name was read out, all fifty-three of us.

Then it was my turn.

'Police Constable Dane Hoopman,' beamed the chief constable. 'PC Hoopman has achieved outstanding examination results, performed to a consistently high standard in all aspects of his training, and has gone the extra mile to assist his colleagues. He has been awarded a certificate of merit.'

More polite clapping from the crowd as I smiled along, listening to this bullshit, all the while pulling my humble winner's face, sad that my armed-robbery days were behind me. Well, probably.

CHAPTER TWENTY-NINE

Starbucks was empty other than two businesswomen sitting at either ends of a long padded bench seat. Sophia and Dane placed their orders at the counter and made their way to the farthest-away table they could manage.

'I'm not sure what I've done,' said Dane, hot drinks collected and cooling in front of them. 'But I feel as though there's something. We can forget all about last night if that's what you'd rather do. I'm in your hands.' He paused, taking a sip of his cappuccino.

Sophia chewed her bottom lip and stared out of the window. 'I don't think I want a relationship at the moment, and don't think for one minute I'm making light of the fact that we had sex last night,' Sophia said, turning to face him, drink untouched.

'It was more than once.' She raised an eyebrow.

'I had the feeling that you were only interested in something casual as well.' She studied his face as she spoke. All too aware that he had been playing her, part of her willing to go along with it, perhaps a small part of her attempting to shield herself if it all went wrong. Wasn't the start of any relationship a leap of faith?

Sophia liked Dane in some ways, though he was extremely arrogant in others.

'Can't we see where it heads?' he said, fiddling with his teaspoon. 'I'm a firm believer in giving things a go and waiting to see what happens.'

'Last night,' she said, 'you told me they'd call us for dinner when the table was ready.'

He stared at her, a quizzical look on his face.

'When I checked, the barmaid said she'd already told you a table was ready whenever we were. We should have eaten earlier; we were drinking on empty stomachs.'

'You struck me as perfectly capable of turning down a drink. You only had to say no.'

'That's not the point,' she insisted. 'You should have told me that we could eat whenever we wanted. You *lied.*'

'All right,' he said, teaspoon clattering back to the saucer. 'Then why didn't you mention this before we slept together?'

Sophia felt her cheeks redden. Was it so wrong to admit that she'd wanted to have sex with him anyway? Had his flippant attitude with Mrs Armstrong put her off him that much, or was she looking for a reason to distance herself from him?

'I misunderstood what the barmaid told me, all right? I thought she said she'd come and get us. Don't try to make out I planned to sleep with you, because I didn't.'

'What do we do now then?' said Sophia.

'Talk about something else, if you want,' he said with a shrug. 'Harry, tell me about Harry and the office politics.'

It was Sophia's turn to fiddle with her ridiculously long latte spoon. 'Harry's a great boss, but he's been under a lot of stress lately. Pierre's death really got to everyone.'

Dane leaned across and placed a hand on hers. 'It does all make a bit more sense now.'

'What does?' she said, pulling her hand back a couple of inches.

'The strained atmosphere in the incident room, everyone appearing much too highly strung for a regular working nick.'

'You really had no idea about Pierre before you came here?' she said, a little incredulous. 'You didn't hear about it on the news when he was killed? It didn't cross your mind that an officer from East Rise had been murdered and you were being drafted into the very same police station?'

He inspected his fingernails, shrugged and said, 'If I'm perfectly honest, I don't take much notice of what's going on in the world if it doesn't directly affect me. And I'm sorry, but I wasn't working here at the time, I didn't know the guy, and the powers that be probably thought it best not to tell me in case it put me off. Not that I had a lot of choice in the matter.'

'Didn't you want to come to East Rise?' she asked before taking a sip of her latte.

'I didn't really know what I wanted, if I'm honest. It seems to be working out okay.'

Sophia smiled and said, 'Harry's a good bloke; no matter what he's going through at the moment, he'll always stick up for his staff. If you'd have joined the department this time last year, you'd have found it a very different place. All the cutbacks haven't helped either. We have twenty per cent more work for twenty per cent less staff. And it's getting worse.'

'Overtime?'

Sophia replied, 'There always used to be endless overtime, because there's too much work, but the budgets are smaller. The money comes in handy, and I'm never one to turn it down when it does come my way.'

'How much were you doing?' he said.

'I was averaging about sixteen hours a week.' He raised an eyebrow at her.

'Sound like a lot?' she asked as she reached for her glass.

'It's an extra two days a week,' Dane said. 'You were pretty much working every single day. How long did you keep that up for?'

It was her turn to shrug. 'As long as I could, and I'd do it again if the chance arose with a new budget on a new murder.'

'Why do you need to? If you're waiting for the fuckwits in government to suddenly wake up and realise that decent officers are leaving in their droves, and those that are staying are at breaking point, you'll be long retired.'

Sophia tore off a piece of her paper serviette and rolled it into a ball before she said, 'Retired? I'll be fucking dead before I see a pension. Thieving bastards.'

'Why did you join in the first place?' he asked.

'To work on murders.'

'Disillusioned?'

'You bloody bet,' she replied, before pushing her drink away from her.

'What are you going to do?'

'I really don't know,' she said, as she settled back into her chair. 'You see, I don't have much choice about the overtime. I owe a bit of money, or rather someone I was seeing *encouraged* me to owe a bit of money.'

'Oh,' said Dane. 'Mind if I ask what happened? Of course, if you'd rather not, I completely—'

'He wanted to start his own business. He said I had a better chance of getting a loan in the steady secure world of policing, and that I'd get a more favourable rate if I . . .'

'Re-mortgaged?' guessed Dane.

'Up to the eyeballs,' she said. 'He got the money and off he went. I thought about letting the house get re-possessed, but decided I didn't want to let the dickhead win.'

'That's a depressing story,' said Dane. 'Some people are low-lives, no doubt about it.'

Sophia felt better for telling him the truth, not because she wanted to share, especially with a man she'd only really just met, but because she actually felt ready to talk about it. She'd kept it from her wider circle of friends, and her family. There was no way she could have told her mum, not with her own financial worries. It felt good to talk to someone about it.

'Shall we make our way back?' said Dane. He flashed her a smile, glancing at his lit-up phone screen as he took it out of his pocket.

'Just got to grab this,' he said. 'Shall I meet you in the car?'

She nodded and headed towards the exit. Pulling her own phone out of her handbag, she realised that she had turned it to silent at Mrs Armstrong's house.

A text message flashed happily on the screen.

Sophia, my name is Hannah. I need to speak to you about Dane Hoopman. Don't trust him.

Sophia read the message through several times, trying to figure out who Hannah might be and how she got her number. How would she even know she was working with Dane?

Sophia glanced back towards Starbucks to see Dane pacing up and down outside the door, features hardened, his grip on the phone turning his knuckles white.

Whatever it was, it appeared Dane had other things on his mind.

CHAPTER THIRTY

It annoyed Sean Turner when anyone took longer than a few seconds to answer their phone. These people were on his payroll. They should jump when he needed them to.

'Oh, you *are* there?' he said, no attempt to keep the irritation out of his voice. 'I was beginning to think you were ignoring me – it wouldn't be the first time, after all.'

He heard a sigh before Dane said, 'I was with someone. I can't simply answer my phone whenever you call.

You are aware of the job I do?'

'Of course I'm aware of it; that's why I'm ringing.' Sean paused, letting his authority hang over the conversation. Dane needed reminding that *he* was the one in charge here.

'We need to speak,' said Sean. 'And I mean in person.'

'That's not going to be possible for a few hours. I'm at some motorway services at the moment.'

'Where?'

Sean heard a change in background noise, the unmistakable sound of someone trying to distance themselves from eavesdroppers.

'We've been running around all over the south coast,

achieving nothing so far,' said Dane. He hesitated. He liked to hold certain things back from his boss; keep a certain level of control. 'It's nothing that would interest you,' he continued. 'Just some old people who were stupid enough to share their financial details over the phone and hand over their bank cards. It amazes me how fucking thick these twats are.'

This news very much did interest Sean, but he wouldn't share that information with Dane yet.

'Get anywhere?' said Sean.

He heard a hesitation before Dane said, 'Not really. The operation seems pretty slick and most of the couriers they've sent to pick up the cards have been untraceable so far.'

Sean took a second to digest this, unsure how much he wanted to tell his police officer at this time, and then said, 'I've got a couple of other matters I need to speak to you about. We need to meet tonight. I've got some transport problems with a delivery guy of mine.'

'I can't keep ducking out of the office,' said Dane. 'I'll probably have to work late, but I'll try to get away this evening.'

'Okay,' said Sean. 'We'll say one a.m., basement club. Don't be late. I hate that.'

With that, Sean ended the call.

For some minutes, Sean stayed where he was, phone in his hand, sat on a cheap wooden seat at the back of the holiday park clubhouse.

It gave him a little time to think. This was a huge cause for concern. He had nearly £500,000 in cash to shift, as well as jewellery he'd defrauded from the dumb-witted public, just like the ones Dane had mentioned. With the police catching on, he'd have to act a lot faster than he'd previously have liked.

There was no room for mistakes.

CHAPTER THIRTY-ONE

EVENING OF THURSDAY 7 MAY

Harry Powell had once again ended up being the last person in the office. As a detective inspector, he wasn't entirely convinced that was the correct order of things. Long gone were the times he would drag out the day as long as possible, simply to avoid going home and spending a couple of hours in front of the television ignoring Mrs Powell.

These days, he was only too keen to get home to his girlfriend, Hazel. She understood that he needed some peace and quiet, more so lately.

One of the reasons Harry was so late leaving was that he wanted to call Frank, Pierre's fiancé. After Pierre's death, Harry had met with him on a number of occasions, each one ending up being as emotional as the last.

Twice Harry picked up the phone and twice he put it down, making excuses to himself that he had to get a coffee or send an email first.

He steeled himself on the third attempt and dialled the number.

'Frank,' he said. 'Hello, mate, it's Harry.'

'Hey, good to hear from you.'

'Are you still okay to talk on the phone?' said Harry. 'Like I said last time, it's never a problem if you want me to come round or meet you somewhere.'

'You've done enough for me, you truly have.'

'You know how much I thought of—'

'I know, I know.'

Harry heard Frank's voice catch.

'There is one thing,' said Frank, hesitation in his voice.

'Name it, whatever you need.'

'I probably shouldn't bother you with this.'

'I'd be annoyed if you didn't.'

'Well,' said Frank, with an audible intake of breath, 'I know that I shouldn't talk about money, and it's not as if I'm hard-up . . .'

Harry felt his brow furrowing, muscles in his shoulders tightening. 'Go on.'

'I'm just going to come out and say it. I've been told that I won't get Pierre's life assurance benefit. He filled the form out years ago, put down his mum's details and never got around to changing it, and as she's got dementia, legally there's nothing I can do about it.'

'What the actual fuck?' said Harry.

'I know we weren't married and didn't have kids, but . . .' said Frank. 'I feel bad even mentioning it.'

'Look, leave it with me,' said Harry, forehead almost touching the desk, hand in his hair. 'This is bollocks. I'll find out and get back to you.'

Once the phone call had ended, Harry sat for a couple of minutes until his temper was under control. In a move to calm himself, he walked into the incident room and wandered from desk to desk, perusing what each of his team had on their workspace.

He wasn't going through their paperwork or checking up on

them, merely being plain, good old-fashioned nosy.

It comforted him to know what they were all up to, and it kept his hand in. It was many years since he'd been a detective constable investigating rather than managing, attending endless meetings and worrying over budgets.

Another of the reasons Harry found himself snooping about in the office at the end of the evening was because he wanted to find out if anyone had any of Pierre's files. He could have asked Sandra or one of the others, but at the mention of him Harry knew he got upset, and tonight's call to Frank wasn't going to help that. He could have tried looking it up on the computer but, truth be known, all Harry wanted to do was sit at Pierre's desk and lament the loss of his friend.

He sat with the CCTV disk in his hand, the one he had picked up at the jeweller's earlier that day. He didn't yet know what it was for, but there was no way he would have refused to collect it, and he didn't want anyone else to pick it up either.

The manager had been quite insistent that he didn't know why Pierre had wanted the footage, but as they'd known each other for years he hadn't even asked.

Harry turned the disk over in his hand and checked the date on the plastic cover. 'WED 29TH NOV' was scribbled on it in black marker pen.

Then the significance of the date hit Harry full on.

He stared at the disk, disbelief at what he was holding in his hand.

Harry quickly powered up the computer in front of him and opened Pierre's drawer in search of his daybook. Any work Pierre had done for a murder, rape or other Major Crime investigation, same as the other DCs, he would have made notes in his investigator's notebook.

At the time of Pierre's death, anything to do with the attempted murder he was working on was seized pending an investigation. His day-to-day belongings, however, were still in his desk, which Harry was currently rifling through.

Holding his breath, Harry took out the notebook and leafed through the pages, flicking between Pierre's last entry a couple of weeks before his death, and Wednesday the 29th of November.

He held a shaky hand over the page, running his finger along the lines as he read them.

The first entry was a reminder to pick up his expenses, and the second was a phone message he took for another member of the team. The rest of the day was blank.

Absent-mindedly scratching at his stubble, it dawned on Harry that Pierre obviously wouldn't have asked for the CCTV to be put aside on the same day as the recording was taken.

He sat at Pierre's desk flicking through the entire book, digesting all the work Pierre had covered, messages he had taken and notes to himself, with small, satisfying ticks next to each task when completed.

Then Harry found an entry for 13 December, which read:
Phone Barry at B's to put aside CCTV.

A neat little tick meant that Pierre had made the call, but Harry obviously knew that he never got round to picking up the footage.

The sound of two officers returning noisily to the incident room distracted Harry from thinking too hard about Pierre's unfinished task.

He looked up and smiled at Sophia and Dane.

'You okay, you two?' he said, attention back on the screen.

'Yeah,' said Sophia as she dumped her paperwork and overnight bag on her desk. 'We got loads of statements and they've warned us how much work there might be coming up.'

This time Harry peered intently at her over the screen. 'You all right with that? You're both off late tonight.'

'To be honest, boss, I could do with the overtime, and besides, the Fraud DS told us we can get in a little later tomorrow if we like.'

Harry scrutinised his newest addition's face. It gave nothing away.

'Yeah, be good experience,' said Dane. 'I'm looking forward to finding out more about it in the morning.'

'So, is it all a bit need-to-know?' asked Harry, keeping an eye on the screen in front of him as he spoke.

'No idea who, where or what we're looking for until the briefing tomorrow,' said Sophia as she walked over to stand behind Harry. 'It's very much being kept under wraps at the—'

'Fucking hell,' said Harry.

'You took the words right out of my mouth,' said Sophia as she leaned in to get a better look at the screen.

'Is that who I think it is?' said Sophia, finger pointing at a grainy figure on the CCTV footage.

'You bet it is,' said Harry, feeling that at last, something was going right in the Jenny Bloomfield murder investigation.

CHAPTER THIRTY-TWO

Sheila Flanagan never had trouble in her pub, so securing the doors of The Boundary at 11.15 p.m. was never an issue. Long gone were the days of lock-ins. They weren't worth the bother, she didn't need to siphon money off the brewery, and she really didn't want to attract any more attention to her pub.

It had been another slow night, but that was of no issue to her. The money was coming in thick and fast from other avenues. Sean Turner trusted her implicitly, and the locals knew that the boozer was under protection from people you simply didn't mess with.

She was as safe as houses.

She helped herself to a double gin from the optics, filled her glass with ice and grabbed a bottle of bitter lemon from the shelf. As she flipped the cap off with the bottle opener fixed to the wall, a sound outside distracted her. Sheila paused, glass in one hand, bottle in the other.

Realising it was only the sound of a van pulling up outside, she poured some of her mixer in the glass and reached for her cigarettes.

She'd risk the smoking ban: she couldn't remember the last

time anyone had paid a visit to check on her licensing hours or make sure she wasn't dealing cocaine from the toilets.

Sheila shook her head, massive gold hoop earrings jangling as she marvelled at what a forgotten part of the world she lived in.

Another noise outside.

For a second, her mind flitted to the contents of her upstairs kitchen: bundles of cash, gold and platinum jewellery, stolen and fraudulently obtained credit cards.

Just who would be stupid enough to try to rip off Sean Turner?

To be on the safe side, she went to the window; the old panes with the lower half frosted meant she had to climb onto the padded bench against the wall to see outside.

As her dyed blonde head, dark roots and all, appeared over the frosted glass, the only word she had time to say before the sound of splitting wood as the doors crashed open was '*Fuck*'.

'POLICE!' hollered a voice. 'Stay where you are!'

More people raced through the doors than the pub had seen in decades, covering every corner, entrance and exit. Each and every one kitted out head to toe in black, several carrying batons and one restraining a very angry German Shepherd.

Sheila stayed where she was, balancing on the bench, gin in one hand, lit cigarette in the other.

'Bit fucking over the top, ain't it, gents? Riot police for smoking on licensed premises.'

'We've got a warrant to search the pub for '

'Yeah, yeah, love,' she said before downing her drink in one. 'No sense of fucking humour, some people.'

CHAPTER THIRTY-THREE

EARLY HOURS FRIDAY 8 MAY

The basement of the club was the sort of place that no one ever needed to or, in fact, was *allowed* to sign in to. There was no name above the door, and if you found yourself in there without an invitation, it was frequently for the wrong reasons.

The entrance was in an alleyway off the main part of town and through a junk shop. A junk shop that didn't sell much in the way of junk. It opened sporadically, mainly to rid itself of too much unwanted attention from other local businesses, and was fronted by a woman in her seventies who gave the impression of being both deaf and batty.

Perfect for the likes of Dane and Sean to meet up in.

As Dane was about to descend the stairs into the club, he paused, sent a quick text to Sophia to tell her he'd see her later, and then made his way down to the bar. The wooden counter took up the length of one of the walls. He leaned against it, nodded to a woman who looked even older than the woman in the junk shop, and pointed to a fridge full of bottled beers.

'A Peroni, please, Doreen, and have one yourself.' He threw a twenty-pound note on the bar, looked across the six or seven tables to where Sean was sitting, and pointed at his own drink.

Sean shook his head and held up a glass of brandy.

Without waiting for change, mostly because he knew he wouldn't get any, Dane crossed the twenty feet or so of smoke-filled floor to get to his employer.

Giving him a wary eye, Sean reached into his pocket and pulled out a large brown envelope.

'Yeah, I know it's a cliché,' he said, 'giving a copper a large brown envelope, but I ran out of thank-you cards.'

Dane put out a hand and, naturally, opened it to check the contents.

'Take it out and count it,' said Sean. 'You know you're in safe company. All the while you're sitting in here, you won't get mugged for three grand. It's outside you've got to worry about.'

They studied each other across the heavy wooden table.

'You look surprised,' said Sean.

'That wasn't what we agreed. We said five grand.'

The chatter from the handful of other members of the criminal fraternity had returned to a gentle hum, leaving them to talk without being overheard, not that it would have mattered much.

'You're right,' said Sean as he picked up his glass and held it to his nose, delighting in the aroma. 'You gave me one piece of info about a fucked CCTV camera and carried out an address check for someone who owed me drugs money. After tonight's turn of events, you're lucky to have got sod all.'

The look of surprise on Dane's face was genuine. He leaned closer to Sean.

At last, after holding his drink up to the bare light bulb, swirling it in his glass and pushing his nose so far inside that Dane thought he was going to ingest it via his nostrils, Sean finally took a sip.

'That's really very good brandy,' he said.

'What's happened?' asked Dane, sensing a change in tone from Turner and expecting the fall-out to head his way.

'A lovely little boozer that houses my business got knocked off barely two hours ago.'

'Christ,' said Dane, picking up his beer to take a swig. 'Rival gang?'

This earned a stare from his employer.

'You could say that, Dane. Only it was *your* gang, so what the fuck are you going to do to make this right?'

Dane slammed his beer bottle down on the table, prompting an immediate reaction from Doreen, who yelled, 'Fucking keep it down or you're out on your arse.'

In response, and suitably chastised, Dane waggled his fingers at her by way of an apology. He knew better than to kick off in here. Some of the hardest villains in the south-east were drinking mere feet away from Dane. And most of them knew what he did for a living, or at least, the wage he declared to the taxman.

'How would I make this right?' Dane said. 'Like I've got an in when it comes to everything that's going on in this county. Where is this pub, for a start?'

'South-east London.'

'*Seriously?*' said Dane a little too loudly. Then, with a little less volume, he continued, 'You are aware that there's more than one police force in the country? You're talking about the Met Police. I don't work for them, remember? How was I supposed to know that was going to happen?'

Sean leaned back in his chair.

'The pub might have been in Metropolitan Police land, but the filth who raided it were your lot. So, you know what that means?'

'I'm to blame?' said Dane, angrier than he should have been. Fear would have been a better emotion.

'They've got my money. Your mates. They've taken my money, equipment and everything I've worked hard for. And you're going to get it back.'

'Me?' said Dane, no attempt to keep his voice down. 'How exactly am I supposed to do that?'

'That's not really my problem. What I do know is that they'll have to store it somewhere, and somewhere safe. Your headquarters? I don't know and I don't fucking care. Now, I suggest you drink your beer, fuck off home, and find out where my money is and how you're going to get it back for me. I'll be in touch.'

Not for the first time, Dane was being dismissed. It wasn't something he was fond of, especially not from Sean Turner of all people.

The nasty bastard.

As Dane pocketed the money and downed his beer, he made for the exit, considering the long day of work ahead of him.

He hadn't been told about the warrant on the pub for a reason. He didn't think his colleagues were on to him or he'd have found himself in a cell. Someone was clearly suspicious of information being leaked, or it wouldn't have been so closely guarded.

All he had to do now was find out where the money and goods were stored and steal them back from the police.

Couldn't be simpler.

CHAPTER THIRTY-FOUR

Sophia's night's sleep had been a very broken one. She was exhausted by the time she got to bed, but felt unable to get to sleep, having too much on her mind.

She had her reservations about Dane. Even though she had slept with him, he didn't seem that keen on her, and the mysterious text message made her wonder about him all the more.

Reaching over to the bedside cabinet, she took hold of her phone and saw with a sigh that it was only 4.30 a.m.

Two new messages were waiting for her.

The first was from Dane. *Thanks for today. Look forward to another long day with you.*

In all honestly, she wasn't sure how she felt about him texting her in the early hours. She had been a bit more open with him today and had spoken more freely than she had in a long time. At the thought of him her heart gave a lurch, the kind of leap she'd felt before, often shortly before it all went wrong, when he turned out to be married, or about to fleece her for £15,000.

She clutched the edge of the duvet up under her chin, for

comfort more than warmth on such a mild May night, and it mopped up her tears.

One thing she really hated was crying. It made her feel weak and pathetic, especially when it was brought on by a bloody man. This wasn't the person she had become over the years – a woman who stood on her own two feet, who didn't need a man to pay her way. No, instead, she had paid for him. All those thousands of pounds she would never see again, no matter what she did.

Dabbing at her eyes with the edge of the quilt cover, she got a grip of herself and accepted she was allowing her emotions to overcome her. Another thing she really hated.

Her hand sought out her mobile phone on the top of the duvet and she read the second message.

It's in your interests that you contact me. There's a lot more to Dane than meets the eye. Hannah.

For a couple of seconds, Sophia stared at the screen. She thought about blocking her, she thought about reporting her and she thought about telling Harry. But reporting her for what? And what exactly would she tell Harry?

Being pragmatic, being a detective, and now being bloody angry, she got out of bed, went to her spare room and sat at her computer.

The desk was strewn with paperwork and was much more disordered that its counterpart in the incident room. She sorted through the chaos until she found the endowment policies – that were her one and only lifeline.

All she had to do was to keep her head above water for a few months and things would drastically improve. The policy was buried beneath bank statements riddled with overdraft charges and credit-card bills with ever-increasing balances. It was enough to pay off everything, and with any luck give her a few extra pounds towards replacing her broken washing machine.

She had been taking her laundry to her mum's house for the past five months, and she had never once complained, but enough was enough.

Clutching the policy like a security blanket, she waited until the panic had subsided and focused next on the real reason she had got out of bed.

She knew it wasn't a good idea to search online about someone she was almost sort of dating, but she couldn't stop thinking about all the little things that didn't add up, and the text messages from the mysterious Hannah. Determined to find answers, she opened up the browser and ran a search on Dane Hoopman.

It hadn't really occurred to her to do it before – the man was a policeman. Surely there shouldn't be much, if anything, about him online.

At first, her search took her nowhere, except down many blind alleys. None of the Danes were the man she worked with and, though she hated to admit it, had far too willingly shared a bed with.

Around five in the morning her patience paid off. But it didn't make her feel any better.

Sophia's hand hovered over the button, unsure what she should do. She knew there was no chance of anyone discovering who she was online; a very useful cyber-crime training course at the Police College had taken care of covering her digital footprint. It simply felt dishonest.

The photograph was on someone else's profile page, and had taken a lot of searching, some of it by making leaps of faith that she was on the right tracks.

She took a deep breath and clicked on the link.

It led her to another page, taking another couple of seconds until she tracked down the originator of the photo. It seemed to be an old photograph at some sort of charity dinner. The women were all in long evening dresses and the men in dinner suits. Dane's face shone out at her even though he wasn't the centre of attention.

What caught her eye was the couple behind Dane: an elegant woman and a good-looking man. Two people who were very much ghosts from the past.

If she wasn't very much mistaken, she was looking at Linda Bowman, the woman who had been murdered in her own kitchen, who Aiden Bloomfield had been convicted of killing, and Linda's husband, former Detective Inspector Milton Bowman.

For reasons she couldn't totally fathom, Sophia's blood ran cold. Dane couldn't have had anything to do with Linda's murder, and Milton had died in a car accident. And yet . . .

Sophia had been very aware of the rumours that had once circulated in their incident room, suspecting that everything Milton had done wasn't always above board. There was speculation that he was involved in the criminal underworld.

The problem was, Sophia didn't know what to do with what she'd found. Being at the same charity event didn't mean Dane actually knew them.

Still, there was the matter of Jenny Bloomfield's disappearance and the discovery of her body. There was no way these things weren't connected.

And right at this moment, the connection seemed to be Dane.

She paced up and down, thoughts of who they'd let into their incident room tormenting her. Not to mention who she had let into her bed.

Furious at letting her guard down, she threw herself into an armchair. For several minutes she tried to run over the conversations they'd had. Had he ever mentioned the Bowmans?

She bolted upright.

Of course, Sophia had told him that Harry had been the one who had found Linda's body. Dane hadn't known Harry and Linda were friends.

Sophia felt her breathing return to normal. It was merely a coincidence, that was all. He wouldn't have acted that way if he'd have known the facts.

This was self-preservation kicking in: she was trying to turn her own mind against Dane in an attempt to stop herself getting hurt again. She shouldn't throw away the start of something because of a completely irrational thought.

She ran a hand through her hair, wondering how she had become so overly suspicious over the simplest and possibly most innocuous of discoveries.

A bleep from her mobile phone brought her back to the present, with the realisation that she had to be up for work far sooner than she would have liked.

A text message from Dane read: *Think I have solution to your problem. I'll drop round before work if that's okay? See you soon gorgeous xx*

The thought of ringing him leaped into her mind, but she quickly shot it down. She didn't want him thinking she was so keen to speak to him, and besides, she still needed a little more time to think.

With weary bones, Sophia took herself back to bed for another hour's sleep, trying to stop her brain from thinking about what Dane could have possibly solved for her, and why he was dropping by first thing in the morning.

CHAPTER THIRTY-FIVE

FRIDAY 8 MAY

Somehow Sophia managed to drop off again, until the alarm rudely intruded on her troubled dreams. She jumped out of bed and rushed to get ready. The last thing she wanted was Dane to arrive and find her still in her pyjamas.

Within half an hour she was dressed and ready at her kitchen table with a mug of black coffee in front of her, mobile phone in her eye-line.

No messages, no missed calls.

For a moment, Sophia felt miserable that Dane hadn't contacted her. Then she became angry. Not so much with him, but with herself.

This was doing no favours to her health or her sanity. The only way to get out of this mess was to work through it.

Sophia stood up, ready to get to work at her normal start time. It wasn't as though she had nothing to do. They had been warned it might be a long day, and as it was Friday, most of the others would be keen to get home and start their weekend.

The noise of a text message alert momentarily stopped her in her tracks as she began to walk away from the table. Sophia resisted the urge to look at the screen.

Instead, she guessed she had a couple of minutes to spare so used the time to make herself a sandwich for lunch and save some money. It seemed like the sensible thing to do.

Once Sophia was ready, jacket on, keys in her hand, she picked up her phone. The lure of reading the message was too great, especially when she realised that there were two texts from Dane.

The first read: *Just outside. You awake?*

The timing of the second one was a couple of minutes later. *Didn't want to wake you by knocking so I've put something through the letterbox.*

Puzzled as to what it could be, and wondering how she hadn't heard him, Sophia peered out of the kitchen door towards the hallway.

A package was lying on her doormat.

Hesitantly, she walked towards it, unsure what she might find. She found herself prodding it with her toe, for some reason fearful at discovering what was inside.

Sophia bent down to pick it up and realised it was full of papers.

She took it back into the kitchen, tearing open the seal as she went.

'What the f—' she gasped as she tipped out the contents.

If she wasn't very much mistaken, there had to be over a thousand pounds spread out across her eighteen-pound IKEA kitchen table.

Turning over the envelope, she saw in Dane's handwriting:

Had some luck on the horses. Thought you could help me spend it. D x

CHAPTER THIRTY-SIX

Harry Powell wasn't the only one to make an early appearance at East Rise.

'Morning, Soph,' he said as he walked through the incident room on the way to his office. 'Thought you were coming in later?'

'Few things to do, that's all,' she answered, taking a sip of her coffee.

Perhaps it was her tone rather than what she said, but Harry found himself retracing his steps. He took a seat opposite her.

'Everything all right?' he asked, only just noticing her bloodshot eyes and slightly waxy complexion.

'Yeah,' she smiled. 'Like I said, I've got a lot on my mind at the moment, what with work and stuff.'

'If you're sure there's nothing else.'

Harry wondered whether to take it any further. He could have left the touchy-feely stuff to his DS, but Sandra wasn't really the type either. The last thing he wanted was a member of staff suffering in silence.

He decided to try a slightly underhand tactic.

'How are you getting on with Dane?'

Immediately, she picked up her coffee mug and took a sip.

'Yeah, he's okay,' she replied, not meeting Harry's eye.

'Look, Soph,' he said, not entirely convinced he should be having this conversation with her.

She met his stare. 'What, sir?'

'Dane seems like a nice enough fella and all that, but . . . we don't know very much about him. Work-wise, he seems solid, despite only having a couple of years' experience, but I suppose . . . what I'm saying to you is . . . would you please let me know if there are any problems at all?'

Sophia remained motionless for longer than Harry would have preferred. She gave his comment far too much thought for his liking.

Eventually, she gave a slow nod of her head, shot a glance in the direction of the door and said, 'As it happens—'

The sound of someone's security pass bleeping against the card reader at the door caused her to break off, and both of them to look towards the corridor.

Dane bowled in, stopped and smiled at them both.

'Sorry,' he said, as he put his security pass away. 'Was I interrupting? You two looked like you were deep in conversation then.'

'Me and Soph were putting the world to rights, as you do,' said Harry as he eased himself out of the chair.

'And don't forget,' the DI said as he walked back towards his office, 'if you ever feel like going for promotion, I think you'd make a brilliant sergeant.'

Walking back to his office, Harry wondered why Dane was sweating quite so profusely for such a mild spring morning. Perhaps he had walked some of the way, but that didn't explain why he looked nervy at the sight of him and Sophia engaged in what looked to be a deep conversation.

If Harry wasn't very much mistaken, he'd say that Dane was

hiding something, and he wasn't sure his incident room could take another battering.

Sophia stared at Dane. 'Why are you looking so worried?' she said.

'What was that about?' he asked, with what appeared to be forced casualness.

'What was what about?' she toyed.

'With Harry just then.'

'He's my DI,' Sophia said. 'We are allowed to talk. Sometimes, in the police, you're *encouraged* to talk to your colleagues.'

'I've offended you,' Dane said, taking the seat that Harry had left seconds ago. 'I knew I shouldn't have just shoved the envelope through the door and left you to open it.'

'It was the most surprising post I've ever received, I'll give you that,' she said, a touch more calmly than she actually felt.

'As soon as we manage to get away from work for a couple of hours I'll tell you everything.'

'I think you'd better,' she said. 'And your explanation better be good.'

CHAPTER THIRTY-SEVEN

Confident that Dane would do as he was told and meet him as soon as he was summoned, Milo walked through East Rise, taking in the sights.

Some of the buildings were beautiful old houses, many converted into flats or bedsits, a number of them still impressive white-fronted buildings that were enormous family homes. Parts of the town left a lot to be desired.

As he walked from the car park towards his rendezvous point, he marvelled at how aspects of the Old Town were so resplendent, yet a matter of streets away the area was a total contrast.

Milo checked the time and sent Detective Constable Hoopman a text: *Half an hour – Seagull Pickings in town.*

Time was running short for Dane, and he was about to find out exactly how little he had left.

Milo had taken a liking to the grotty cafe with its good old-fashioned British service with a grimace.

He sat at the same table as their last meeting, farthest from the door with his back to the window, white ceramic mug of strong tea in front of him. He clocked the orange waitress, brand-new tattoo on her neck, eyebrows visible from a considerable distance, and thought how perfect she'd be as a drug mule.

He had such happy memories of working this town.

The misted-glass door opened. Dane ran a wary eye over the clientele and made for Milo at the back of the café.

He pulled out a cheap metallic chair, lighter than the sandwiches the mottled waitress was dishing out with her own unique flair. His face told Milo he was less than impressed with this turn of events.

'I'm supposed to be at work,' hissed Dane across the table.

'Technically, you still are.'

'You know what I mean.'

Dane moved back in his seat, prompting the waitress to come over.

'What can I get you?' she said.

'Just a tea, please,' said Dane with a wasted smile.

She was gone before his dimples had even appeared.

'What?' said Dane as he caught Milo's expression.

'You want to watch your girlfriend doesn't find out you're flirting,' said Milo. 'Hear she's quite the looker.'

'Get to the bloody point.'

'Calm down,' he tutted. 'Stop being so touchy. I've got a message from Mr Turner and he wanted it delivered personally. He doesn't want to risk our phone conversations being tracked, recorded or intercepted.

This is the safest way to get things done.'

'For you, perhaps.'

'For all of us.'

Milo paused while the waitress spilled Dane's drink over the table then waddled off.

'Mr Turner's found out that the stuff that was seized from the pub is at the police HQ in Riverstone,' said Milo as he pushed his own drink away from him. 'I don't have to tell you that he's not very pleased at having to do his own research. He does pay you, you know.'

Dane turned his head away from Milo, prompting him to rap his knuckles on the table. 'Wake up, will you?

You need to get on with this.'

'I can't! It's impossible. How can I ever pull this off?'

'Firstly, you need to keep your voice down, and secondly, you'd better find an answer.'

At this, Dane allowed his shoulders to sag, and began to drum his fingertips on the table. 'Any clue as to how long I've got?' he asked with less enthusiasm than was actually good for his health, and that Milo would have liked.

'Hard to tell exactly,' he said as he began to push his chair back. 'From what we can gather, you've probably got until after the weekend before it's moved.'

Milo stood up, walked around the table and placed his hand on Dane's rounded shoulder.

'I have to say,' he said, as he placed his mouth close enough to Dane's ear that only he could hear. 'I've very much enjoyed our chat.'

Milo slapped him on the back and walked off in the direction of the door, leaving Dane wondering how on earth he was going to get away with burgling police headquarters without being seen.

CHAPTER THIRTY-EIGHT

As he pushed his tea away from him, Dane knew with sinking heart that it was now or never.

He took out his phone and jabbed at the buttons before he could change his mind. He forced himself not to disconnect the call before Sophia answered.

The surprise in her voice was evident. 'Dane?' she said. 'Aren't you in the office?'

'No, Soph,' he said, smiling to try to keep his voice as light as possible.

'Is everything okay? You sound strange. Where are you?'

'I nipped into the town after we spoke. I had to catch up with an old . . . acquaintance. I'm all right though, don't worry.'

Dane took a deep breath. 'You free tomorrow night? I've got something very important I need to ask you.'

He heard it then: the hesitation in her voice. Sophia had no idea of the magnitude of what he wanted to ask her. He assumed she would think it had everything to do with all the time they'd been spending together outside of work. In a way it did, yet not quite how Sophia could ever have foreseen.

'Any hint of what it's about?' she asked with a drop in

background noise, leaving Dane to guess she'd stepped outside the incident room.

'Not until tomorrow,' he said, sounding more mysterious than panicked, which was the exact opposite of how he felt. 'It'll give me a chance to explain about the money too. Like I said this morning, it must have been weird, me dropping that through your letterbox.'

There was a hesitation and Sophia said, 'Are you coming back to the office? Do I need to let Harry know you're not—'

'No, no, don't tell him anything.' He took a deep breath and looked up to the yellowed ceiling. 'I'll be back in a bit. I'm getting my head round a few things first. I've had some family news, that's all. It's thrown me a bit, but I'm definitely fine. See you soon, okay?'

'Okay,' she said after a couple of seconds' hesitation. 'You sure you don't want me to come into town and find you now?'

'No, don't do that. I need to book us a table somewhere. How about a meal at The Grand, on me, of course?'

'Bloody hell,' she said. 'The Grand? What did you do? Rob a bank?'

Dane supposed that the most natural reaction for a police officer was to laugh. So he did, albeit a very hollow sound, to his ears anyway.

'Let me give them a call, book a table for say eight o'clock tomorrow and I'll pick you up at half past seven.'

'Well,' she said, 'that sounds fine, but you said that as though I won't see you for the rest of the day. We've been warned it might be a long one.'

'I'll be back soon and we can get over to headquarters then.'

'In case Harry asks, how much longer do you think you'll be?'

He felt a headache coming on. What was it with detectives

and all their fucking questions? Why couldn't they be like everyone else and accept what people said to them?

'I'm really not sure, Soph. Let's call it half an hour.'

'All right,' she said. 'I'll see you when I do.'

'Nice one,' he said as he ended the call. It didn't give him very long to plan what he was going to do; something that might affect the rest of his life, which was possibly a very short amount of time if he didn't get this right.

CHAPTER THIRTY-NINE

Sophia hung up the phone and sat for a second thinking about her conversation with Dane. She liked him more than she thought she would at this point, but as she sat in the incident room, the hum of a murder enquiry surrounding her, she had to admit that there was more to him than met the eye, and not necessarily in a good way.

Her thoughts were going round and round, questioning what she was even doing with Dane. She was so distracted that she didn't immediately hear Harry calling her.

'Earth to Sophia?' Harry said, after his first two attempts to get her attention had failed.

'Sorry, boss,' she replied, twisting her head towards her DI. 'I was miles away.'

'What time are you due at HQ?' he asked, a look of concern on his face.

'I've got a bit of time,' she said, looking at her watch. 'Sooner or later the DS will probably be wondering where Dane and I have got to.'

'Where is Dane?' said Harry, glancing around the room, which, for once, had more than a handful of people in it.

Sophia hesitated. 'Er, I think he said something about nipping into town before we went to HQ.'

'Really?' Harry paused, contemplating his next move.

'Could you come along to my office for a moment, please, Sophia?' he said, his expression giving nothing away.

'Yeah, of course,' Sophia said, immediately and illogically concerned that she was in trouble.

Seated in Harry's office with the door closed, Sophia said, 'Have I done something wrong?'

He raised an eyebrow at her. 'Why would you think you've done something wrong?'

Sophia shrugged. 'Guilty conscience, I suppose.'

'Not at all. Listen,' Harry said, leaning across the desk towards her, 'I've asked you a couple of times if things are okay. Every time you tell me they are, so I won't keep prying, but if there is anything I can do to help, you will let me know, won't you?'

This was her chance: she could tell Harry about the money Dane had posted through her letterbox. Not to mention the photo of Dane with the Bowmans,

She bit her lip. All that would do was worry and upset Harry without further proof it was anything more than a coincidence and make her DI wonder why a virtual stranger was giving her cash, and in exchange for what? She didn't want Harry to think Dane had paid her for sex, even if, at the moment, that was what it felt like.

'You okay?' said Harry. 'You've gone a bit red.'

'It's still not the menopause.'

It was Harry's turn to redden.

'The thing is,' Sophia said, 'money's been a little tight lately, that's why I like to do overtime whenever I can. Things are massively looking up for me with some investments I've got put aside. It'll be much better in a few months or so.

Thanks for being so concerned. It's why people like working for you.'

She moved in her chair, unsure whether that was the right thing to say.

She watched Harry as he rubbed a hand over his face, fingertips scratching at his stubble. 'Everyone's leaving since Pierre died.'

'It was a terrible shock,' she said. 'The only person to blame is the person who killed him. No one else.'

'That's another thing,' Harry said. 'If it isn't bad enough he died, they won't pay Frank the police life assurance.'

'Why the hell not?'

'Pierre hadn't made Frank the beneficiary, and Pierre's mother, who currently is, has dementia.'

'Seriously?' said Sophia, voice almost a shout. 'And what about Pierre's pension? Shouldn't Frank get that too?'

She watched Harry give a slow, sad shake of his head. 'They weren't married. Frank gets nothing.'

Momentarily stunned, Sophia forgot her own financial troubles.

'Sometimes,' she said, 'this job boils my piss. I've got a pension that's worth fuck-all now. I've got to work an extra twelve years at least and still won't get as much as I should've got. Makes you wonder why you bother.'

'Because we want to do the right thing,' said Harry. 'Talking of doing the right thing, want to work on murders again? We need some more staff on the Jenny Bloomfield job if you're interested. That's really what I called you in for. As you saw, the CCTV I got from the jeweller's needed enhancing and some ANPR work carried out, but we're hoping to have that back any minute. Might be some arrests.'

For a moment, Sophia was torn: she very much wanted to get back to the incident room, yet she'd heard a whisper of a working rest day if she stayed with Fraud, and that meant money.

'I think they've got plans for us today, sir,' she said. 'Perhaps I'll catch up with you on Monday if the offer's still there?'

'Well, you know where I am if you need me,' said Harry.

Taking her cue, Sophia got up and made her way back to her desk. As she got within a couple of feet, she heard the bleep of a text message.

Hi love, don't want to hassle you but any chance of that money? Love mum x

With a sigh, she stared at the year planner on the wall, counting the days until payday.

Harry needed to get some fresh air. He grabbed his jacket from the back of his chair and left the office by the rear staircase.

A walk along The Leas usually did the trick, especially on a warm, bright morning.

As Harry turned out of the police station towards the clifftop promenade, he spotted a figure about thirty yards in front of him. If he wasn't mistaken, Dane Hoopman was walking towards him, and even at the distance he was, Harry could hear him shouting into his phone.

Seconds later, the distance between them somewhat smaller, Dane looked up and saw Harry. His face was a mixture of surprise and annoyance as it dawned on him that his detective inspector had heard him hollering and swearing at whoever was on the other end of the line.

Harry stopped walking, forcing Dane to do the same. With what seemed to be reluctance, Dane ended the call.

'Family,' said Dane with a frown. 'What you going to do with them?'

'They can be tricky,' said Harry. 'Anything I can do?'

'No, cheers, it's sorted, but thanks.'

With a nod, Dane stepped around him and carried on walking back towards the police station.

For a second, Harry remained where he was, his only movement putting a hand up to scratch at his stubble.

Harry's first conversation with Dane Hoopman sprang to mind, the one where he told him that he had no family of any kind.

He wondered how many other lies he'd told them.

CHAPTER FORTY

AFTERNOON OF FRIDAY 8 MAY

Not long after Sophia and Dane left the incident room, Tom Delayhoyde's overexcited face appeared at Harry's office door.

'All right, Tom,' said Harry.

'Guv, come and see this,' he said, almost hopping from one foot to the other. 'We've got the enhanced CCTV back from Digital Forensics.'

'Blimey, that was fast work,' said Harry, as he pushed his chair out to follow Tom to the incident room.

A small, eager crowd had gathered around Tom's desk, all waiting to see the footage, willing the DI to get a move on so they could get a much-needed morale boost, finally feeling like they were making progress.

'Right,' said Tom, back in his seat, playing to the crowd. 'As you know, the footage showed Jenny Bloomfield standing in the doorway of the jeweller's, before moving out towards the road as a car came along. It was all a bit grainy from there on, but it's a lot clearer now.'

Tom relished the moment, everyone hanging on his every word. 'Well, we could tell it was Jenny: the dates matched, we knew that Pierre would have had a good reason for asking for the footage, and we're all familiar with what she looks like. But, what Digital Forensics have been working on is getting a clearer picture of the car and driver, which, thankfully, has now been enhanced.'

He paused again, total silence in the room as he pointed to the top right of the screen. 'This is where the vehicle approaches from. Now watch.'

With a flourish, he pressed play and sat back.

A few seconds later, Harry stood open-mouthed, staring at the computer screen as he watched footage of the late Jenny Bloomfield huddled in the doorway of the jewellery shop as a car approached her, snaking its way along the street.

The car, which they could now see was a Range Rover, pulled to a stop and the driver's window opened, bringing a man's face into view. His identity was partially obscured by the shadows, but Jenny stepped out of the doorway to speak to him, before jumping in beside him.

The team knew they were probably looking at the last person to see Jenny Bloomfield alive, and most likely her killer.

CHAPTER FORTY-ONE

'I've never seen so much jewellery,' said Sophia, as she stood next to Dane in the middle of a conference room on the first floor of police headquarters. It was a large room with huge sash windows on one side and wood panelling on the other three.

An exhausted-looking sergeant from the previous night's search paused with his hand on the door handle. 'Right, then. I'll leave this lot to you. Now we've gone through the handover – the cash, the gold, the credit cards – they're all yours to log and find the owners.

Good luck. I'm off to bed.'

Sophia and Dane looked at one another.

'There has to be over two hundred grand's worth here,' said Sophia, eyes struggling to take it all in.

'Bit more, I expect,' said Dane as he walked over to the nearest table and picked up one of the exhibit bags. 'This looks like a diamond solitaire ring. The stone's fucking huge.'

He sat on the edge of the conference room table, held the bag and its contents up to the light and said, 'Would anyone even notice if we took one?'

'No, shouldn't think so,' said Sophia, 'apart from the lads

who brought it all in and made us sign for it, the evidence gatherer who videoed the warrant the entire time and the Fraud DS who's already told us how many bags of exhibits there are. Other than that, we should get away with it nicely.'

'Makes you think though, doesn't it?' said Dane.

Sophia's head turned in his direction. 'Makes you think what?'

'How easy it would be to take a few of these bags, set yourself up for life.'

Dane was still holding the ring up to the light, a look of concentration on his face.

'Apart from the getting caught and going to prison bit,' Sophia said as she took a seat and began to rifle through her paperwork. 'We've got a lot to do here so we really should get on.'

A minute or two later, Sophia glanced up from her notes and ran an appreciative eye over the packets of cash, the illegally gained watches, rings and bracelets.

For a second – only a second – she thought how much easier her life would be without her ex-boyfriend's loan to pay off, without worrying about taking care of her mum and without having to chase overtime.

Sophia tried to shrug the feeling off, but it was already there. If ever temptation was being put right within her grasp, this was surely it.

Her sweep of the room saw Dane casually throwing packets of cash and jewellery from the pile on his right to the growing pile on his left.

After watching him for several seconds, she took a deep breath and then said, 'Dane, I need to ask you something.'

He looked up, exhibit bag of bank notes in his hand. 'What?'

'How well did you know Linda Bowman?'

'Linda who?' he said, face impassive.

'Linda Bowman?' said Sophia. 'The woman I told you about; the one who was murdered. She was a friend of Harry's.'

'Oh, that Linda,' he said, one hand smoothing out the side of the bag so he could read the reference number on it, other hand busy scribbling down the number. 'Didn't know her at all. Why do you ask?'

Sophia paused before she answered. She had known all along that no matter what the answer, she wouldn't have liked it.

'I found a picture online. You were in it, along with Linda and her husband.'

He shrugged. 'So what? You said he was a copper.

Where was this picture taken?'

'I don't know.'

He shook his head and carried on sifting through the piles of contraband. 'Then how am I supposed to know how I ended up in a photo with them?'

'It looked like a charity event,' she said, biting her lip and turning her attention back to her own work.

'Am I supposed to have done something wrong because I once went to a charity event at an unspecified date and location, and had someone, who I also don't know, take a photo of me?'

'Sorry. Forget I mentioned it.'

He got up and walked over to her, perching on the edge of the table.

'Did you stumble across this photo or were you trying to find out more about me?' he said, peering down at her.

Defensively, she crossed her arms and pushed her chair back. 'As it happens, I did look you up,' she said.

This was met with a raised eyebrow and the beginning of a smirk.

'Go on, Soph. I'm fascinated.'

'Well,' she said, biding her time, 'I've had a couple of text messages about you.'

He leaned back as if she was a physical threat to him.

'Me? Who from?'

'Hannah.'

For one second, he sat perfectly still, and then he laughed.

'What's so funny?' Sophia said when his merriment was getting on her nerves.

'What's the spiteful, delusional bitch been saying about me now?'

Sophia paused. She wanted an explanation from him, but as she hadn't responded to any of Hannah's messages, she didn't actually know what it was she wanted to tell her, meaning that she had no information to question Dane about.

'Tell you what,' Dane said as he stood up and walked back over to his seat, 'please be careful if you ever happen to bump into her. She's volatile. She had a few mental health problems, and I wouldn't put it past her to be dangerous.'

'Why would she text me out of the blue about you?'

'Aren't you listening? She's dangerous, Soph, and she can't be trusted. She got kicked out of the job for her behaviour. Now, that wouldn't have happened if she hadn't been up to no good. Take it from me, leave well alone.'

Sophia couldn't be sure, but in that moment she thought Dane looked more worried than angry.

Perhaps she would meet with Hannah after all.

CHAPTER FORTY-TWO

'Say that again,' said Harry, struggling to stop his mouth from hanging open at Tom Delayhoyde's revelation.

'It's all to do with the cutbacks, boss,' said Tom, several other members of the team nodding in agreement.

Someone muttered, 'Fucking disgrace,' although no one looked as horrified as Harry.

'So, let me get this right,' said Harry, frown so deep on his forehead he could have hidden a biro in it. 'The council have got fuck-all money, and as well as taking out most of the cameras in the town, there are also no operators to view anything that goes on. How did I miss this?'

A few of them looked away and some even stepped back to return to their own seats.

'Oh,' he said, the penny dropping. 'This was one of the many changes after Pierre died.'

'I think you were on leave when it was announced,' said Tom. 'Lots of stuff changed in a small space of time. They announced it, kept it quiet and didn't want to let the public know too much about the possible dangers or cost-cutting.'

Harry accepted the DC's lifeline.

'So how do we view it?' said Harry.

'I can access it from here,' said Tom, pointing at the screen. 'I've got access and can match it to ANPR too, so if this Range Rover was to enter the town again, not only can I search for it, I can try to track it on CCTV.'

'Only a total fuckwit would drive round the same town with the same number plates still on it,' said Harry.

'Fortunately, there are enough fuckwits around to keep us gainfully employed, sir,' said Tom, as he turned his attention back to the computer screen.

He began punching numbers into the keyboard and switched between the ANPR, live CCTV in the town centre and an enhanced view of the Range Rover as Jenny Bloomfield climbed inside.

Harry watched Tom as he punched the registration number into the ANPR, unsurprised when no matches over the last three months appeared.

'Look at this,' said Harry, leaning forward to get a better view. 'Is that something on the front of the dashboard? It looks like a parking permit of some kind.'

Tom's fingers hit the keyboard at a rapid rate, enlarging the section of the screen Harry was pointing at.

'That's a parking permit for guests staying at The Grand,' said a voice in Harry's ear, making him jump.

'Bloody hell, Sandra,' he said. 'Didn't hear you creep in behind me. And I didn't know you stayed at The Grand.'

She peered across Harry's shoulder and said, 'Yep, I'd recognise it anywhere. I do have a life outside of this job, you know.'

Harry stood up from where he'd been perched on the edge of the desk. 'Okay, what I need is someone to get over to The Grand. Speak to the manager there. Get a list of every guest staying there over Wednesday the twenty-ninth of November, going back as far as the twenty-third just to make sure, and up to the first of December. I particularly want to know their vehicles and registrations and anything else we can find out about them. I want their CCTV if it goes back that far. The image of this bastard's face isn't entirely clear, but it's good enough to match him when we find him. Tom, you carry on with the ANPR and town centre CCTV. Have a word with Sandra if you need anyone to help you with it. We've got a murderer to find.'

CHAPTER FORTY-THREE

EVENING OF FRIDAY 8 MAY

Sophia wanted a chance to speak to Dane before their night out. Her attempts to find the right words continually failed her, and their exchange about Hannah hadn't gone quite as well as she'd hoped. She was still having reservations about him, not helped by the fact that he seemed oddly focused on what they were doing. Although their brief was to painstakingly log and catalogue every item, Dane appeared to be doing so as if his very life depended on it.

At one stage, from her seat at the far end of the conference room table, she glanced over and saw he had his mobile phone in his hand, jewellery laid out before him.

He was holding his phone in his left hand, an evidence bag in the other.

'You look like you're about to photograph that,' she called out.

Annoyance flitted across his face before he lowered the phone and said, 'Course not. That's already been done by uniform.'

Then he smiled and pushed his chair out, walked towards

her and said, 'I'm going to nip out and get us some food. Want anything?'

'Yes, please. I don't mind what. I could do with a break myself, but I suppose we can't leave this here.'

'Not really,' said Dane as he picked up his keys and wallet from the table. 'You'll be all right here? I don't think there's anyone else left in this part of the building. So much for security.'

'Makes you think, doesn't it?' she said, standing up to stretch her legs and yawning.

Dane stopped on his way to the door. 'Makes you think what?'

'How vulnerable all this is. Jewellery, cash and cards left here like this with us.'

'We're hardly going to take it, are we?' said Dane, hand now on the door handle. 'Or will I need to search you when I come back?'

'I've never taken a penny that didn't belong to me,' said Sophia, 'and I don't intend to start now.'

'Honesty is a virtue only the rich can afford.'

'That's very profound,' said Sophia, fingers massaging her neck. 'Besides, lots of rich people are crooks.'

'True, but where did being honest and playing by the rules ever get you, Soph? Here we are on a Friday night working until who knows when and you're considering working tomorrow too. After tax, what are you going to get in your pocket for two fourteen-hour shifts? A couple of hundred quid if you're lucky.'

She removed her hands from her neck, stiff from hours of bending over the table logging the items in front of her.

'What should I do then?' she said. 'Take Mr Rodriguez's credit card here and go shopping? Grow up.'

'Fish and chips it is, then,' said Dane as he opened the door and walked out.

Sophia threw herself down in her chair. She was tired, and although she didn't like him having the last word, she was too worn out to shout after him.

A text from Harry lit up the screen of her phone, temporarily taking her mind off the frustration of being stuck at headquarters logging stolen goods.

Soph, overtime tomorrow if you're interested. Let me know, H.

Murder was definitely more interesting than what she was doing. She hesitated only a moment before she replied:

Thanks but can't really. Dane and I are likely to be here til late and I'm back at 8am. Anything good?

She saw that her DI was typing a response, yet it took a long time for so few words to appear on her phone.

Bit hush hush ATM. H.

Was it her imagination, or was Harry reluctant to share information with her?

CHAPTER FORTY-FOUR

SATURDAY 9 MAY

Fortunately for Harry, his girlfriend Hazel didn't ask too many questions. She clearly trusted him implicitly, not that he'd ever given her any reason to be concerned about his behaviour.

He knew he'd been a bit distant lately, not to mention quiet on their evenings at home together. It was why he thought she wouldn't probe too much about why he was disappearing off to Sussex on a Saturday morning, when the incident room was on the cusp of arresting someone for Jenny Bloomfield's murder. Harry had thought long and hard about whether he should go, but he simply couldn't shake the feeling that something wasn't right about Dane Hoopman. No one else seemed to notice.

He gave Hazel a hug and a kiss on the cheek, told her he'd be back in East Rise incident room within a few hours and drove towards the motorway that would lead him in the direction of Sussex.

An hour later, Harry pulled up outside a small detached cottage. At first glance it was a picture of perfection with its country garden on the cusp of blooming, green land stretching out behind, cottage itself like something from the front of a chocolate box.

Only as Harry began to walk towards the house did he see the rotting wooden window frames, the peeling paint on the walls and the guttering full of moss and leaves.

He rang the bell and waited.

The door was flung open by a woman he knew to be in her mid-fifties, although she could have passed for ten years younger. She was five foot ten, of generous build with long dark-brown hair, a hint of grey barely visible.

'You must be Carrie,' he said, showing her his warrant card.

'Please come in,' she replied, voice matching her height and size.

He stepped inside, marvelling at how modern the interior looked and the amount of work that must have taken place. He ran an appreciate glance over the front room, which stretched the length of the house.

'Yes, the inside's finished, it's the exterior that's drained our money and energy levels.'

'Been here long?' he said.

'We bought it several years ago, but it's only since I retired from the police last year that I've had time to do much,' she said, indicating towards an armchair. 'It's been a lot of hard work, as you can imagine. The place was empty when we bought it, hadn't been lived in for years, so it really was a lot of hard graft.'

'I love it,' said Harry with genuine enthusiasm.

'Anyway,' Carrie said, 'I know you didn't drive all this way to talk about interior design. You were a bit mysterious on the phone about why you wanted to make such a journey to visit me. It was as if you were worried someone was listening to us.'

'I don't think anyone was listening to us talk, but it saddens me to say that I don't feel I can trust anyone at the moment. It's all too easy to record a phone call only for its contents to fall into the wrong hands.

'I'll get to the point: I'm here to ask you about Dane Hoopman.'

The silence that followed allowed Harry the chance to really appreciate the solitude of the Sussex countryside.

'Dane Hoopman,' Carrie repeated, pronouncing each syllable as if relishing the sound. 'He was quite the rising star.'

She let out a long sigh.

'I was about to put the kettle on, but now I think I'll make it a beer. Want to join me?'

'As tempting as it is,' said Harry, 'the drive back's a bit of a problem, especially with my lack of breakfast. I'll stick to a coffee if you don't mind.'

'Dane Hoopman,' she said again with a shake of her head as she made towards the door. 'I'll get the drinks sorted and then I'll tell you all I remember about my young protégé.'

A couple of minutes later, she was back, bottle of Stella in her hand.

'Yours won't be long,' she said. 'Sure I can't tempt you? I'll even make you a sandwich to soak it up.'

'It's kind of you, but no thanks. Getting back to Dane.'

He watched her lift the bottle to her lips and swallow down half of its contents in one mouthful. He waited while she used the sleeve of her sweatshirt to wipe the beer from the corners of her mouth.

'You can take the girl out of Riverstone,' she smiled at him. 'Now you've seen my classier side, what exactly is it you want to know about Dane?'

'You were one of his trainers at Police Training College?' said Harry.

His question was answered with a nod, followed by another swig of beer.

Harry carried on. 'Is there anything you can tell me about him? Particularly anything that didn't sit comfortably with you.'

Carrie peered at him, blue eyes piercing into him.

At last she said, 'It was never anything, you know, *definite*.'

She pulled the sleeves of her sweatshirt down over her wrists until only her fingers clamped around the top of the bottle were visible.

Carrie's fingers teased the corner of the label from the glass surface.

'He seemed under the radar,' she said. 'And he was always one step ahead of everyone else. I like to think that I was switched on. I'd been a response officer for years, but I was finding the hours and shifts a struggle, so for my final couple of years I went to Training School. I loved it. At least until I had Dane Hoopman in my class. He didn't seem to work very hard, but he achieved great results in exams, stuff like that. I didn't like him: he had attitude, but never enough to get him in bother. It was the looks I sometimes saw him give people when he thought no one was watching. Mostly, it was just this feeling I got, you know?'

Harry wasn't sure that this was getting him anywhere. Carrie jumped from her seat and said, 'I'll get your coffee. And another beer.'

From the look on her face when she returned with his coffee and another bottle of Stella for herself, Harry could tell she was stealing herself to reveal something that was clearly playing on her mind.

'Right then,' she said when she had settled back, legs tucked under her. 'There's little I could tell you of any substance until right at the end of training. Dane seemed to produce good results when it mattered – exams, arrests, getting himself noticed by more senior officers. On our last night out, I watched him in the pub, eyeing up a really lovely young girl called Hannah.'

The second beer looked as though it would have the same life span as the first.

'I know she's not in the job any more; I was never sure of the reason why, but it seemed to be kept quiet. Anyway, I saw the way Dane was looking at her that night, and the way another lad in the class, Clive Cavanagh, was also looking at her. I'd noticed over time that Dane had never become particularly friendly with anyone, but especially not the blokes. He didn't seem to talk to any of them, although he made a point of taking Clive to the bar with him and buying him drinks the rest of the night. Dane couldn't stand him, he used to call him "Numb-nuts", so it made me suspicious that they were suddenly drinking together.' She paused, deep in thought.

'And then there was the accident.'

'Accident?' Harry asked, sitting forward, finally feeling like he was on the verge of getting answers.

'Clive . . . *fell* . . . in front of a car that night on his way home. Most of the group, including me, had already left, but according to the door staff, Clive was pissed as a fart and had to be helped out.'

Harry had a sinking feeling where this was going.

'Guess who helped him out of the door?' she said, smacking her empty bottle down on the coffee table. 'Dane Hoopman.'

This made Harry move to the edge of his seat to take in what she was saying.

'There must have been witnesses, CCTV, Clive having some recollection of it?' said Harry. Her next words made Harry's mind whirl.

'Clive hit his head on the kerb. He never woke up. It was in a part of town with no CCTV and the driver said it was as if someone launched themselves under his car. A driver going in the other direction said the same thing. Clive didn't stand a chance.'

'Bloody hell,' said Harry, a throbbing in his temples taking hold.

'Clive's family were convinced that someone must have spiked his drinks in the pub,' said Carrie, 'as it was very out of character for him to drink so much. The alcohol in his system was off the chart.

'We all gave statements about what happened in the pub and everyone denied buying Clive anything other than a few pints of lager. It never sat right with me, not even the bar staff could remember Clive buying a drink. It was packed in there. Three deep at the bar, most of the time. Anyone could have slipped something into his drink.'

'Christ,' said Harry. 'What have I let into my incident room?'

'The only one who said they'd seen Clive drink vodka that night was Hannah,' said Carrie, a scowl on her face. 'A young impressionable woman. If you ask me, she succumbed to Dane's charms. I expect a lot of women did. No doubt they still do.'

Carrie's eyes met Harry's. 'I hope there aren't any women working in your department with Hoopman who fit that criteria.'

CHAPTER FORTY-FIVE

Unlike Sophia's dreary day at work, Dane's Saturday rushed by. Before he knew where he was, he was back at his flat getting ready to leave for their date.

He paused in front of the mirror, four of his favourite shirts pristinely ironed and suspended by their coat hangers, dangling off the end of his index fingers. None of them seemed suitable, yet he failed to remember a single time when he hadn't had a good night wearing any of them.

He threw the clothes on the bed behind him and ran his hands through his hair.

He had very little choice about what he had to do: he couldn't ignore Turner's demands, and using the police database to find out information for him was becoming more and more difficult. His last posting had given him access to all sorts of information he could easily divulge, without a finger of suspicion ever being turned on him.

Times were changing in the police, and auditing was severely restricting his unauthorised secondary employment.

Dane sat on the edge of his bed, head in his hands, and knew that there was only ever going to be one way out of this.

He couldn't stay and play at being a detective any longer when he was being forced to break into police headquarters to steal an organised crime group's ill-gotten gains.

The big question was whether Sophia could – and more importantly *would* – help him pull it off.

CHAPTER FORTY-SIX

Grateful that he hadn't joined Carrie in throwing beer down his neck, Harry made his way back towards East Rise, paying little heed to the speed limit. He had called Hazel to let her know that he was unlikely to be home for several more hours and not to wait up for him.

As he negotiated the roads, he thought about what Carrie had told him, what his own instincts had told him and, more worryingly, what he had suspected was going on in his own incident room between Dane and Sophia.

This called for absolutely no bollocking about. Harry called the head of Anti-Corruption and explained all of his concerns about Hoopman, plus what he knew about Clive Cavanagh's death.

Half an hour later, when he ended the call, he didn't feel any better for it. Just more of the same sinking feeling in the pit of his stomach.

This wasn't going to end well, and his incident room couldn't take another beating. Whatever the outcome, he was moving on from East Rise. Even if his hand wasn't forced, he no longer felt the same about the place any more.

He swore loudly when he saw the traffic queue on the motorway, but with little option than to sit it out, he formulated a plan in his head about what he would like to do with the rest of his life after Major Crime.

Hazel, the absolute love of his life – after his children, of course – was the most important part of his future. If he was thinking of retiring, he should probably run it by her first. Being at home all day might not be part of her plan for the rest of her life.

While he thought about it, fingers drumming on the steering wheel as he sat staring at the boot of the car in front, he should probably have a conversation with her about Dane Hoopman. It had crossed his mind, and not for the first time, that Hazel might well have been on Hoopman's radar if things had been different. Harry didn't put it past the creep to try it on with her anyway, even though he was certain she would have told him if that had happened.

The realisation dawned on him that maybe she wouldn't have told him, what with him being the DI and in a position to make Hoopman's career – and life – miserable if he dared make a move.

'Fucking bastard,' shouted Harry, drawing some looks from the family of four in the stationary car beside him.

'Sorry,' mouthed Harry to the woman in the front passenger seat, who gave him a less than impressed look in return.

Harry ran a hand over the stubble on his chin. Keeping his temper in check was going to be more of a problem than usual, only this time he knew he was going to have to play the long game.

First things first, he would have to get out of this traffic, make sure that his team were making progress with Jenny Bloomfield's murder, and then get on his way to headquarters at

Riverstone to have the first of what would no doubt turn into dozens of meetings of the talking heads.

As long as they actually dealt with Dane Hoopman once and for all, he could live with the hassle. What he couldn't tolerate was another complete disaster in his office.

Nearly an hour after he was supposed to arrive, Harry screeched to a halt at the front security barrier at HQ. It took him another minute to find his security pass to get in.

He bit his lip as he fumbled in his pockets, his wallet, his warrant card and the side pockets of the car doors. Eventually he found it down the side of the seat. He cursed softly under his breath, aware that the surveillance camera was capturing his every move.

At last he drove in, made his way to the chief officers' corridor of power and steeled himself for what was undoubtedly going to be a very long evening.

CHAPTER FORTY-SEVEN

EVENING OF SATURDAY 9 MAY

Dane and Sophia sat at the bar at The Grand, East Rise's best, and in fact only, star-rated hotel. There was a smattering of customers: a family, a couple of businesswomen sitting alone banging on the keyboards of laptops, and a few tourists. Dane and Sophia, however, were the only two perched on stools at the black marble bar.

'I fancy a martini,' said Dane as he glanced through the drinks list.

'Very James Bond. Is this the part where you tell me it's all been a ruse and you're a spy?'

'You wouldn't believe me if I told you the truth.'

'Ah, the "You can't handle the truth" speech,' she said with a wry smile on her lips.

'I was about to tell you how hot you look in that dress,' said Dane as he put the drinks list back on the bar. 'But the barman's coming now so it'll have to wait.'

'Good evening,' said the barman, Eastern European by his accent, Tamas according to his name badge.

'What can I get you?' Dane looked across at Sophia.

'Martini sounds like a good idea,' she said. 'We'll take two, please.'

Drinks ordered, with a promise from the barman to bring them over if they wanted to sit at a table, they made their way over to a booth in the far corner. The nearest person three tables away was one of the business-women, who was unlikely to notice a bomb go off from the expression on her face and the velocity with which she continually hammered the keyboard.

'So, what's your big secret?' said Sophia, ensconced in her seat, head resting on the high-backed sofa.

'What makes you think I've got a big secret?' he said, laughter lines showing around his eyes.

'Hasn't everyone? And what exactly did you want to speak to me about? Yesterday you made everything sound very mysterious.'

She sat poised, waiting on his explanation. For a brief, horrendous moment, she thought this was the part where he told her he had a wife and kids stashed somewhere, but not to worry because Mrs Hoopman had never understood him, and he knew he'd found his soulmate on that first day, when their eyes met across the front counter at East Rise police station . . .

Dismissing the idea from her mind, she waited, watched the barman as he removed disposable paper coasters from his tray, slid them on the table with a flourish, set down their drinks, added a bowl of cashews and, with a smile, made his way back to the bar.

'Must be about a fiver's worth of nuts here,' Sophia said.

'Cheers,' said Dane, holding up his drink.

'Cheers.'

'Talking of money,' said Dane, with a shift in his seat, and what Sophia thought was a reddening to his cheeks. 'Tonight's on me.'

'I know. And if you think you're getting away with a bowl of nuts and an envelope full of cash through my letterbox, you're very much mistaken, young man.'

He threw his head back and gave what she assumed was a genuine bark of laughter, and not the sound of sympathy minutes before bad news. She had nothing to base it on, yet it didn't stop her from thinking something must be up.

'So, what's this all about?' she said, Martini in hand, preparing for a large gulp to steady her nerves.

As Sophia tipped the glass towards her and studied Dane's face, she thought she saw confusion run across it.

'I'm having a good time with you, Soph. Are you telling me you're not?'

It was his turn to lift his drink up and take a swig that wasn't conducive to Martini-drinking.

'I must have been overthinking things,' she said, with a gesture towards their surroundings. 'I wasn't sure what tonight was all about. And what made you think I should have so much money spent on me, let alone *given* to me.'

'I wanted to take you out for a meal, and I wanted to help you. The money was cash I won gambling, so I don't want it back and there are no strings attached.'

'There's a lot you don't know about me,' she said, 'but let's start with the fact I don't do charity or handouts.'

'Well, I guessed that. From what you've told me, you do way too much overtime.'

'Apart from the fact the police wouldn't function without everyone doing overtime, I need the money. It's no secret and I've told you why. I have to work at least twenty hours extra every month to live comfortably, and anything over that is a bonus.'

'But you still live alone, no roommate or lodger?'

Sophia took another sip of her drink, a smaller one this time.

'This wasn't where I thought we were heading, I have to

admit,' she said, her eyebrows raised partly due to the alcohol hitting the back of her throat. 'Are you trying to tell me you want to be my roomie?'

'Don't be daft, it's only that I may have an answer to your money troubles,' said Dane. 'But let's eat first and I'll tell you more after dinner.'

CHAPTER FORTY-EIGHT

Sean Turner settled down in his seat at the back of The Grand's restaurant. He had really missed this place: not the run-down seaside town, but this hotel, where he'd spent many sex-filled afternoons with a fair few women.

The hotel didn't have the same air of desperation much of the town had, with its drugs, unemployment, immigrants and crime. No, this place was much more in keeping with his lifestyle. A bolthole within his working environment.

Pleased as he was with himself, bottle of Sauvignon Blanc in front of him, swordfish on its way (which he presumed hadn't been locally sourced from the Channel), he was mostly looking forward to the peace and quiet.

The thought of booking a room had crossed his mind, but he had a lot to take care of, so he'd had Milo drop him off at the entrance with orders to wait nearby.

The waitress was a young beauty who melted his heart every time she brought something to his table. He gave her one of his winning smiles as she topped up his wine, and glanced at her name badge, which revealed that her name was Anna.

'Everything okay, sir?' she asked with a look that said she really cared what he said next.

'Thank you, it is,' he said. 'I like being here at the back of the room away from anyone else. Don't want to be made to feel conspicuous.'

He saw her face drop at his last word, a look of panic take over. Clearly, it was a word she was unfamiliar with, in fact, from the look of concentration on her face, every English word probably was a struggle.

'You know,' he said to help her out, 'like everyone's looking at me, the sad bloke on his own.'

'Of course, sir,' she said, a blush coming to her complexion.

And that was how Turner liked to spend his time alone: secure at his table at the back of any room, but able to see everyone coming and going in the restaurant.

Best of all, he was still visible to the other guests.

Sean had seen the two of them at the bar when he'd made his way to his table.

Surely two police officers making their entrance involved a recce of the place before they sat down. They were bound to see him. The young lady Hoopman had in tow wouldn't know who he was, yet that didn't matter. The important thing was that Hoopman saw him.

Some people deserved what they got in life; Hoopman was one of them.

Turner had never liked his arrogance, and his usefulness was quickly coming to an end.

He watched the bent copper swagger through the restaurant's entrance, a brief pause at the maître d' and a hand on the small of his date's back. The exchange of a few words, pleasantries, laughter. All false, all bollocks.

He had to hand it to Hoopman: he had good taste. She was a very good-looking woman, stylish dress, great figure.

He took a sip of his wine.

He watched Dane's date as she walked across the wooden floor, three-inch heels clicking their way to their table. Her walk was confident, her posture fine. Here was a woman at ease in the world.

From where he sat, Turner wondered how she was going to feel when she found out she'd been involved with a police officer on the payroll of a crime syndicate.

Guilt by association.

And if she managed to keep her job, perhaps she'd even think about coming to work for him. He was very much an equal opportunities employer and, come to think of it, he didn't have many women on the books.

CHAPTER FORTY-NINE

Tom Delayhoyde had drawn the short straw again: he didn't mind working late because the overtime always came in handy for his young family, but his eyes hurt from staring at the CCTV screen for so long.

Sat on his own in the incident room, trying to follow black Range Rovers around East Rise, was not his idea of fun. The Grand had whittled down their list of guests with black Range Rovers during the dates to a Mr Sean Turner, but unhelpfully hadn't been able to provide his registration number. Despite all the computer databases Tom had access to, he couldn't find anything on Sean Turner. It was as if he didn't exist.

'Exciting life of a detective,' he muttered to himself as he scribbled down the camera's recorded time on the CCTV viewing log.

With a glance at his watch, he was about to call it a night when his mobile phone rang.

'Hello,' said the man's voice in a reasonably well-spoken accent. 'I'm the shift manager at The Grand. Is that DC Delayhoyde?'

'Yes,' said Tom sitting up, all traces of tiredness gone. 'What's happened?'

'When I took over a couple of hours ago from the day manager, she told me to let you know if a Mr Sean Turner should return to the hotel.'

'Yes,' said Tom, impatience barely hidden.

'He's here, well, he *was* here.'

'What do you mean? Where is he now?'

'I'm so sorry, officer, but he was in the restaurant and now he's gone. The person taking the booking didn't know what he looked like, so we only realised it was him when we went through the night's bookings.'

'Oh, f—. Give me ten minutes and I'll be there.'

Shaking his head at how easily they might have let a murder suspect slip through their fingers, Tom grabbed a stab-proof vest, a police Airwave radio and ran out towards the police station car park.

Within eight minutes, he had called the control room and let them know that all patrols should be aware of a black Range Rover in the area belonging to Sean Turner, possibly using false plates. He had also let his wife know that he would be home late and he had called Harry.

The last call was the toughest and undoubtedly had the most swearwords in it.

'Sir, there's been a development,' said Tom into his handsfree as he pulled out of the car park. 'There was only one possible name of guests with a black Range Rover at The Grand, and that name was Sean Turner.'

The air in Tom's car was filled with the sounds of Harry swearing.

'I'm not sure if that name means something to you, sir, because I can't find anything on him.'

He waited for a response from Harry but when he didn't get one, he carried on. 'The Grand's manager just called me and said that Sean Turner was in the hotel tonight . . . only he's gone.'

'For fuck's sake.'

'I know. I'm on my way there now. I'll call you later.'

Tom pulled up outside the hotel main entrance, got out and ran up the steps towards reception.

He waved his warrant card at the nervous-looking middle-aged man on reception who introduced himself as the shift manager and then led him to the back office.

Secured within the small windowless room, Tom said, 'When did Sean Turner leave?'

'It was probably about an hour ago.' He looked worriedly down to the floor. 'I'm sorry we didn't call you earlier. It's only that no one was monitoring the names in the restaurant, only the rooms. I have the CCTV footage ready for you to view.'

The shift manager indicated towards a large screen split into six camera views. He took a seat and pressed the button, speaking over his shoulder to Tom.

'It's interesting, because there was a couple eating in the restaurant. The man left the woman at the table briefly to get up and talk to Mr Turner.'

Fascinated by what he was watching, Tom leaned across to get a better view.

He need not have worried about the quality of the footage: it was evident to him who else was in the restaurant with the suspected murderer.

Sophia Ireland and Dane Hoopman were a stone's throw from Turner's table.

Tom was sure that his jaw was hanging open as he watched Dane get up from his table, walk over to Turner, lean down and say something to him.

Whatever it was, Tom stared as Turner sprang from his chair, threw a handful of notes on the table, and all but ran from the restaurant towards the hotel's foyer.

CHAPTER FIFTY

When Harry's meeting with the senior officers at HQ ended, he left the building, grateful for the cool May night air.

He stood for a minute or two next to his car enjoying the sensation of his lungs filling with fresh Riverstone oxygen.

He wished he smoked: he could really enjoy it then.

Lost in the idea of buying himself a vape, he was rudely plunged back into reality by his phone ringing.

Harry was all the more surprised to see the name that came up on his screen was Sophia Ireland.

'Everything okay, Soph?' he said, frown creasing his forehead.

'Harry, I'm . . . er . . . sorry to call you so late, especially on a Saturday night. You're probably at home with Hazel . . .'

'S'all right, girl. What's up?'

Hesitation, then: 'I feel stupid now . . .'

'Listen,' he said, 'if it's important enough for you to call me, it's important enough for you to let me know why.'

Apart from being tired and desperately wanting to get home, having just left a meeting with a gutful of people talking shite, which he thought would never end, Harry was also aware that anything he now said to Sophia – in fact anything *anyone* said to Sophia – was no doubt going to be monitored in some way. He cut to the chase.

'Has this something to do with Dane?' he asked.

Sophia's voice caught as she tried to speak. It sounded to Harry as though she was on the verge of tears, and the slight slur to her voice probably meant she'd been drinking. When she eventually managed to get her words out, there was a tremble to her voice.

'I'm so confused, Harry. I can't think straight at the moment. I could do with someone to talk things through with.'

'Soph, you're no fool, but I'll always be here if you want to chat. You know that.'

There was silence on the line for several seconds until Harry said, 'Look, are you on your own now?'

'Kind of.'

'I'm not sure what you mean by that, but if you want to come over now, or if you want me to come and get you, I can call Hazel and let her know you'll be popping in for a late drink. You know her, she won't mind.'

There was something that sounded like a short laugh from Sophia and she said, 'You're about the kindest, most decent person I know, H. That's why I love working for you. The world could do with several more Harry Powells.' She paused, Harry assumed to take in his offer. 'Look, that's very sweet, but could I come over tomorrow instead? I'll bring some pastries. I need to talk to someone, but tomorrow's fine.'

Harry screwed his eyes shut, leaned against the side of his car and said, 'Course. We'll see you around, say, ten tomorrow.'

He ended the call, pocketed his phone and wondered if there would ever be a convenient moment for him to tell Sophia that minutes ago he had sold her out to almost every chief officer in the force.

CHAPTER FIFTY-ONE

EARLY HOURS OF SUNDAY 10 MAY

I woke up with Sophia next to me in bed. And by bed, I meant her bed. It had taken a bit of persuasion on my part, but if I knew nothing else, it was how to manipulate people.

I preferred her place to mine. She had a much nicer home. I knew she was struggling to pay the mortgage, but so was I on my run-down one-bedroom flat.

I would have felt sorry for her, but her life was simple: she went to work and got paid for the hours she put in. How I'd love that as a way of living now.

Instead, I was sneaking around while she slept trying to find something to blackmail her with. It was a dirty way of operating, but how else was I supposed to get by? I'd managed on my looks for a long time, which had become middle-aged attractiveness. Now, rapidly approaching forty, I understood that what was once seen as virile, would soon be seen as past it.

There would be no more Sophias or Marions. No more Jills, bloody Chardonnays, even once there was almost a Jonathan. I had to admit that I was running out of time. There would have been a point I'd have waited it out on my police pay: that was no longer an option with Sean Turner making less than idle threats. Things were simply too risky for me to hang around.

As I rifled through Sophia's paperwork in the desk drawers in her spare bedroom, it saddened me to think how much the police had tightened up on access to information.

It was as if those in charge no longer trusted us.

Leaving that thought aside, I found a couple of photos tucked inside a diary. One was of her and that bloody red-haired old fool of a DI. He had his arm around her, but sadly, they were both fully clothed and the old twat didn't even have anything near a lustful look on his face. It was clearly at some sort of Christmas function. Still, I suppose it was touching that she kept a photo of her detective inspector. I had always thought of most DIs as dickheads.

At the point where I thought I was either going to have to sneak out of the house or nip downstairs to put the kettle on, pretending I'd been waiting for Soph to get out of bed and join me, I struck gold.

My fingers lingered over the paperwork in front of me. I couldn't quite believe my luck.

I had tears in my eyes as I silently read the words that would change both my life and Sophia's.

I didn't have to throw her to the wolves after all.

CHAPTER FIFTY-TWO

SUNDAY 10 MAY

Feeling oddly nervous in his own home, Harry made himself busy making sure that the coffee was brewing and the glasses for the orange juice were sparkling. Hazel had already laid the table for the three of them with serviettes, cutlery and plates, but it didn't stop him fussing.

He saw her look at him once or twice, probably wanting to ask why he was pacing. They had been a couple for long enough now for her to know when something was up, yet she rarely asked. Instead she let him get it out of his system, always ready to listen and give advice when he needed her.

And he did – every single time.

Except this time, he hadn't told her what was bothering him, and it was highly likely that he wouldn't. Not with so much at risk.

He had learned the very hard way after Pierre's passing that he needed to talk to Hazel when things got too much, but the situation with Sophia was so bloody sensitive. It could cost Soph her job, the department its very being, and what was left of Harry's reputation.

The one thing he knew it couldn't jeopardise was his relationship with Hazel. That was simply not worth losing.

Right on time, Harry heard a car pull up across the driveway.

From the corner of his eye, he saw Hazel step back slightly to allow him through to the hallway first.

Harry opened the door wide and stood with a grin on his face as he waited for Sophia to get out of her car.

She walked down the driveway, enormous white cardboard box in her hands.

'Morning, Soph,' he hollered at her from the front step. 'What you got there, girl? A bloody birthday cake?'

He watched her face relax, saw her break into smile and give a genuine laugh. Though it didn't distract him from the rings around her eyes, with their purple hue, or her unusually pale complexion. Still, at least she was laughing.

'Hiya, Harry,' she said, as between them they manoeuvred the box out of the way long enough to give each other a hug and kiss on the cheek.

'Watchya, Haze,' Harry heard Sophia say as they stood, one arm around each other, box precariously held to the side.

'Morning, Soph. Harry, are you going to let her go before you knock that box out of her hands?'

He stood back, held her at arms' length and said, 'Course I am. There's food in there and I'll be fucked if it's going to waste.'

Sophia handed him the box before making her way to Hazel and giving her a more modest embrace.

'Come through,' said Hazel. 'We've only this minute put the coffee on.'

Harry followed the pair of them to the kitchen. Once they were seated around the table, the aroma of the coffee filling the room, Harry pointed over towards the counter.

'Come on, then,' he said. 'What's in it? It was heavy enough.'

He watched Sophia force a smile, shrug and say, 'I got three of everything they had. I wasn't sure what you both liked.'

'Must have cost a fortune,' said Harry. 'You didn't need to get so many.'

Sophia's face reddened.

'Start without me,' said Hazel as she pushed herself up from her seat. 'That's my phone ringing.'

Harry wasn't sure if Hazel was telling the truth or had found the easiest way of leaving the two of them alone.

As soon as she was out of earshot, Sophia said, 'Is she okay with me crashing your Sunday morning?'

'Haze? Bloody hell, yeah. She's sound as a pound. Now, what's going on? And no bullshit.'

Her bloodshot eyes filled with tears. He put out a hand, gently placing it over her trembling fingers clutching the table's edge.

After a minute or so of biting the inside of her cheek and scrunching a tissue in her free hand, Sophia said, 'You'd be a very poor detective if you hadn't noticed the amount of time I've been spending with Dane lately.

On and off duty.'

He gave her hand another squeeze before letting go of it.

'I had noticed.'

'Well, I'm not sure what I'm getting myself into, if I'm honest. He's been a bit . . .'

'Bit what?'

'I don't know how to explain it. He's been intense and then he disappears. We had a great night out last night. Well, to a point anyway. I nipped to the loo and when I came back he was arguing with some fella in the restaurant.'

She paused and looked away. More chewing on the inside of

her mouth. He could tell she was still keeping something back, but Harry wasn't sure he actually wanted to know what that was.

'He came back to mine, which was probably a mistake, and then, well, just before I called you, I thought he'd gone.'

Sophia took a deep breath and said, 'I was ready to chalk it up as one of those things, but when I opened the bedroom door I saw him in my spare room. He didn't see me, but he was going through my paperwork, my private stuff. There was absolutely no need for him to be in there, and what he was looking at was personal.'

Harry asked, 'Any idea what he was looking at?' A slow, sad nod.

'Yeah. I'm broke, completely broke, and I've been hanging on, waiting for a couple of endowment policies to mature. I was set to get around twenty-five grand over the next few months. It's the only thing that was keeping me going.'

'Was?' said Harry.

He watched Sophia's shoulders tense up to her ears.

'Turns out, they're not really worth anything. A letter arrived yesterday morning telling me the news that I'm going to get back a lot less than I paid in, about five grand tops. What with that and what you told me about the job refusing to pay out Frank after Pierre's death, I know I have absolutely no financial security. Harry, I'm screwed.'

Once again, he leaned across and gave her hand a squeeze. 'We can sort this, girl. We'll make an appointment for you to go and see Welfare. There's always a way out, trust me.'

Sophia stared at him with sad, exhausted eyes.

'Even worse than that,' she said, 'I didn't really want him staying the night in the first place. He talked me into it, against my better judgement. I could have said no, I did say no at one point.'

Harry put his head in his hands.

'Soph, if you didn't want him to stay the night, why did you let him?'

'I don't know what I'm doing,' she said, tears in her eyes. 'I can't think straight any more.'

'You're sensible and smart,' he said. 'You can surely see what you're doing, where this is heading?'

'Thanks for nothing,' she shouted as she threw herself back in her seat. 'Even you're judging me now. Christ, I knew coming here was a mistake.'

Sophia pushed her chair back and grabbed her handbag, her bloodshot eyes now spilling tears down her cheeks.

'Soph, I'm sorry. Please stay. Talk to me.'

'You think I'm stupid and vulnerable,' she sobbed. 'Of all people. I thought I could count on you.'

Harry watched her walk towards the kitchen door, Hazel's worried face appear in the doorway, and Sophia push her way out and into the hall.

Before he knew it, he was on his feet after her.

Only a hand on his chest from Hazel stopped him grabbing Sophia and dragging her back into the kitchen.

'Leave her,' whispered Hazel. 'She'll be back when she wants to talk.'

He made his way to the front door as Sophia reached her car, hands over her face. His heart was breaking at the sound of her crying.

CHAPTER FIFTY-THREE

AFTERNOON OF SUNDAY 10 MAY

Time was running out and I had to get Sophia on board soon or I would have to cut my losses. The endowment policies I'd seen were due to pay out, and if I couldn't persuade her to help me pull off my next job for Turner then I'd settle for taking her money.

I had managed several hours' sleep since getting home from her house, and since then I'd paced up and down in my depressing little flat, trying to plan a robbery of police HQ. I had an idea about how to pull it off, but Sophia was pivotal to what I had in mind, and one way or another I would make her help me.

As soon as I had a vague plan in my head, I sent her a text asking her to meet. I knew this would be the most delicate part of the entire operation.

I needed to make the text seem as though I was being thoughtful, but not desperate. The last thing I wanted was for her to get wind of anything being wrong. I had learned from my mistakes in the past and knew only too well how one false step could jeopardise an entire operation.

I need to see you this evening. There are some things I really should explain xx With luck, that would do it.

Barely fifteen minutes had gone by when I got a text from her.

Busy at the moment. See you at work.

This wasn't good at all. I was desperate and couldn't see any way out of my predicament that didn't involve Sophia. I suppose I was fond of her, in a desperate kind of way.

Not one to sit idle, I showered, dressed and drove towards her house. I made a quick detour on the way to pick up some flowers. I hoped she would appreciate the gesture, especially since I avoided buying them at the petrol station forecourt. I had gone out of my way to visit the only florist in East Rise that was open on a Sunday and didn't mean parking in the town centre. Sundays were always particularly busy, not to mention two pounds for an hour in the multi-storey.

Pleased with my purchase, I drove to Sophia's house.

The first thing I noticed was that it seemed like she wasn't home: the driveway was empty, the curtains were open and, despite the warmth of the Sunday afternoon, all the windows were shut.

To be fair, she had texted me back to say she was busy, but I thought she was still sulking with me for whatever reason had set her off that morning.

I sat and pondered whether I should wait or give her a call, not impressed that I'd wasted my time, not to mention twenty quid on a bunch of bloody roses I would never reap the benefits of.

I took out my phone, not entirely certain that calling her was going to work if she wasn't in the mood to be persuaded. Again.

Then, as luck would have it, I saw her car turn the corner.

Should I let her see me and know I'd been waiting, or should I watch her get out of the car and follow her inside?

My life was full of these dilemmas.

Someone was smiling on me today: as she got out of her car her next-door neighbour came outside. I saw them exchange pleasantries and saw Sophia lean over and pat some small, pointless, hairy little dog.

This was my moment.

I jumped from the car, grabbing the flowers as I did so, and strolled over to them.

Flowers held in my arms, I gave Sophia my best winning smile. It was the same one that had won her over at East Rise police station front counter.

As she turned to me, I saw her face harden and then the corners of her eyes wrinkle as she smiled, and her mouth turn from cat's arsehole to grin.

My timing was perfection as the nosy next-door neighbour said, 'Oh, are those for you, Soph?'

'Course they are,' I said, trying my best to look modest, only it didn't come naturally.

I held them out, saw her hesitate.

She took them a little gingerly, with some reluctance it seemed.

'What a gorgeous dog,' I said as I bent down to pat the little bastard on the head.

'Thanks,' said the annoying woman. 'We're just off to the park.'

'Have fun,' I said, as if I really cared.

'Well, bye, then,' said the neighbour, with what I suspect was supposed to be a surreptitious wink, which failed spectacularly.

The walls in these houses were probably fairly thin; I guess she'd heard us.

I was so busy watching her walk away that it took a second for me to realise Sophia was already at her front door.

Concerned that she might try to go in and close the door behind her, I covered the short space between us and made sure I was within leaping distance of the threshold.

'Listen,' I said, hand out to touch her shoulder, 'I'd love the chance to make it up to you.'

She turned, a new gleam in her eye.

'Make what up to me, Dane?'

I hesitated, glanced down at my feet. An attempt at being bashful.

'Whatever it is I've done.'

She was still staring, so I tried a different approach.

'And there's something I really need your advice about. You see, I need an expert.'

Her reaction made me think she was at least curious, so whatever I had done, it couldn't have been that bad.

'Come in, then, but I've got a lot to do today.'

I grinned at her back as she walked towards the kitchen, and followed her in.

CHAPTER FIFTY-FOUR

EVENING OF SUNDAY 10 MAY

Sophia knew that the weakness she felt for Dane was clouding her judgement, yet she simply couldn't help herself. Was having someone in her life who made her forget about the sheer drudgery of the daily grind such a bad thing?

Yet she had to admit it – Dane had entered her life at a low point, and he'd seemingly sensed her vulnerability. She hated herself for that.

She looked across to where he lay in her bed. He was good-looking, funny, he had a job, his own place and sex wasn't something she was going to be complaining about any time soon.

Now she thought about it, how exactly had they ended up in bed that evening? She was sure he hadn't charmed her with the flowers: she wasn't that easily persuaded.

Sophia put a hand up to her lips. It had started with him kissing her. That's right, they were in the kitchen, she was about to tell him that he couldn't get around her that easily. Then he had.

She let her hand drop back down to the duvet.

'You okay there?' Dane said.

'Sorry,' she said. 'Did I wake you?'

He rolled on to his side and propped himself up on his elbow.

'No, I only nodded off briefly.'

'I wasn't sure whether to let you stay there or wake you up. We've got work in the morning.'

He gave a sigh, eased himself on to his back and said, 'What if we didn't have work in the morning?'

'Yeah, funny,' Sophia said. 'What are we going to do? Throw a sickie? Both have a duvet day?'

'I'd make it worth your while,' he said with a wink, and inched his hand towards her under the covers.

'Stop,' Sophia said as she smacked his hand away.

'How about we never had to worry about getting up for work ever again?'

'Ever again?' she repeated. 'What are we going to do? Knock off a bank?'

Dane hooted with laughter, a little too hard, Sophia thought.

'Weirder things have happened,' he said when he managed to stop himself from finding her flippant remark quite so funny.

'So, you're an expert on bank robberies now?' she said, starting to lose interest in the conversation and focus on what she needed to get together for the week ahead at work.

As she grabbed the corner of the duvet to get out of bed, he placed his hand on hers and said, 'Think about it: we're the police. If we did robberies, how bloody good would we be at it?'

For a second, she held his gaze, seeing such intensity in his eyes. Sophia knew she had hesitated for a fraction longer than she should have.

She sensed that was going to come back to haunt her.

'You're thinking about it,' he called as she slipped her hand from his and reached across for her dressing gown on a nearby chair.

With her back to him, she shrugged into the gown, pretending not to listen to him as he outlined his reasoning to her.

'They've taken the piss out of us for years,' he said. 'And you more so: everyone's fucking with us. The government, the Police Federation, senior officers. I've heard enough conversations about them taking away the pension, and I haven't even got one. I can't afford it, and I'd have to work until I'm ready to die of old age before I saw a penny of it. Why shouldn't we take back what we're entitled to?'

Sophia looked over her shoulder, not wanting to meet his eye any longer.

'Because we're the police, that's why, and we're not thieves. We should be better than that.'

She stormed out of the room, full of anger and fury.

It wasn't so much that she was livid with Dane, it was because she thought he was right.

The financial situation she was in was dire, and there was little she was going to be able to do about it.

Little that was the right side of the law, anyway.

Surely nobody could say they wouldn't have their heads turned by the prospect of walking away from all the grief and problems in their life, and simply starting again, putting everything bad that had happened behind them.

Would people really blame her? Wouldn't they do the same in her position? Thoughts of her murdered colleague Pierre flashed through her mind. He had done the right thing and look at what happened to him.

A single tear ran down her cheek.

She wasn't over Pierre's death . . . none of them were. And while two wrongs didn't make a right, she was damned if she'd end up the same way: sold down the river by a failing organisation that couldn't protect her.

Whatever happened though, Sophia was certain she couldn't break the law she had upheld for so many years. So why then was her head now full of thoughts of how she could make her existence much, much easier?

Life wasn't fair, but perhaps she could tip the balance back to where it should have been had she not been dealt such a rough hand.

CHAPTER FIFTY-FIVE

Tom Delayhoyde had spent another day in the incident room, mostly by himself, while his colleagues raced around East Rise and the surrounding areas, following every lead they had on Sean Turner and black Range Rovers.

Painstakingly, Tom watched the town centre CCTV over and over again, watching as a black Range Rover pulled up outside the hotel. Turner jumped in the back seat and it drove off. No amount of enhancement of the footage was ever going to reveal the number plate. The camera was at the wrong angle.

For hours, until his eyes felt as though they were full of grit and his back was screaming at him as he hunched as near to the screen as he could get, he switched from camera to camera and back again.

At the moment he thought he might go insane, he pressed pause and sat upright.

'Oh, you beauty,' he said to himself in the empty room. 'It's a bus. It's only a bus.'

Never in the history of the number 238 bus, had anyone been as happy as Tom was to see it edge its way around the corner and into view.

He grabbed his coat and made his way to the bus depot.

CHAPTER FIFTY-SIX

Sophia stood in her kitchen, mug of coffee in her hands, listening to the creak of the floorboards as Dane got out of bed. She guessed from the moving around he was getting dressed and ready to leave.

Her feelings weren't entirely clear to her. She knew she would much rather be single than with the wrong man, yet she enjoyed having company. Not to mention the sex.

By the time he appeared in the doorway, Sophia was perched on one of her breakfast-bar stools, finishing her drink.

'I can put the kettle back on,' she said, aware that her tone was flat.

He leaned against the doorframe.

'Want to talk?' he said, more enthusiasm in his voice than she had managed.

'I'm not sure what there is to talk about? Some sort of heist? Armed blagging? What exactly was that about?'

'That's a lot of questions,' he said as he pulled out the stool beside her.

Aware that his hand was inching towards her thigh, she stood up and moved to the kettle.

'I'm having another one, even if you don't want one,' she said over her shoulder, voice louder than necessary over the noise of the running tap as water sloshed into the kettle.

'Soph, please come and sit down.'

She set the kettle down and slid back on to the stool beside him.

'We've just spent several hours in bed and then you come out with ludicrous crap like that.' She stared at him.

He laced his fingers together, left his hands on the breakfast bar and slowly shook his head.

'I'm not sure where to begin,' he said, still looking down at his hands. 'I'll level with you . . . I've had financial difficulties, all right? It's something I didn't want to bring up and burden you with. It's not your problem, it's mine.'

Dane gave a miserable shrug and peeked out at her from under his hair.

For a moment, Sophia almost fell for the little-boy-lost look, then she remembered that she had put her days of being won over by good looks alone well behind her.

'So, go on,' she said, 'what's the great plan that'll get us a new life on the Spanish coast?'

'Don't be glib. If you want me to tell you how we can change our fortunes, I will, but not if you're going to take the piss.'

Sophia had to hand it to him – he did look genuinely hurt.

'Sorry. Go on.'

They sat side by side, staring ahead for several seconds before Dane started to speak.

'I've not always been a completely decent person. I've done some stuff in my past that I'm not particularly proud of, but that stopped when I joined the police. I wanted to help people, lock up criminals. You know, the sort of stuff most people join for.'

Sophia said nothing. She'd had her own reasons for becoming a police officer.

'Well, I turned a corner,' Dane said. 'I put everything behind me and threw myself into the world of fighting crime. And if I do say so myself, I'm bloody good at it.' She couldn't resist a giggle at this part. 'Don't laugh at me, please.'

'I'm sorry. Go on,' she repeated.

He gave a rather dramatic sigh before continuing. 'All my life, I've worked so hard, put in the hours, but even with working like a dog, well, I got into debt, lots of it.

'A bit like yourself, no matter how much overtime I did, I couldn't get ahead of the game. Like a mug, I tried gambling. I won a few times, of course, although it hardly swelled my bank balance. I've managed to get by, and I had to sell my house to pay off what I owed. It's left me with virtually nothing, but at least I've got a roof over my head.'

'So, the flat you're in isn't yours?' Sophia said.

'No, I rent. It's a crap-hole, but it's home.'

'And what's your plan?'

Dane gave a wry laugh and turned on his stool to look at her. He put his hands over hers.

'Love the way you said, *"Your* plan".'

'Well, I have to distance myself from the conspiracy to commit burglary somehow.'

'Interesting,' said Dane. 'You've gone for a classic burglary rather than a robbery.'

'Robbery means violence and I don't want to hurt anyone.'

His eyebrows all but disappeared under his hair.

'So, you're saying what?' he said. 'You're actually thinking about doing this?'

'Doing what though, Dane? I don't actually know what it is you're thinking of doing.'

He let go of her hands to push his hair back from his face.

'I need to know that you're really going to help me take part in this before I tell you what it is,' he said. 'There'll be no going back once I make you a part of it.'

She took a long slow breath and said, 'I know, I know, but what have I got to lose? Apart from my freedom, job, friends and family?'

'At least you have a home,' he said under his breath. 'Just about.'

She watched his face intently as she said, 'Fortunately, I have endowment policies about to pay out, even though they're now worth nowhere near what they should be. If it wasn't for them, within six months I'd be homeless. I've had to re-mortgage twice to cover my own debts. You're not the only one with piss-poor finances. I'd say we were well and truly suited.'

Was there a flicker of disappointment? It was hard to tell. So practised was Dane's performance that Sophia knew she would have missed any deviation from his usual manner if she hadn't been looking out for it.

'You too, hun,' was all he had to say.

'Too right. Too bloody right.'

For a second, they sat in miserable solitude until Dane broke in on her thoughts and said, 'So we take what they owe us. It's that simple.'

'How do we right this wrong?' she said.

It was as if someone had switched a light on behind his eyes, illuminated his entire face. He came alive in a manner Sophia had never witnessed before.

'We take enough to tide me over and what you'd have got if you'd never paid into their bloody pension in the first place. Imagine if you'd taken the amount you've put into a pension you were mis-sold and invested it in property. You'd have a house that you'd bought for something like a hundred and twenty grand, now worth nearly half a million.'

He sat back, arms crossed as if the job was done.

'Yes, but I didn't, although I could have,' she said.

She held his stare.

'Headquarters has a safe,' he said.

'As it happens, there are a number of them.'

'One of them in particular has a lot of money in it,' said Dane. 'And it's money that shouldn't be there.'

In spite of all the conflicting feelings she was having, she did have to admit to herself that she was more than mildly interested.

'Are you talking about the money and jewellery we've just put in there?' she said, getting up to make the abandoned coffees.

'Pour me a whisky to go with that and I'll tell you.'

Sophia reached up to the cupboard to grab a couple of glasses and pointed Dane in the direction of the meagre selection of spirits she had in another cupboard.

With a bottle of cheap booze, two glasses and two mugs of strong coffee between them, Dane sketched out a crude map of police headquarters on the back of a piece of kitchen towel with a pen he'd found on the worktop.

'The safe is here, on the top floor.' He jabbed at the cross he'd made with the end of the pen. 'And we go in here.'

'Are you crazy? In the front? Trust me on this, through the back across the fields is definitely the better option.'

He stared at her, head on one side. 'There are less cameras at the front.'

Sophia took the time to enjoy her moment. She sat back and positively beamed at him. It was her turn to take the pen and stab at the map.

'This camera here at the back,' she said, 'doesn't work and won't record. This one here is permanently pointed at the chief superintendent's car since someone dented it last year and failed to own up, and this one here is a dummy.'

With a sly smile, Dane topped up both of their glasses, held his up and said, 'I guess I underestimated you, young lady. Here's to our success.'

'Here's to us,' she said, as their glasses clinked together. 'And so I'm clear, how much money's in the safe?'

Dane took a sip of his whisky, leaned across and whispered in her ear, 'Eight hundred and fifty thousand pounds.'

CHAPTER FIFTY-SEVEN

MONDAY 11 MAY

The start of the working week in the incident room had its usual stresses and strains: too much work and not enough people to do it, another busy weekend meaning everyone who had been on duty had accumulated an average of ten hours of overtime in two days, and Harry had no idea when he was going to get his staff back from the newest investigations to raid his workforce. He had already told the Fraud Department that they were taking the piss and he wanted his two detectives to return immediately.

He was relieved to see Sophia walk through the door after she'd stormed out of his house. She looked exhausted. As if she'd had a very late night.

Dane walked in barely two seconds behind her, stifling a yawn as he swaggered to his desk.

Harry had to hand it to him, he looked as tired as Sophia, yet he appeared to be more worn in than worn out.

Unsure whether to make too much of it, Harry thought it best to leave them to it: if he was right and Sophia had spent the rest of her Sunday with Dane, he was far from certain what

Dane now knew of Harry and Sophia's conversation. That was a depressing thought.

For now, he decided to sit back and watch what they did.

Harry made himself busy at the photocopier nestled in a far corner. He tried his best to make copying a memo five times take as long as he needed to so he could surreptitiously watch Sophia.

He saw her check something on her screen and a frown crease her forehead as she leaned closer to read it, her mouth hanging slightly open.

He didn't want to let her see him studying her every move and was even less keen that anyone else in the office should catch him observing her.

From the corner of his eye, he saw her jot something down, rip the piece of paper from the pad and push it into her handbag.

It wasn't only her rapid movements that gave Harry cause for concern, it was that the whole time she was doing so, Sophia was keeping one eye on Dane to make sure he didn't see what she was doing.

Despite the conversation Harry and Sophia had had the previous morning, he couldn't fight the feeling that she was about to land herself in serious trouble. And Harry knew he could only help her so far when the time came.

CHAPTER FIFTY-EIGHT

To describe Sophia's morning as emotional would be an understatement. As soon as she checked her messages, workload and emails, she knew that the day was about to take an unpleasant turn.

Initially she had paused over opening the email, coming from a source she didn't know, the sender listed as Hannah Reeves. The name made her breath catch in her throat. The only Hannah who had contacted her recently had warned her to stay away from Dane. It had to be the same person, so she opened it.

With a casual glance or three in Dane's direction, Sophia tried to remain calm as she read the words.

Hi Sophia, you probably got my texts and haven't replied, so here goes. My name is Hannah and I used to be Dane Hoopman's girlfriend. I was also in the job, but thanks to him, I'm now not. Here's my number again if you want to find out the truth about him and why I'm no longer a police officer.

For a few seconds, Sophia sat and read through the email another couple of times. Harry was making a mess of photocopying one page, Gabrielle was being as weird as ever at her desk, and Dane seemed preoccupied with himself. Nothing seemed out of place for a morning at Major Crime.

As soon as Harry had stopped jamming the copier and Dane was occupied trying his best to get Tom or one of the others to make him a cup of tea, Sophia slipped out of the office, taking her handbag with her.

Standing under the stairwell leading down to the custody suite, Sophia stood chewing the inside of her mouth, mobile in one hand, paper with Hannah's number in the other.

It took her a second before she punched the number in and waited for the call to connect.

A voice said, 'Hello.'

'Er, hello,' said Sophia. 'My name's . . .'

'Is that Sophia?'

'Yes, I'm . . .'

An awkward silence followed until Hannah said, 'I think we should meet. I've got some things I need to tell you.'

'I'm so busy at the moment. I'm not sure I can take the time to meet up. Please, whatever it is, tell me.'

There was another pause until Hannah eventually said, 'I'll come to you. Name a place in East Rise and I'll see you there later today. It's not as if I'm busy.'

There was a short bark of laughter Sophia was unsure how to react to.

'I'm not sure this is going to work,' Sophia tried to protest. What could this woman possibly want?

'Listen, love,' said the voice, now with a much sharper edge to it. 'This isn't for my bloody benefit, so I suggest that you meet me later today. Shall we say midday, so you can look as though you're slipping out for lunch?'

A little taken aback at the abruptness, Sophia found herself agreeing with the snarly woman barking orders at her.

'We'll meet at a café. Do you know the Seagull Pickings?'

'Unfortunately, I do,' said Sophia, common sense kicking in. 'Have you been there before? It's a bit grim.'

'That's what makes it ideal. I'll see you there in a few hours. And it goes without saying, I hope, don't bring Dane.'

Sophia found herself with a phone to her ear, listening to a disconnected signal.

In a little under four hours, she might be able to put some more pieces of her Dane-shaped puzzle together.

CHAPTER FIFTY-NINE

Because I was bored, not to mention worked up, I made an excuse and left the office. I drove to headquarters, firstly to check out what Sophia had told me the night before, but also to get out of her way.

She was still acting a bit off with me and I didn't really know why. No doubt, she didn't fully trust me, and for good reason. I was a criminal, a bent copper. They didn't come any lower than me. And she didn't even know about the shit I'd pulled in the past, despite my heavy hints.

I pulled out of East Rise police station, heading in the direction of the motorway. The shitty little Ford Focus I was driving wasn't going to get me any speeding tickets, and besides, I wasn't in a hurry.

As I drove along, I thought about how Sophia and I could actually have a future together. I had completely cocked things up with every woman I had met. My ex-girlfriends all hated me, usually for very good reason too: encouraging them to spend money on me they didn't have and stealing from them usually did the trick. Some I'd done worse to. I really should think about jacking this all in and heading abroad.

I fancied Spain or Italy.

It all boiled down to whether I threw Sophia under the bus or took her with me. I really was undecided. Perhaps I'd merely see how things panned out when we had the money.

It wouldn't be too difficult to make an anonymous call, leave some of the money at her house, and leave something of hers behind at the crime scene. With several years of criminal activity under my belt, plus a couple as a copper, if I couldn't fit someone up, I really hadn't been paying attention.

It would probably be about the lowest thing I'd ever done to a former girlfriend, actually send them to prison. I'd come close a couple of times, but usually left them a get-out-of-jail-free card. Sophia was different though. Sophia was intelligent, and I saw in her that she had the ability to bring me down.

That's why I liked her so much.

Still pondering the difficulties of keeping her around against sending her to prison, I pulled off the motorway and drove through Riverstone towards police HQ.

It was important to be seen at headquarters, and besides, I had expenses to collect. I wanted to pick up my £27.58 before someone emptied the safe.

I was still smiling at my own joke as I parked the car and wandered towards the finance department on the top floor.

As casually as I could, I took my phone out of my pocket and stopped a couple of times as if I was checking messages, all the time making sure there were no internal cameras or extra security installed since I was last there.

Eventually, I made it to the top floor, got my form signed and approved in one office and then took it to where the money was kept.

Not for much longer.

I smiled at the woman who took my form from me, stamped

it and seemed only too pleased to get me my money from the safe. I liked her.

When she had her back to me, going through the money, counting out the notes and coins, I ran an eye over the back of the safe. It had three shelves, all stacked high with note-shaped bundles and piles of jewellery. In those bundles was the rest of my life.

The other three people in the large open-plan office had their heads down and were working away, not even appearing to be fazed by the small fortune that was sitting feet from them.

Why weren't they plotting to steal it? I simply didn't get people and their keenness to work themselves to death when they could take what they wanted and not have so much stress in their lives.

Then I was signing my expense form and handing it over in exchange for my £27.58.

The nearest bookies to headquarters was less than half a mile away.

With any luck, my horse would come in and I'd have enough to last me until payday having already blown Turner's money gambling online.

If not, I'd have to see how much money Sophia had on her.

CHAPTER SIXTY

Harry had set the briefing time for 10 a.m.

A meagre number of people took their seats in the conference room, watched by Harry from the top of the table as they spread themselves thinly around its edges.

'Thanks for coming,' he said, counting six people and remembering the days a murder would mean twenty-five-plus at his briefings.

He was greeted with murmurs, the odd nod.

'Okay,' he continued, 'the murder of Jenny Bloomfield. As you probably all know, Pierre had the foresight to ask the jewellers to put some CCTV aside. From Pierre's notebook, he had some of her belongings to return to her and when he couldn't get hold of her, it seems he tried to track her down. It shows Jenny getting into a car, a black Range Rover. Tom can talk you through the next part and the developments he's made over the weekend.'

All eyes turned to Tom Delayhoyde.

'Well, boss,' he said as his hands smoothed out the investigator's notebook in front of him on the table, 'the registration on the Range Rover was impossible to see and the driver's face was partially obscured. However, there was a car park pass for The Grand hotel. I asked them to check all records for anyone registering a black Range Rover with them around the time of Jenny's disappearance and they came up with a list that we worked our way through.'

He paused, took a sip of water and said, 'It wasn't a very long list and we eliminated every one of the cars except one – it had tenuous links to a Sean Turner.'

Tom paused again and looked at Harry. 'Go on, Tom. Tell them,' said Harry.

'Prison intelligence has confirmed that Sean Turner visited Jack McCall in prison, Jack being the former cellmate of Aiden Bloomfield, Jenny's son.'

A few incredulous looks greeted this latest update.

'That's not all,' said Tom, glancing in his DI's direction. 'We've recently discovered through Witness Protection and Intel that Sean Turner was Linda Bowman's brother.'

'What?' said Gabrielle Royston, one of the DCs who hardly ever said a word even when her colleagues were talking directly to her.

'We do know,' said Harry, 'that this is a fuck-up of epic proportions and there's already a serious case review of Linda's murder. Leaving that to one side, we need to find Sean Turner Tom, go on.'

Harry stole a glance at the members of his team, all open-mouthed and wide-eyed at this revelation. That they could have worked so hard to lock up a completely innocent man was beyond comprehension, yet possibly they had.

'Getting back to The Grand,' Tom said, trying his best to be diplomatic, 'the staff were briefed to call us if he should turn up. We expected him to book a room as he usually did. Although they were asked to let us know if he came in for any reason at all, they failed to realise that he was in the restaurant on Saturday night until he had already paid and left.'

Harry found himself unable to look at Tom for the next part.

'I've printed off stills of Sean Turner from the restaurant's CCTV,' said Tom. 'I've also put a very short clip of it on the shared drive so you can see him as he gets up and leaves the restaurant, followed by the footage of him getting into the car.'

'Why can't we watch the whole thing?' asked Gabrielle.

Harry knew her question made him look annoyed. The last thing he could risk was anyone seeing CCTV of Dane and Sophia in the restaurant, especially seeing Dane speaking directly to Sean Turner.

'It's something to do with Digital Forensics,' said Tom. 'They've had some bollocking from the Crown Prosecution Service about too many people viewing original footage or something. No one's got to the bottom of the problem yet, so I've copied the important bits and locked the original footage away. Come and let me know if you need anything.'

It was the first time that Harry had ever asked a member of his staff to lie, and Tom seemed to have taken to it like a duck to water.

'Getting back to the Range Rover,' prompted Harry.

'Oh, yeah,' said Tom. 'I spent a lot of time trying to track it from The Grand on Saturday night. Again, the camera wasn't brilliant, and I couldn't get the registration number clearly. I only had a partial number. After hours of trying to track it around East Rise, I hit a break late last night when a bus pulled out going in the opposite direction.

'I went straight out to the bus depot and, long story short, the bus camera will be downloaded first thing this morning. I'm going straight there to pick it up after this briefing. As long as the camera was recording properly, we'll have a brilliant view of the car, its number plate and its driver.'

'Arrests are imminent then,' said Harry with an encouraging smile at his staff. 'As soon as we have it, we'll get the number plate circulated to all patrols, on PNC and ANPR. We'll find Turner and then the hard work will really start.'

The only problem was, Harry knew that any arrest of Sean Turner was going to affect every member of his team. Not only was it a possibility that they had sent the wrong person to prison for Linda Bowman's murder, but he suspected Turner had also managed to infiltrate East Rise incident room through Dane Hoopman.

CHAPTER SIXTY-ONE

Sophia had a ridiculous amount of work to do and she was well aware that, as well as developments in the Jenny Bloomfield murder, there had been a rape overnight along the seafront, meaning that officers were being deployed to carry out CCTV and house-to-house enquiries. Officers were also needed to interview the distraught young woman who had been attacked.

As a Major Crime detective constable, or merely as a human being, Sophia knew how important those early enquires were, yet all she could do was watch the clock tick round towards midday, so she could make her excuse and slip off into town.

She was curious to meet Hannah, one of Dane's cast-offs. The usual questions ran through her mind – was she fat? Old? Plain? Absolutely gorgeous? Was she a threat to Sophia?

The last question seemed unlikely, yet she had no idea what her motive was for texting and emailing her like this.

Sophia fidgeted in her seat and checked her phone for about the hundredth time that morning, earning yet more glances from her colleagues who were all quietly trying to look busy and avoid being sent to another major incident before they'd cleared up the last one.

When at last it was time for her to slip away, she made sure her phone was in one of her jacket pockets and the last few pound coins she had were in the other. She couldn't bring herself to spend any of Dane's money.

If Hannah was thinking of eating, she was paying for herself.

With as much of a hasty exit as she could manage without drawing attention to herself, she made it to the door.

The fastest way to the town was out through the front counter, where Sophia was pleased to see that a small queue had formed, meaning she wouldn't be stopped by Ian behind the desk, and asked how Dane was getting on, as he had on two previous occasions.

Sophia made her way to the Seagull Pickings and stood twenty yards or so along the road. She tried to get a good look at who was inside, but the windows were largely covered on the inside by menus and posters, and on the outside by birds' mess. At least she hoped it was that way round. It was largely regarded as a terrible place to eat, another reason why she didn't want to squander what little money she had.

After several seconds of feeling like the most conspicuous person in the town, Sophia went towards the door.

There were a handful of people dotted around the tables, many sitting alone, most of the clientele eating with little joy and their mouths open, possibly willing the food to make a last-minute break for it.

At a table in the farthest corner sat a woman, similar age to Sophia, pale pink summer dress, long brunette hair hanging loose around her face. She was an attractive woman, although dark circles under her eyes and a slight red flush to her cheeks made Sophia think she drank a little too much and suffered from a lack of sleep.

Hannah raised a hand from the table in front of her and

waggled her fingers in Sophia's direction, who in turn gave a curt nod.

She made her way over, both women watching each other intently.

'Take a seat,' said Hannah, the beginning of a smile on her face.

'Thank you,' said Sophia. 'I see you've got a coffee. I'll just get myself one.'

She walked the few feet back towards the counter and placed her order with an angry-looking woman with amazing eyebrows, before taking her drink and sitting down opposite Dane's former girlfriend.

'I won't pretend that this isn't weird for me,' she began. 'Firstly, I don't normally meet up with the exes of men I'm seeing, and secondly, you seem to have something you want to get off your chest.'

Tears sprang into the corners of Hannah's eyes; she opened her mouth to speak, caught on the words and looked down to her fingers, drumming on the tacky tabletop.

'Oh, boy,' Hannah said. 'This is so hard, even after all this time, this is still so hard.'

Her intense blue eyes focused on Sophia's.

'Does he ever mention me?'

The silence was too long for it to mean anything else.

'No, no,' Hannah said. 'Of course he didn't. Why would he? He had what he wanted, so why remind himself of it. Christ, I've been so bloody stupid.'

Fighting the urge to put a hand on Hannah's arm, Sophia was unsure where to go next. Whatever she said was bound to be the wrong thing.

'Okay,' said Hannah, taking a deep breath. 'I wanted to speak to you, let you know what happened between me and

Dane. Please don't for one moment think that I'm a lunatic raging ex who wants him back, because I most definitely don't, or that I'm trying to jeopardise things between you. That's the last thing I'm trying to do. All I want to do is give you the facts and leave it at that.'

'Right,' said Sophia. 'I appreciate that, but I have to ask, why would you do that? Help me out like that?'

Hannah's eyes narrowed, an instant hardening of her face. 'Because I don't want to see what happened to me happen to anyone else, that's why. Let's just say the only friend I've got left in the police told me Dane was on the move and I've made it my business to keep informed of what he's up to.'

Whatever Sophia's opinions or thoughts, she was going to try her best to keep them to herself. Did this woman have her own agenda?

'What did happen to you?'

Instantly her features softened. 'I fell head over heels for Dane Hoopman, that's what happened. He charmed me, no doubt thought I was a soft touch.'

Here, Hannah's demeanour changed. She leaned across the dirty table towards Sophia, the tiny red veins around her nose and across her cheeks more visible now. Her mouth tightened into a mean straight line, skin puckered at the edges of her lips.

'It's what he goes for, you know. The lonely and the weak.'

Sophia guessed that some spitefulness was inevitable.

'And don't look at me like you pity me,' said Hannah. 'He hasn't ruined your life yet. I know that much or else you wouldn't be sitting here now in your work suit, nipping out for lunch.'

She threw herself back in her cheap, silver, lightweight chair, tucked a strand of hair behind her ear.

'Oh no,' she continued. 'He would have had you roped into

his next get-rich-quick scheme by now, and like me, you'd have been out of a job.'

Not for the first time, Sophia wondered if perhaps the woman was a bit crazy.

'Why did you leave the police?' said Sophia.

Her question was met with a look of utter bewilderment.

'Bloody hell,' she replied with a shake of her head, hair falling back over her shoulders. 'You really don't know what happened and why I'm no longer a police officer.'

The short pause should have given Sophia time to think, but instead her mind was whirring with so many questions.

'He really never told you?' Hannah chewed the edge of her thumbnail. 'I suppose there's no reason why he would. If he had, you might have wised up to him by now, done your own research as to how I came to leave the police after a very short career under a very dark cloud. All of it caused by Dane bloody Hoopman.'

Even though she knew she didn't want to know the answer, Sophia found herself saying, 'What did he do?'

Hannah held up a finger, bitten nail and all, to silence Sophia. 'Has he ever taken any . . . *photos* of you?' Sophia felt her own eyes narrow at the question.

'Photos? Do you mean, well, *photos*?'

Hannah raised a well-plucked eyebrow in response.

'You're quick,' was the accompanying reply.

Sophia felt a headache coming on. 'So, are we talking revenge porn?'

This time, the retort was a snort of laughter.

'No, love,' said Hannah. 'If only it was that simple and mucky. No. Dane's capable of so much more than that. His entrepreneur skills are out of this world.'

Her eyes misted up again and she looked away at her nails, bitten and cracked.

'So, he blackmailed you?' said Sophia.

'No,' Hannah said, unable to stop a tear from escaping down her cheek. 'He pimped me out, put me on a website and sold me for sex.'

CHAPTER SIXTY-TWO

I got back from headquarters in good time. That stupid old sod Powell was still moping around in the incident room. Did the old boy really have no proper work to do? I was busy, and I was running on half-capacity. Still, I expected that the ploddy git always did the right thing. He struck me as the sort to tell the truth, no matter the consequences. I'd like to get the chance to put that to the test, though I didn't think I'd be about that long.

Sophia wasn't there when I got back, which was fortunate. It gave me time to think if nothing else.

I'd seen the money at the back of headquarters' safe, and from hanging around listening to conversations as I did (which had often come to stand me in good stead in the past), I knew that we had to act fast.

Tonight would be the best night to do it while the money was most definitely there. Tomorrow, it might be gone.

Planning under pressure was never a smart move, but in all honesty, I was desperate. If I didn't get hold of some money and make a break for it, with or without Sophia, Turner was going to have my nuts on a platter. I was either going to prison, or most likely hell, with bits of my anatomy missing. I'd rather take my chances on the run. I reckoned I'd get away with it too.

No one was watching so I took a map of headquarters off the wall, photocopied it and circled the top floor, roughly where the safe was. Then I folded it in half and slid it into the bottom drawer of Sophia's locked pedestal next to her desk.

That should do for starters. It wouldn't be enough to hang her, but I was working on that.

I looked up as I walked away from her desk. What I was doing wasn't that suspicious, apart from the latex gloves I'd slipped on. I couldn't risk fingerprints on the page. A complete lack of prints might look odd, still, that was better than incriminating myself.

From the corner of my eye, I saw Harry coming towards me. He was getting on a bit, although not completely unobservant. I dropped the gloves into the bin next to my desk, certain he hadn't seen what I'd done right in front of him.

'Dane,' he said, standing a couple of feet from me, 'I've been meaning to ask how you're getting on. You got time for a chat in my office?'

Well, I did, but I didn't want to.

'Sure, boss. Why not?'

I followed him down the corridor to his boxy little office, turning down his offer of coffee on the way.

He shut the door as I sat down, and then took his own seat and gave me a half-hearted smile. I thought, not for the first time, that a couple of his front teeth looked as though they were false and questioned whether the man ever shaved. Every time I saw him, he had ginger stubble all over his bloody face. I might be a light-fingered bastard, but at least I was smart.

'You settling in all right?' asked Harry.

'Fine, thanks. Everyone's been very friendly, shown me the ropes, you know.'

I nodded and smiled, feeling that was the reaction he wanted. He eased back in his chair towards the open window, the annoying noise of the seagulls whizzing around, probably crapping all over my car.

How could anyone bear to live here? This place was getting to me and I'd only been here a matter of months.

'As long as you know where I am if there's anything you want to ask me, speak to me about,' said Harry with what I suppose he thought was a reassuring smile.

'That's very much appreciated, sir,' I lied, with my own winning smile. 'I most certainly will.'

An awkward pause followed which I think he thought I was going to feel obliged to fill. I failed.

'Okay,' he said, unable to resist filling a silence. 'I wanted to let you know where I am if there's anything you want to talk to me about . . . Perhaps something you're not sure whether you're heading in the right direction, that kind of thing.'

Heart-warming, but I had things to do.

'I'm great, thanks,' I said as I stood up to leave. 'You take care of yourself too.'

He was still scratching at his stubble when I got up to walk out. The screen on his phone lighting up grabbed my attention, especially because the name that jumped out at me was Sophia Ireland.

I wondered what she could possibly be calling him about.

CHAPTER SIXTY-THREE

EARLY HOURS OF TUESDAY 12 MAY

Sophia had never felt so wretched in her entire life. She had done a couple of unfavourable things in the past – she'd once got a friend to write an essay for her at school, told a couple of lies to get herself out of trouble and had even embellished the odd fact when trying to get a prisoner remanded to prison – but she had never come close to getting involved in any kind of criminal activity, especially the type Dane had somehow managed to talk her in to.

Her hands were trembling as she tried to tie her shoelaces. She was dressed from head to toe in black, something Dane had been most specific about. He'd got annoyed with her when she'd joked about using camouflage paint.

Dane had planned the whole thing with very precise timings of where and when they were to meet, and the route they were to take. Between them, they'd pooled the information they could about the security system.

They'd been helped out enormously by an innocent conversation Sophia had had with an old friend who worked at the Force Control Room, telling her how funny it was that half of the cameras weren't working as the maintenance contract had run out. It seemed that they really did have everything worked out to the nth degree.

As instructed, she had left her phone switched on and on the work surface in the kitchen, along with her security pass. Her pockets were empty and all she had in her hands were her car keys and house keys.

Resisting the urge to throw up, Sophia sat on the edge of her bed, calming herself down with long, slow breaths. She wasn't sure she could go through with this. She knew Dane was relying on her, and once tonight was done, it would all be over.

That's if she could even live with herself and what she was about to do.

With little option but to finish what she'd started, Sophia stood up, ready to break into police headquarters and steal what Dane insisted was rightfully hers.

CHAPTER SIXTY-FOUR

EARLY HOURS OF TUESDAY 12 MAY

I watched Sophia's car headlights as she pulled off the road and into the space behind the hedge. I'd chosen this spot because I knew there were no cameras, no number-plate readers and no houses around. It was unlit and shielded from the road, which had no pavements. It was pretty perfect, if I did say so myself.

She parked her Honda Civic behind my car, which I'd been sitting in for the last twenty minutes, trying to steady my nerves. I was a bit out of touch, and this wasn't my usual sort of job.

Still, I needed the money if I was going to get away and make a clean start of things, not to mention put things right with Turner. Even though I'd promised to keep him updated with everything I could after seeing him in The Grand, I knew he wouldn't hesitate to put an end to my favourite pastime of breathing.

'Hi,' said Sophia through the window when she'd turned the engine off. 'You want to jump in and we'll go over it one more time?'

That annoyed me: we'd been over this several times already. If she couldn't pay attention, she shouldn't have fucking well got involved in the first place. If I could have done this without her, taken more of a cut, then I wouldn't be putting up with an amateur. Still, I could only carry so much cash and was going to take most of hers anyway.

'Sure, darling,' I said with a smile as I walked round the car to get in beside her.

She looked across at me as I leaned over and took her hand in mine. She seemed absolutely petrified.

'It'll be okay,' I said. 'No one expects headquarters to get knocked off, do they? No one'll be in the main building at this time of night, just the squads in the outer buildings. We've got the alarm codes, we've got recently stolen passes from my trip to HQ Finance to get us in and out, and I've got the tools to open the safe in case we can't find the key.'

Her middle-aged forehead was still creased, despite my comforting words.

'I'm not sure how I let you talk me into this,' she muttered, chin almost touching her wrinkled neck.

'Hey, listen,' I said, moving my hand over to lift her chins up so she was looking me in the eye. 'This will all be fine. I'm not forcing you to do anything, but if you chicken out on me now, I'm going to be bloody annoyed with you.'

I tightened my grip on her face enough to let her know what I meant. I saw her eyes widen as I squeezed. She had to understand I wasn't bluffing.

'Okay, Dane,' she said without conviction. 'I'm absolutely petrified; let's get this over with.'

'We'll be fine,' I said as I let go of her and pushed open the car door. 'We'll be in and out without anyone even knowing what's happened.'

Ten minutes later we were creeping though the fields at the back of headquarters, watched by Riverstone's wildlife. I was grateful that it was a cloudy night, with little moonlight to illuminate us as we traipsed across the mud and fox shit to get to our location.

When we reached the wire fence that ran across the back of the perimeter, I hesitated, not sure whether to cut a hole in it as I'd intended or to pull the fence up where something had clearly been digging itself a pathway.

'I think we can crawl under,' whispered Sophia, echoing my own thoughts.

I grabbed the bottom of the wire fence with both hands and pulled. It came away from the concrete post with ease.

I couldn't help but laugh at my good fortune. I'd always known that budget cuts would be a blessing.

I dropped down to the ground, shoving the holdalls in front of me, wiggled in on my belly and waited for Sophia to do the same. We had chosen a spot to the side of the sports field, so we wouldn't be seen by anyone glancing out of the window in the dead of night. Headquarters had offices overlooking our entry point, though I didn't reckon many people would still be at work at two in the morning, and if they were, they were unlikely to either be staring out of the window, or able to see hundreds of yards in the pitch-black.

We stuck to the side of the field that was secluded by trees and bushes, making slow but steady progress until we reached the beginning of the car park. This was the most worrying part. Other than the holdalls, we could be two detectives returning to headquarters after a late finish, there was nothing out of the ordinary about that.

What made us conspicuous was our gloves, black clothing complete with hoods, and bag of tools for breaking and entering.

The route we had to take was one we had worked out around the motion sensors and live cameras.

Taking a deep breath, adrenalin through the roof, I stepped

out of the shadows, feeling Sophia do the same. This was the part that carried the most risk.

For about ten seconds, as we made our way across the tarmac, we were completely exposed.

It was exhilarating.

We reached the first door, a stolen pass card at the ready, which I swiped on the sensor. The catch released and we were in.

Some of the corridor lights were motion-sensored so we knew they'd come on; I still jolted when the first one lit up the way to the main reception area, fifty yards or so away from the three flights of stairs we needed to climb.

Keeping to the wall furthest from the front of the building, we made our way along the corridor, getting ever closer to the bottom of the stairs.

Thanks to yearly fitness tests, neither of us was going to have a problem getting up three flights of stairs in reasonable time.

We reached the top, having been sure of seeing no one until this point. The landing areas were sealed off on the first and second floors, and even during business hours it was rare to see anyone come or go from these quarters.

I looked over at Sophia whose face was an absolute picture. She looked absolutely petrified. Crime clearly wasn't her thing.

The next part was the easy bit. Once we were inside, it was plain sailing.

I grinned at Soph as I held some other poor sod's security access card up against the door swipe. It clicked open.

I wasn't expecting to see a light on, but it was only a desk lamp in the far corner that someone had obviously forgotten to switch off before going home at four o'clock. I could picture the fella who sat there, having been here only yesterday watching as he worked away at his keyboard, crunching numbers.

I walked over to the locked drawer I'd been reliably informed contained the safe key. I didn't even need to force the lock. A paperclip usually opened standard police pedestal locks without too much fuss. I'd done it many times before and was a little bit sad to think that I wouldn't be doing it again.

I supposed I'd soon get over it.

Sophia stood beside me as I bent down to put the key in the lock of the huge metal safe. The lock released, and I turned the handle.

Both of us froze as we heard the unmistakable sound of the toilet flushing.

Panic was only a split second away. I felt it course through me as I watched it run riot across her face.

I put a finger up to my lips and grabbed her arm with my other hand.

'We have to leave,' she mouthed at me as I held her arm.

'No, it's too late.'

This time, her eyes were as wide as saucers, her face completely grey in the soft light.

I dragged her over to the far side of the room, close to the number-cruncher's desk and near to the door he was about to come through.

I pulled her down to the floor, hidden from view as I heard the sounds of the door being opened.

With a sigh, he threw himself back down in his chair and began tapping at his keyboard.

I knew it was now or never. If we ran, he'd be able to call the police and we wouldn't get out with the holdalls and tools.

I didn't want to do it, but I was left with no option.

Since Christmas 2005 I hadn't done a job without back-up in my pocket, and today my reinforcement of choice happened to be a socket wrench.

Whether the screaming came from Sophia, the number-cruncher, myself or was a combination of all three, I couldn't tell.

I was up and around the desk, weapon in hand, before I had a chance to change my mind.

He looked petrified, as of course he had every right to be. I was dressed all in black leaping out at him in the early hours of the morning swinging a wrench at his head.

A sickening crunch killed the sound in his throat, as I raised my arm to hit him again.

Momentarily, I couldn't work out why I wasn't cracking him across the head for a third time. Then I remembered that this was why I'd always worked alone.

'No,' shouted Sophia, pulling my arm back, trying to get the wrench off me.

When she realised I wasn't going to let it go, she pushed herself between the guy and me.

'For God's sake,' she sobbed, 'stop it, stop it now.
You'll kill him.'
Sophia reached across the desk to his phone.
She wasn't going to stop me now, not after this.
I smashed the wrench into the phone.

'Don't fucking think about it,' I shouted back at her. 'Get the fucking bags and start filling them.'

For a second, I thought she was going to cry. Then she backed away with a nod. She was trembling all over. She was now another problem I had no idea how I was going to take care of. I'd use her to get the money out of the building, then worry about the rest later.

I watched her take a few tentative steps towards the discarded holdalls, then she glanced at me before reaching out to pick one up.

I suppose I shouldn't have underestimated her.

With no prior warning, Sophia ran for the door. I wasn't

even aware there was a big green release button on the inside of the office. I had wrongly assumed that we'd need the pass to get out.

'Fuck,' I shouted, wavering as to whether I should run after her and bash her head in there and then, or grab some money and run.

Whatever happened, I wasn't going to prison now.

I dropped the wrench, ran over to the safe and started to fill the holdalls.

Sophia would have to wait.

CHAPTER SIXTY-FIVE

Sophia ran down the stairs on legs she thought would give out on her at any minute. She felt the bile rising in her throat, unable to believe what she'd seen. This was beyond anything she had ever wanted to get mixed up in.

She was only aware she was crying as hard as she was when her vision blurred to the point of her running into a door.

Somehow, she'd managed to find herself on the ground floor, unable to remember her escape down three flights of stairs. Memory told her there was an emergency exit somewhere near to where she was, as she chugged on, past the conference suite, towards the public meeting room and the canteen.

This wasn't the arranged meeting point in case of an emergency abort of the plan, but under the horrendous circumstances, it would have to do.

She needed to get to a phone. Someone had to help that poor guy in the office with his bashed-in head covered in blood. She'd stood by, frozen to the spot while Dane hit him again and again.

The emergency-exit light was glowing in the distance at the end of the longest corridor she had ever run down. With outstretched hands, she fumbled for the metal bar to see her to freedom.

She was through and on to the rear of another building. Surely an emergency exit was supposed to take you to safety, not the back of a building and a car port. The fresh air filled her lungs as she heard the alarm sound, triggered no doubt as she forced open the door and ran towards the front of headquarters.

Legs aching, chest burning with the surge of adrenalin, forcing her onwards, she ran towards the main road.

Suddenly, a figure dressed in black, just in her periphery, ran from behind a parked van and grabbed her with both hands, the momentum forcing her knees to buckle. As she tried to scream, a hand clamped across her mouth, and another on her throat, before her head hit the tarmac and she blacked out.

CHAPTER SIXTY-SIX

MORNING OF TUESDAY 12 MAY

Harry Powell shook his head at the sight of the crime-scene tape all over the front of police headquarters.

This was bad, very bad.

He was feeling his age today more than ever.

With heavy heart, he got out of the unmarked surveillance car, walked past two surveillance officers dressed in black, seemingly explaining to their guv'nor why they'd thought it necessary to take an unmarked female detective constable to the ground head first, especially one who was wearing a tracker around her ankle so they knew her location at any given moment.

Harry didn't stop to talk to them, afraid he might twat them, and made his way over to the ambulance with its rear doors open. He could see two paramedics talking to someone on the trolley, a uniformed officer standing guard close by.

As one of the paramedics moved aside, Harry saw the deathly pale face of Sophia propped up on the trolley, her eyes shut as her head was examined.

With a nod at the uniformed officer and a wave of his warrant card, Harry called out, 'Soph.'

Her eyes snapped open and instantly filled with tears.

'I'm here, girl,' he said. 'I know, I know. It'll be all right.'

'Sir,' began the officer who stood between Harry and his responsibility, 'I really—'

'Yeah,' sighed Harry. 'You're under strict instructions not to let me talk to her. That on?'

Harry gestured at the body-worn camera strapped to the top of the officer's stab-proof vest.

'It's recording, sir, yes.'

Harry leaned forward, lowered his head so he was looking straight at the lens and said, 'Detective Constable Sophia Ireland spoke to me yesterday about Dane Hoopman and his plans to break into headquarters to steal money. After he had explained what he was going to do, she called me and told me everything. I passed the information on and I was told by senior officers, who I'm not afraid to name, that she should go with him and take part so we could get him once and for all, along with whoever he's been working for. Something, I notice, which has failed to happen at this exact moment because someone messed up and he's legged it. I pointed out that only one evening's planning was not enough to carry out the research, get officers briefed and in place before he attacked the safe. No one listened to me and my concerns.

'Sophia had absolutely no idea that anyone would be there tonight in the office and that anyone would get hurt.'

With that, Harry walked away from the camera, and probably from his career.

CHAPTER SIXTY-SEVEN

For the first time in several days, Sean Turner was feeling more optimistic. He was due to meet with Dane in a couple of hours and take all his ill-gotten gains from him, not that Dane knew that. If he told him, he wouldn't show up. Dane was no fool, yet Turner had backed him into a corner. Caging an animal such as Hoopman wasn't always a good idea, not unless he was prepared to keep him in that cage.

For once, Turner had wanted to come alone and deal with Hoopman himself. He'd thought about using Milo or one of the others to accompany him, and then had dismissed the idea. Siphoning a bit of cash off the top would be much easier on his own and he wouldn't have to pay off the hired help to turn a blind eye.

Unimpressed that he was having to wait around in a field of all places, with only a cheap Toyota hire car for company, Turner sat back in the driver's seat, scanning the road for any sign of movement.

The plan, if everything went well, was for Dane to meet him and hand over half of the money. Turner had other ideas.

Time was now getting on: the clock on the dash read 4:14

a.m. By now Turner should be heading away from Riverstone, looking to set up shop somewhere else.

The sun would be up in an hour or so and Turner wanted to be tucked up in a hotel somewhere far away, with a *Do Not Disturb* sign on the door. Instead he was sitting in a field, waiting for a career criminal and police officer who had ripped off the safe at headquarters.

That last part made Turner smile.

Headlights came into view from the direction of Riverstone. Turner sat upright before easing himself out of the car.

He watched as the approaching car slowed and pulled off the road, now only lit by its sidelights, and coasted to a stop.

The door clicked open and Dane got out.

'Took your time,' said Turner, watching Dane's every move.

'Ran into a spot of bother.'

Even though he wasn't in the slightest interested in the answer, Turner felt obliged to say, 'Where's the woman?'

Dane put his hands in his jacket pockets and took a step forward, closing the gap between them considerably.

'Yeah, that was the spot of bother I mentioned.'

'Is she going to cause us a problem?' asked Turner, also taking a step closer.

'No, she knows better, and she's as much in the shit as I am, so we can forget about her.'

'You're trying my patience now, Dane. If she's not with you, where's the half of the money she was supposed to be carrying?'

'That's a bit of an issue.'

'Give me the fucking money, now,' said Turner. 'If you haven't got the two hundred grand you're supposed to hand over, I'll be the least of your problems. Understand?'

Dane held out his hands. 'Search me, if you like. You won't find anything else on me, only what's in the car. And you can have it all. All I want is the passport you promised me.'

'One thing at a time,' said Turner.

He pointed a finger in Dane's face. 'You were due to do the job at three a.m. You said it'd take no more than half an hour to get in, get out and come and meet me.'

'I've told you, there were hold-ups. Now, are we going to do this exchange, or talk about it?'

Dane gestured in the direction of his car and walked towards the boot, remotely releasing the catch as he went.

Keeping a gap between them, Turner fell into step beside him.

'Look, here,' said Dane as he leaned into the dark boot and unzipped a holdall.

He plunged a hand inside and pulled out a wad of £50 notes. He held them out for Turner to see in the weak interior boot light.

Turner moved his head forward, tipping him off-balance enough to slow his reaction to the object looming towards his temple.

The last thing Turner saw before he lost consciousness was what looked very much like a socket wrench.

CHAPTER SIXTY-EIGHT

I wasn't sure how it had come to this: I literally had nothing. The low-life criminal whose safe I had once knocked off was blackmailing me, and now I'd knocked him unconscious, gone through his pockets for the promised passport, and left him on the ground. I couldn't blame him for trying to stitch me up – after all, if the boot was on the other foot, I'd have done the same.

I turned the car towards the docks. I had a passport in my pocket, plus as much cash as I could carry. The holdall next to me on the passenger seat was only really for show. I thought I'd look a little less conspicuous strolling on to the ferry with a bag than without one. The socks I'd grabbed didn't even match. Still, Spain sold socks. I'd worry about it when I got out of this shitty little one-horse town.

My heart lurched when I saw a flashing blue light in my rear-view mirror. Would I actually get away if they were coming for me?

The relief hit me when the marked police car behind me turned down a side road, giving me a new concern. Were they trying to head me off at the docks?

Surely they wouldn't be stupid enough to let me know they were behind me and then try to cut in front of me.

Not willing to take the risk, I put my foot down and drove towards the top of the cliffs. It was a clear and bright afternoon, people milling about, going about their business as if they didn't have a care in the world. I'd never felt like that in my life.

I pulled into a car park that was rarely used at this time of day. It was too far from the port, too far from the town, and the dog walkers usually came along later. I knew the footpath down the side of the cliff could be a bit heavy on the calves, but it cut valuable minutes off the journey, not to mention the CCTV in the car park still wasn't working so no one would know at what time I'd walked away from my car.

I even bought a car-park ticket valid for twenty-four hours to make it look as though I'd meant to come back.

Then I picked up my bag of meagre belongings and trotted towards freedom.

The pathway was fairly steep, but wide enough for me to avoid the edge. East Rise council didn't want to be sued for some careless day-trippers plummeting over the edge.

I tried to peer over to see how far away the fall to my death would be. I couldn't even see it. No danger of that today then.

Stopping to look at the sea, I wondered if I'd ever be back this side of the Channel again. I supposed it was unlikely, unless I wanted to see out my days banged up constantly wondering when Turner or his cronies would get to me.

The noise of cars turning into the car park, fifty yards or so above my head, made me hurry on down the path. There was a chance they were police cars, so the sooner I got completely out of sight and on a ferry, the better.

I started to run. I knew they'd catch up with me if they really wanted to, head me off at the bottom, but what else could

I do? Stand there and wait for them to put the cuffs on me? That wasn't going to happen.

At times, I stumbled; I was getting closer to the terminal building and where I needed to be. Once I was off the side of the coastal path, I was there. All I had to do was buy a ticket, show them the passport I'd taken from Turner's pocket, then I was away.

Of course, I knew that I wouldn't be completely away until my feet touched French soil, yet still, I was getting closer.

The noise behind me from the car park grew ever fainter with the sea breeze and the distance I was putting between us, so on I stumbled, stepping aside a couple of times for walkers and joggers as they made their way past me.

At last, I reached the building, sweating more than I would have liked. It was instinct to want to look round, make sure I wasn't being followed. I fought the temptation to check who was watching. Apart from being a pretty good criminal, I had an idea how surveillance worked and I wouldn't see them before it was too late.

Steadying my breathing, calming my heart rate, I strolled to the ticket booth, ready to act as though all I wanted from life was to head to Calais, buy a baguette and stagger back with as much cheap booze as I could carry.

Ticket in hand, someone else's passport in my pocket, I felt good. Even the slow, steady stream of passengers I joined to get on the boat made me reckon that this was actually going to work out.

As soon as I got on board, I made my way to the bar. A celebratory pint of over-priced lager was in order.

Nursing the only one I knew I could allow myself, I sat in the far corner, cradling it, while I watched the other passengers come and go.

For the first time since abandoning her, I thought about

Sophia. That was how self-centred I'd become. I stared into my pint. Or had I always been this way?

There must have been a time when I wasn't such a selfish bastard. Strange thing was, I don't ever remember being really happy, just elated when I was committing crime.

For the first time in years, I was without a phone. It was probably for the best. Who was I going to call anyway? Sophia? Tell her I was sorry for running out on her, and for fitting her up for stealing half a million pounds from police headquarters?

She'd probably be all right. She wasn't violent, didn't have any other convictions and could take care of herself. Prison probably wouldn't be too bad for her.

I took a swig of my beer. Who was I kidding? She was as likely to get shanked inside as I was.

Still, better her than me.

Yeah, I really had the morals of a polecat.

A glance at the clock above the bar told me we were about halfway to France. I thought I'd take a wander around the deck, make sure no one had followed me. I'd been keeping an eye on who was in the bar area, looking out for anyone under sixty who didn't have kids with them. I'd never know if a surveillance team were anywhere close to me and could only rule them out by old age and children. Even Turner didn't stoop low enough to employ toddlers or geriatrics. It didn't mean to say that they weren't hiding somewhere else on the ferry.

I'd go and buy some chocolate, make myself look like a proper tourist, then take a leak.

The next few minutes passed without incident until the moment in the shop when I saw what looked like someone wearing an earpiece. It was more the fiddling, finger-poking to the ear that did it. He fitted the bill: white, mid-thirties, five-ten, looked like he worked out, casually dressed, but in a way that said 'police officer'. He looked clean too, both literally and free of alcohol and drugs. And a dead giveaway was that he wasn't like most of the fucking clueless sheep who were following each other around the shop in the hope of two pounds off cheap vodka.

I knew this was a risky journey, leaving me like a sitting duck, but I'd had no other choice. I couldn't afford to panic, yet I couldn't afford to pretend that this bloke was going to be anything other than my undoing.

With a glance at the queue with a huge bar of Toblerone in my hand, I sauntered towards the exit. It led to one of the seating areas with doors to the deck.

If it came to it, would I have the bottle to throw myself into the sea?

The weather was mild, I was a strong swimmer and the bundles of notes in my pockets would dry out eventually in the Spanish sunshine.

I decided to test the waters – not the English Channel waters, but the ones that would tell me if I was being followed or not.

I chucked the bar of chocolate on the nearest shelf, not wanting to add shoplifting to my misdemeanours, and idled through the door.

There was a slow but deliberate movement behind me, confirming my worst fears. The celebratory pint had been too early, and had no doubt numbed my senses slightly, numbed them enough that I only saw him lurch towards me when it was too late.

In my last few seconds, I could have sworn he came out of the disabled toilet. I hadn't even thought that danger could lurk there. How many others could claim that the most defining moment of their life came from a disabled toilet on a fucking ferry?

I fell to the floor for some reason. It took me a moment to

realise why my legs wouldn't work and what the burning feeling was in my side. Then I saw the blood.

Fucking typical. I was going to die closer to France than England. That was one of my last thoughts as Milo's face began to blur as he was grabbed by the bloke with the earpiece from the onboard shop and a couple more of his colleagues.

My meaningless life had one more surprise for me as I lay shivering in the warm May weather, bleeding to death on the Calais-bound ferry. A figure dropped down beside me.

'Dane,' he said, 'hang on. Help's on its way.'

The pain was beginning to subside, as was everything else, but still I managed a smile at my detective inspector.

'What you doing here, Harry?' I said with a voice that sounded so very quiet and unlike my own.

'Listen,' he said. 'I need to put pressure on the wound. You've been stabbed. The medics are here on board, so you're going to be fine.'

'Hey, don't bother. I'm not worth it.'

He was leaning in so close to me. His face was next to mine. I could only focus on his stubble.

'There's one thing I have to tell you,' I said. 'I need to tell you about Sophia.'

Harry moved his head so close, I could feel his breath on my skin, his ear touched my lips as I spoke.

'It was all her idea – the safe at headquarters, the theft, the plans she drew up were in her drawer in the office.

She's a wrong 'un. I had to tell you.'

CHAPTER SIXTY-NINE

Harry fought to get Dane's jacket open to stop the bleeding from his chest. He knew it was futile, but it didn't stop him trying. Arms grabbed at him, pulled him away before others took over.

Once again, he was aware he was sitting by and watching his colleagues try to save another fallen comrade's life, even if that comrade wasn't worth saving.

As he moved back out of the way, Harry was aware that Dane's holdall had been dropped by his side as he fell to the ground. Moving it aside with his foot, he unzipped it, trying to conjure up an excuse if anyone ever questioned why he'd opened it.

He crouched down, pulled the sides open and came up with the best excuse that if it contained a firearm, it needed to be made safe before it was moved.

What greeted Harry were several bundles of twenty-and fifty-pound notes and a two-inch bundle of papers. At least, at first glance, it all looked like papers. He leafed through Police National Computer checks, private bank and personal details from police intelligence data bases, and one name jumped out at him – Jenny Bloomfield.

That stopped him in his tracks. Harry looked back over to where police and security were trying to save a man who appeared to already be dead.

There was no way that Hoopman could be responsible for Jenny's death, so what was he doing with all this paperwork?

That was the point that a colour photograph pushed into the black-and-white pages caught his eye.

It was a photograph of Linda Bowman standing next to a man who bore a striking resemblance to Linda. If Harry wasn't very much mistaken, he was looking at Linda and her brother, a career criminal and someone who had never been located in Linda's murder investigation. This was the information he had been missing all this time that would link the murders of both Jenny Bloomfield and Linda Bowman.

And that link was Sean Turner.

CHAPTER SEVENTY

AFTERNOON OF THURSDAY 14 MAY

Quite what Sophia was supposed to do with herself while suspended from work, she couldn't fathom. Her mind was whirring and most of her colleagues wanted nothing to do with her after she'd been arrested and interviewed for her part in a burglary at headquarters and the attempted murder of a colleague.

Could she really blame them? Still, everyone was being very cautious whenever they did speak to her. The only one who truly didn't seem to care was Harry.

Sophia hated to think what kind of place the incident room would be if they didn't have Harry. He had taken them through so much over recent years, and she knew he had no idea how much he meant to them all.

As she trudged from the town centre car park towards the Seagull Pickings where Harry had asked her to meet him, she thought about how bloody foolish she'd been.

Walking through the door of the seedy eatery, she saw the unmistakable figure of her detective inspector waiting for her.

Tears pricked her eyes as she fumbled through the tables and handful of grumpy diners, until she reached her friend.

His arms were around her, grabbing her in a bear hug and crushing her until she had to pull away to catch her breath.

'How you doing, girl?' he said, with damp eyes staring down at her.

She managed a shrug, despite still being encased.

Harry let go and waved at the counter.

'Two teas, please, De Niro,' he said to the waitress whose face relaxed into the beginnings of a smile, only didn't quite make it there.

Harry pulled out a chair for Sophia and took the seat opposite her.

She opened her mouth to speak, then closed it again.

She took a deep breath, waited until 'De Niro' had unceremoniously plonked two mugs of strong tea down on the table, and moved away.

'Even after everything he did,' she said, voice faltering, 'I can't believe Dane's dead.'

'None of this was your fault,' said Harry, placing his hand on her hers. 'He was rotten to the core.'

She noticed Harry glance at the other customers, a frown flashing across his features.

Following suit, she stole looks at the couple sitting next to them, meeting Harry's eyes with a raised eyebrow.

'You can't be too cautious,' he said in lowered tones, accompanied by a conspiratorial wink.

'Look,' he added, leaning across the table, 'it would be wrong of me to tell you too much about his background, but he wasn't a good person. What he was, was charming, and like others before you, you fell for it.'

Harry gave her hand a squeeze and produced a tissue from his pocket.

'Here,' he said, 'have this. I've only used it once or twice.'

She couldn't help but smile through the tears as she dabbed at her bloodshot eyes.

'Thanks, Harry. You don't know how much this means to me. Most people have shunned me, and I can't say as I blame them.'

She hesitated, not sure whether to tell him, then figured she owed him a full explanation.

'You remember me telling you about Hannah?' she said, blinking through the tears.

'Course I do. An ex of Hoopman's.'

She nodded. 'Well, when I met her, here, she told me that he got her into bad ways. I've told you some of it, but she said that he . . . sold her online for sex.'

Sophia choked up, the words catching in her throat. 'He said that we'd disappear away together, forget everyone else. In the back of my mind, since she told me her pitiful story, I worried I'd end up like Hannah. If he was prepared to do that to her and steal from me, I don't doubt that'd be next.'

There was an awkward pause, Harry pulled his tie away from his throat as if it was cutting off his air supply, and Sophia tried as best as she could to hold it together.

'Whatever's happened, you would have come to me or someone else and told them. I know you, Soph. You wouldn't have let things go on. What we need to concentrate on now is getting through this.'

'What's going to happen to me?' she said. 'Will I go to prison?'

With a shake of his head, Harry said, 'You know the criminal investigation takes priority. You've been interviewed. They had no choice. At best they've got a conspiracy to commit burglary; you came straight to me about it, so please don't worry. Then of course, they'll want to talk to me.'

'What? You're not—'

He held up a hand to stop her. 'I don't have anything to worry about, and neither should you. It'll be unpleasant, but you have to keep it together, all right?'

Sophia gave a wretched nod. 'I'm sorry I stormed out of your house on Sunday.'

'You came back though,' said Harry. 'That's the main thing.'

Sophia paused while she steeled herself to ask her next question.

'Can you tell me one thing?'

Harry's hand went up to scratch his stubble.

'Go on,' he said.

'The man in the office. Was he . . . Is he likely to get better?'

'We think so.'

One second-hand tissue was not going to be enough to stem her tears. Harry fished in his pocket for another.

'He's not in a great way, but he's alive,' Harry said when the crying had subsided.

'He just kept hitting him, again and again. We didn't know he was going to be there, or we wouldn't have risked it, not that night. Well, I certainly wouldn't have done. I can't guarantee Dane wouldn't have been there.'

They both sat staring at their mugs of tea, united in their misery.

'There is one other thing though,' Sophia said. 'If Dane was being set up, and I was sent in to go along with it all, why was someone sitting at his desk working in the early hours with us about to knock off the safe?'

Harry loosened his tie again and ran a hand through his hair.

'That simply doesn't make sense,' she added. 'Even when I went through the humiliation of being arrested and interviewed, no one's been able to give me an explanation of what that fella was doing there.'

'That's because, Soph, it was what they call a good old-fashioned police fuck-up.'

'And I'm supposed to face the consequences of that, am I?' She felt something which she hoped was anger – at least it meant she had some sort of energy left in her.

'It's a murky world,' said Harry. 'One that Dane lived in and one that he dragged you into.'

'At least he did the decent thing in the end,' she said, a tight smile on her face.

The questioning look Harry was giving her forced an explanation from her.

'It was one of the things they told me in the interview,' Sophia said as she wrapped the sodden tissue round and round her fingers. 'He must have had some modicum of decency about him. You know what I mean?'

She gave a genuine smile. 'The officers that interviewed me told me what Dane's last words to you were as he lay dying on the ferry deck. "It was all down to me. I forced Sophia to help me, so please leave her out of it. Tell her I'm sorry."'

She leaned across and kissed him on the cheek.

'Thanks, H. I'm glad it was you he told.'

'Me too, girl, me too.'

CHAPTER SEVENTY-ONE

Sean Turner watched Sophia walk out of the cafe and away from the town centre. He'd love to follow her home and then tidy her away, but he was running out of time. He would follow her round town until he found her in an isolated spot and make his move. The most useful thing Hoopman had told him was at The Grand and was no doubt to encourage him to leave town. Even so, hanging around after being told the police had CCTV of him picking up Jenny Bloomfield in his car, was enough to make him rethink his plans.

He wasn't even sure that Sophia actually had any of the money from the safe. If Dane had been prepared to rip off Sean and any of his hired help who might come after him, why would he worry about the financial security of the latest in a long line of expendable women?

It was more to do with being had over. That was a feeling Sean really didn't like. He'd take care of Sophia next.

It had been unpleasant dealing with his own sister, not to mention Jenny Bloomfield, so a woman copper of all things wouldn't stop him sleeping at night.

He kept his distance as she walked back towards a car park

on the far side of town. He noticed with amusement that she had chosen to leave her car as far away from the police station as she could without actually being in the next town.

He saw her get into her Honda Civic, wondering briefly why the police had given it back to her so soon after her arrest. Dane had happily fed back to Sean and Milo everything about this woman's house, car and way of life. Tracking her wouldn't have been easy without the inside information. He wasn't sure she had any of his money stashed away somewhere, but he'd enjoy trying to get its location out of her.

His fingers flexed around the pliers in his pocket.

Still, following her would be fun. His old skills never failed him.

He would have liked to bide his time, watch her, wait until she was alone and vulnerable. That would be the most rewarding. If only he had a little longer.

Whatever it took to get his money back and get shot of the girl.

The only trouble was, his favourite place to bury a body was still being searched by the police. Sometimes life was unfair.

CHAPTER SEVENTY-TWO

With too much on his mind and too little energy, Harry walked back to his office. He knew that he was fortunate not to have been moved, suspended or at least get slapped with restrictions. His only guess was that his angry rant to the poor young officer's body-worn camera two days ago had had some effect.

The shit storm that was coming now would be like nothing he had ever encountered.

Harry was so fucking angry that Sophia had been used in the way she had been. What with her and Pierre being tossed aside like leftovers, he wasn't sure he wanted much more of this rotten organisation.

His pace back to East Rise nick got faster, his stride increased, and he felt his shirt start to stick to him in the unexpected afternoon warmth.

Harry flung the door of the incident room open and was met with a wall of laughter. People enjoying themselves at work was one thing, but this was simply too much. If they had time to piss about, they had time to knuckle down. It wasn't as if there was a shortage of work to be done.

He muttered, 'Hello, everyone,' as he stomped off to his

office, away from all forms of human interaction. Why hadn't he become a zoo keeper or tractor driver? They couldn't have had much in the way of conversation all day. Lucky bastards.

Not for the first time, he knew he had to shake himself out of it. The thing was, he was lost and, if he was being perfectly honest, he didn't want to get over it. He'd had enough of the job that simply kept on taking. And it was taking and taking. Mostly the piss.

Harry jabbed at his computer's keyboard, printed off some emails he was sure were important, although he couldn't for the life of him think why, and made his way back out to the office to get them from the printer.

Already seething at the general injustice of life, he stepped into the incident room and felt as though someone had lit the touch paper.

Someone had dumped bags of exhibits on Pierre's chair, left a tray of dirty coffee mugs on the desk and, if he wasn't very much mistaken, it looked as though the night before, someone had sat and eaten a takeaway, leaving yellow staining all over the surface.

'Who the fuck has done this?' shouted Harry, apoplectic with rage, his already red face turning a health-warning purple.

Silence dropped into the room. A couple of the older, wiser members of staff looked away. Those that were daft enough to gawped at Harry and the debris on Pierre's desk.

'He was a fucking better detective dead than you shower of shit are alive, and you've the ill manners to leave his desk like this. What is the actual fucking matter with you dickheads?'

From the back of the room, Hazel stood up.

Harry watched her walk towards him. A shining light in this atrocious job he found himself doing with no love or enthusiasm any more.

She stopped in front of him.

'Can we talk in your office, please?' she said as quietly as she could, although without any doubt, everyone else in the room heard it.

A nod and he turned and walked away.

Harry was aware that she was following him: her footsteps on the worn and torn carpet tiles sounded as loud as tap shoes on a stage in the team's deathly hush.

They sat opposite each other in his office, she a detective constable of many years, carrying her own misery, he a battle-weary detective inspector, not doing such a good job at hiding his torment.

'I've lost it, Haze.'

She smiled, perhaps to break to him gently what she was about to say, or maybe because she was stalling for time and didn't actually know how to say it. An ordinary conversation couldn't emerge from his latest outburst.

'Perhaps it would be best if you took a couple of days off,' she said.

A simple solution to a very complex set of emotions.

Harry rubbed at his eyes, felt the first signs of tears forming, so he simply shook them away. He didn't have time for sentimentality.

'No one, H, and I mean no one, has had such a bad time of it as you have in the last few years.'

She paused as he opened his mouth to say something; he never established whether it was to agree or disagree with her because the thought froze, and the words refused to form.

'When we met, your wife had recently left you, then you found your friend's body, and then Pierre was murdered. By anyone's standards, that's a lot to deal with. Your head must be a mess. I know mine is and I've had much less to contend with than you have.'

Slowly, the cogs began to move, and the fog cleared.

'You're right,' he said. 'I need a bit of time away, but the arrest of Sean Turner is our current priority. We just have to find the murdering fucker and it'll all be over.'

'I'll ring the DCI and tell her you've had to take some last-minute leave. She'll be fine with it; you know she will.'

Mirroring each other, they now stood on opposite sides of Harry's desk.

'Thanks, Haze. And I'm sorry for shouting at everyone back there. I'll get home, get my act together and make it up to you.'

She nodded wisely at him and said, 'Not really me you need to apologise to.'

The nod turned into a tilt in the direction of the incident room.

'Oh, yeah,' said Harry with an absent-minded scratch at his stubble. 'Good point, well presented.'

He took a deep breath, buttoned up his jacket and walked to address the rest of the team with a display of more authority than he felt.

It was amazing how much Harry's spirits lifted once he was at home, showered, changed out of his work clothes and had a plan forming in his mind.

Half an hour of research on the internet and he was sure all would go according to plan and, most importantly, Hazel would go with it. They both had a terrible time of it lately and they needed something to look forward to, something to celebrate. He was certain this was what was missing.

By the time his girlfriend had come home from work, hung up her jacket and joined him in the living room with a cup of tea, he had convinced himself that he had the answer to all their ills.

'How was the rest of your day?' he asked, tentative question accompanied by a tentative sip of his own drink.

'It was okay,' she said, putting hers down to cool on the side table between them. 'Usual ridiculous amount of paperwork, but there's nothing out of the ordinary about that. I've probably got to do a set of nights in the next few weeks.'

'Sounds delightful, love.'

He paused, moved in his seat to get a better look at her face, to take in her expression when he delivered his latest idea.

'I've been thinking . . .'

'You've been home for hours now, H, I should hope so.'

'We've both got passports, and we've never been abroad together. How about it?'

Hazel's eyes softened; the corners of her mouth turned up.

'Why not?' she said. 'Where were you thinking?'

'How about America?'

'America?'

'Why not?' said Harry. 'I've never been, you said the other day you hadn't been, and I've always fancied seeing the Grand Canyon.'

'Grand Canyon? Could be interesting.'

Harry felt like rubbing his hands together at Hazel's enthusiasm. Well, perhaps it wasn't the right word to describe her emotion, but when they got there and happened to wander past the chapel next to their hotel, she was bound to get as caught up in the moment as he was.

After all, there was little point in going all the way to Las Vegas and coming back without getting married.

CHAPTER SEVENTY-THREE

EVENING OF THURSDAY 14 MAY

It took a moment for Sophia to fully grasp what was happening: the fear that gripped her momentarily rendered her speechless, frozen. She was unable to move, powerless to do anything.

And then she remembered – no, she wasn't.

She'd be damned if she'd let this shit of a man get the better of her in a deserted alleyway in the dead part of town.

'Who the hell do you think you are?' she all but shouted at him.

'You wanna be careful,' said Sean Turner as he took another step towards her, the tips of their shoes almost touching.

'Do I? And has it occurred to you for one second that your threats don't intimidate me?'

Sophia leaned towards him, so close she could smell his breath. She wasn't going to show this man any fear.

Despite the volatile situations she had found herself in, the training, the expectation that any day at work could end with her being beaten senseless, it still came as a shock to her when Turner's hand shot out and he grabbed her around the throat.

She supposed that, for a second, she must have looked

absolutely petrified. She only guessed that by the smug look of satisfaction all over his face.

That made her angrier than she had ever been in her life.

Instinctively both of her hands came up in a single movement, straight against his arm, forcing him to do one of two things. Sophia counted on him squeezing her neck tighter.

Grateful that the violent bastard was so predictable, as his fingers dug into her windpipe, she brought her right knee up with as much force as possible. The impact with his testicles was short and sharp, just like his breathing when the pain kicked in.

As Sean doubled over, she knew she didn't have long before he was on her again, so she used what she had to hand – literally.

Policewomen were still women so didn't tend to walk about without an awareness of who might be lurking around corners. That was why Sophia clutched her door key in between her knuckles.

A perfectly legal and explainable weapon. It paid to know the law. And how to jab someone in the eyeball.

One swift movement was all it took to make her tormentor's screams pierce the air.

Sickened by what she'd done, yet relieved it wasn't her thrashing around on the ground in the alleyway, Sophia felt her way along the wall towards the street. Her fingers felt numb as she pulled herself along the brickwork, bile rising in her throat.

She knew she couldn't run away from this. Apart from someone most likely hearing Turner's wailing, her front-door key was wedged in his eye socket. There was little hope of the police failing to catch up with her; besides, she would rather face her colleagues than spend the rest of her life looking over her shoulder.

Now safely in the street, close to a nearby shop window, she made her way on shaky legs to the centre of the pavement. With trembling hands, she reached into her pocket and pulled out her phone.

As she kept watch on the entrance to the alley, she rang 999.

ALSO BY LISA CUTTS

EAST RISE SERIES

Mercy Killing

Buried Secrets

Lost Lives

ACKNOWLEDGEMENTS

This book was inspired by my time in the Professional Standards Department. During my time there, no serving police officer was found to have committed a string of burglaries and armed robberies, it was quite the eye-opener. Legend has it that years before my time in the job, a former police officer was caught carrying out a raid on a bank on his way to work. He was caught because witnesses recognised his police uniform under his coat.

Most police officers and civilian employees do a very difficult and demanding job, day in, day out. All with the public pointing cameras in their faces waiting for them to get it wrong. To all those continuing to do their upmost to uphold the law and protect the public, thank you. I expect it's more difficult today than it has ever been.

Huge thanks to the wonderful team at Bloodhound Books. My thanks especially to Betsy Reavley, Fred Freeman, Tara Lyons, Hannah Deuce and Lexi Curtis for being just absolutely fantastic.

A NOTE FROM THE PUBLISHER

Thank you for reading this book. If you enjoyed it please do consider leaving a review on Amazon to help others find it too.

We hate typos. All of our books have been rigorously edited and proofread, but sometimes mistakes do slip through. If you have spotted a typo, please do let us know and we can get it amended within hours.

info@bloodhoundbooks.com

Printed in Dunstable, United Kingdom